eyes

like

mine

A NOVEL BY

Paul Cody

BASKERVILLE
PUBLISHERS, INC.

Baskerville Publishers, Inc.
7616 LBJ Freeway, Suite 220
Dallas, TX 75251-1008

Library of Congress Cataloging-in-Publication Data

Cody, Paul, 1953-
    Eyes like mine : a novel / by Paul Cody
    p. cm.
    ISBN 1-880909-44-8 (hard cover : alk. paper)
    I. Title
PS3553.0335E97   1996
813'.54--DC20   96-1397
                                                        CIP

Manufactured in the United States of America
First Printing, 1996

FOR *Maggie,*

FOR *Mary, Michael, Shawn and Gretchen,*

FOR *Jane Howle*

Also by Paul Cody

THE STOLEN CHILD

If he had smiled why would he have smiled?

To reflect that each one who enters imagines himself to be the first to enter whereas he is always the last term of a preceding series even if the first term of a succeeding one, each imagining himself to be the first, last, only and alone, whereas he is neither first nor last nor only nor alone in a series originating in and repeated to infinity.

ULYSSES

THEY WOULD BE TALL, *Ann says. They would be tall and thin, and they would have questions about everything. Any son or daughter of ours. They would want to know this, and they would have to know that, and it would be constant. Their presence, their being here.*

Ann is tall, and she has brown hair that is almost blond, and blue eyes, and she has on black shorts and a white blouse and no bra. I can see the outline of her breasts through the blouse, the nipples, the pale smooth skin of her arms and neck, her face.

The living room has grown mostly dark, here in Ithaca, New York, in late summer. We can hear people walk past on the street, their voices murmurous for a moment or two. We can smell the moisture of the trees and bushes outside the windows, and here on the couch, Ann puts her hand on my arm, and her fingers are long and white, and they touch my shoulder, then go lightly over the skin on my arm.

They'd like ice cream, I say, like their mama, and they'd be smart like her. Ann smiles and puts her hand on the side of my face, at my neck. She pushes my hair back from my face, and then her fingers move over my forehead, my cheeks, my nose and lips.

They'd say, Daddy, tell about when you and Mommy met, Ann says, and her fingers go over my lips. Tell about when you were little. What was your Daddy like?

I lick her finger, and Ann smiles, and says, What do you say, pal? What would a body tell them?

one

This is what it was like in there, near Boston, when I was twenty-four years old and skinny as sticks and wire. They walked down the halls at night, at two and three, when the bats were outside and blind, and the white circles from their flashlights bounced on the floor and ceiling and walls like a thought inside—rushing and growing fat, then knocking the walls, glancing into corners and thinning to a ghost. And none of it would stop.

In there, when I was twenty-four, it was night, and cars passed outside, a long way off. A half mile or a mile in the distance, and I saw the headlights inside, saw them rushing around the curves in roads, rushing past trees and under the leaves on branches. They went seventy and seventy-five and eighty miles an hour, and the steering wheel and dashboard must have begun to vibrate with the speed, and in the dark, at the sides of the roads, the trees were dense and dark, and the stone embankments were gray like smoke, like something you couldn't really see.

In there, the halls were long and shiny, and sounds echoed for a long time, echoed until I wasn't sure when the sound had begun and when it had ended. It was a ping on the far side of the ward, was somewhere in the pipes, or in the ceiling. It was a thrum in a wall, in a vent, and then it whirred, but so softly, so low, that it was hard to tell if the sound was inside or outside my ear. I lay in bed there, when I was twenty-four, and tried to figure which side of the building, the pipe, the wall, the ear, it had come from.

When I was twenty-four I pulled the pillow over my head, and heard someone on the hall move, and thought it was Rolfe, who was fat as a couch, and moved slowly. Rolfe couldn't cross a room, Rolfe was on enough Elavil to lift a building.

They locked the door, and I walked up and down, up and down, up again and down again, a hundred times during the day, and the clock behind the cage on the wall ticked so slowly that a minute was a day, a day a month, a month a decade.

When I was twenty-four they came with the needle, and I swung at them, and there were voices and rushing footsteps, and the needle bit my hip, and I was a cloud, I floated and drifted, and they said, You don't have to be here. You could have a life out there.

There are things, they said. You're just twenty-four.

Their voices echoed, and grew loud and soft. Someone was shifting the volume, someone was fooling with the speakers. The sound came from the front, the side, the back, then from all directions, then the voices wavered, the voices were from underwater.

I stayed where I was, at the base of the wall. There was a thin mat like in gym class on the floor.

The room was white and had one window, and the mesh was doubled, was painted white. The door had a square panel, and there was a glass eye in the upper half. The eye was clear, was looking, and I could hear them on the other side.

What's he doing? they whispered.

Where is he?

Lemme see, they hissed.

I could feel them, and I didn't move, didn't blink, didn't breathe. I felt my chest rise, and air came out, and I breathed like a monk in a cell, a monk on a mountain, a monk who could stop his heart.

I was a monk, and I was a weed, and I was mold on a wall—the dark spot, the speck near the ceiling, the thing they almost couldn't see. I'd gone away, and they'd send in an old man with a broom, with trembling hands and watery eyes, and he'd sweep up what was left.

What was I then?

Ash?

Dust?

Dirt?

Twigs?

Leaves?

Air?

Nobody would see, nobody would come toward me, eyes black. Eyes that were small glittery spots.

The dark deepened outside, and I heard the door, and three men came in, wearing jeans, wearing keys on their belts, with fat wallets in back pockets, and the one on the right had the needle, and the middle one had thinning hair, had black frames on his glasses, and he was bored, he was a man cleaning a toilet.

I stayed at the wall, and the wipe was cold, and the needle hardly pinched, hardly burned.

They went out, and the lock clicked, and the eye watched me for two minutes and an hour, and I was twenty-four.

A man said, You're just a boy.

He said, You're a child.

I tried to stay close to walls. The walls were cool, were solid.

DAYS WERE LONG as death, sitting in the dayroom in front, and sitting in the dayroom in back, and standing up, walking, sitting, standing again. Men with keys walked by, and nurses in blue jeans stayed in the nurses' office, and came out to say it was time for shots or pills.

I sat the way Rolfe sat, with his beard and size, in the orange chair with chrome armrests. Rolfe didn't move. A fly came and landed on Rolfe's cheek, and he didn't twitch or blink or even breathe.

Rolfe wore black and red shirts that hung down the outside of his pants, and he wore blue painter's pants wide as a lake, and brown corduroy slippers, and the heel was crushed down, was flat as a thong.

Rolfe weighed three hundred pounds, and he never smiled, never sneezed, never said a word to anybody. He sat in the back dayroom, and I watched him.

I went twice to his room to check the name printed on the card on the door. The card said, Rolfe, Thomas J., and the J was for James or John or Joseph.

Sometimes Rolfe was gone, to some life in Medford or Arlington or Boston. Rolfe was riding streetcars and buses, and people watched Rolfe and wondered who he was and how he got so big, and how hard it was to move all that size, that weight.

I WALKED, AND TRACED the wall with my fingers. My fingers were long and skinny, and there were small white scars on the back of my left hand, just above the knuckles, and I thought of the way the doctor in the emergency room looked at me, then looked at the hand, then lifted the small flaps of skin.

Nice, he said. Clean.

He injected my hand with Novocain and began to sew with black thread, saying the whole time, Clean. Pretty. Very nice.

He had blond hair, and wore glasses with amber frames.

I WAS SKINNY AS WIRE, and stayed in a chair in the back dayroom, then walked the halls for ten or twenty minutes, and watched the hands on the clock never move. I came in a police car, with a heavy grate between the front and back seats, and I asked the police for a cigarette.

At the emergency room I swung at a man who said, Too bad, and they all came in. Then an ambulance came, and there were small buildings spread over hills, and a green, rusting water tower.

The doctor wore a robe, and had a red spot like a ruby on her forehead. The robe was maroon and had peacock feathers on it. Men with keys were outside, in the hall.

She smiled, and the ruby in her forehead didn't move. She had black hair in a braid that hung to her waist, and her skin was brown. She had teeth like piano keys.

She said, What brings you to us, and smiled.

She said she would be grateful if I would answer a question or two. Would I be willing? Could I do that for her?

She said, Strike when the iron is hot. What does that mean? She said, The grass is always greener on the other side of the fence. She said, A rolling stone gathers no moss.

She wanted me to name the last five presidents, and asked me what I did for fun. Do you have a sweetheart? A special someone?

Is your mother living? Is your father alive?

I wanted to sleep in a bed that drifted over water and clouds.

We would like to help, she said. She shifted the robe on her shoulder.

The man was at the door. She signaled with her hand. Her hand lifted and moved like a handkerchief on a clothesline.

I was air and sticks and things that grow on walls.

She said, Thank you very much.

We drove, and it was raining, was drumming the hood and the roof, was tapping the windows and running down.

7

They smiled, and put things in an envelope. The watch hadn't worked in weeks. A social security card, a key ring with three keys, and two dimes, a penny, a quarter, a rubber band.

They said, Sign down here, and pointed. The woman wore a wedding ring. She brushed her cheek with her hand.

I signed three pieces of paper. Will Ross, Will Ross, Will Ross.

They said, Stand up, and took my belt and shoelaces.

They said, Okay.

We went down the hall. Here, they said. Inside was a bed, a chair, a wardrobe.

I stepped out of the sneakers because they flapped around my feet. I took my pants off, and sat on the edge of the bed.

There was wire mesh on the window. The window was open a few inches, was open enough for air.

He said, You're set, and shut the light off, and I stayed on the bed, and listened and heard rain outside. It fell like it meant to drown the world, and way off, on roads that curved past trees and walls, the water made everything fast and slippery, and windshield wipers went back and forth and back and forth, and water streamed down the glass, and sheets and blankets of water crossed the road, and it was darker than midnight, darker than two a.m.

I PUT THE PILLOW on my head, and saw them pass outside in the hall, the light bouncing over the ceiling.

Hey, I almost said.

Hey, I nearly whispered.

THE NIGHTS WERE SLOW as erosion, as the movement of glaciers, as the formation of rock. I whispered in the dark, to the wall next to the bed, and I could see sound waves leaving my mouth, and crossing to the wall where they broke and dissolved like pond water.

The footsteps came, stopped at my door, and I was invisible as air.

A man stopped and shined the light on me.

What, I asked, and he said, Shhh, in a slow voice, a voice of sleep.

Then he padded away, and I pictured Jasmine, her brown eyes, her nose and lips. Jasmine crawled into bed with me, naked as stone, her skin cool and smooth, her breasts and hips against my side. I could feel nipples, elbows, chilly feet. Her fingers were feathers, everything was swimming.

Will, she whispered, and her breath was fingers.

Where you going? she whispered at three a.m.

She sipped gin and tonic, and ice clicked the side of the glass, and a slice of lime floated on top like ice, and her lips and tongue were cool.

Hey Will, she whispered, and licked my lips.

Hey, old pal, why you here? she wanted to know. Why'd you come this way?

Her mouth was a bruise at three a.m.

How come? she asked, and she touched my ear with her tongue.

Water flowed darkly and silently past the window.

Hey, Will Ross, she whispered. You miss me?

WHEN I WAS TWENTY-FOUR, they swabbed the skin on my arm with alcohol, popped the needle in, pushed, drew it out, put a cotton ball on the spot. They did it so fast I wondered if they'd really done it, then I walked.

There were other people. There were two men named Angus, there was a Bill, a Matthew, an Ethel, a Maureen. There was a Julian who had dark hair, and wore canvas loafers and never spoke.

Lillian spoke all the time, spoke in floods of words, for hours and hours, up the hall and down the hall, in the front and back dayrooms. In baggy dresses with flowers, in a white cardigan.

They stole her house, they stole her kids, they'd implant listening devices where her ears used to be, but she wouldn't let them, she didn't care who said so or who didn't say so. This was America, where the buffalo roam, where Davy Crockett died so that we might enjoy the fruits of freedom, and she didn't care if President Carter or J. Edgar Hoover or Eleanor Roosevelt said so.

Her hair was gray, and a clump was gathered into a squirrel's tail at the side of her head with ribbon, but the ribbon was trailing onto her shoulder. She'd been at a party, at a parade.

DURING THE EVENINGS, the rooms were unlocked, and the small clicks from fingers and doors and locks traveled the halls. Rolfe sat in the dayroom, in a Hawaiian shirt, and he looked, but I couldn't tell what he saw.

I was near a window, and Angus flicked his cigarette. It landed on my arm, and I watched it burn through my shirt, and burn my skin.

Angus smiled. He had wet eyes. He watched me.

I stood up and went over to him. I kicked him in the thigh, in the side, in the shin. He dropped to the floor and crawled to the wall.

Hey, someone shouted. Hey, they yelled.

I was in the room again, and the nurse with glasses said, You want Bridgewater? You think you'd like that? She closed the door and clicked the lock, and I stayed where I was.

My mother and father didn't know, and Martha and Eric and Seamus and Greta didn't know either. They were my brothers and sisters, and they had no idea.

There were five of us, and if I went to Bridgewater there might be four of us. Bridgewater was ten or twenty miles away, and Bridgewater was for baby killers, for people who needed thirty days or five years before they stood trial.

Bridgewater had dripping water and bars. Bridgewater had guards, and naked people would squat in corners and sing and cry and masturbate at the same time.

I would have sympathy cards, and my arm patted. Long looks into my eyes, black suits, dark ties.

We're sorry. We're very sorry. We're awfully sorry.

Hey, I whispered at night, after the lights were out. Hey, hey.

Jasmine was trying to come to me, and Rolfe was there. Rolfe had pajamas with cars on them, and crushed slippers. Rolfe didn't move. Rolfe didn't blink or breathe.

THE POLICE WORE GUNS that were so black they were blue. They wore thick belts, they had handcuffs, radios, pens, cigarettes.

I went quietly, softly, silent as stone, down the front stairs, in blue sneakers, a sweatshirt, in shorts that flapped around my thighs. The car was sitting in the driveway, and a woman across the street stood and watched.

A cop opened the door, and I got in, and the radio squawked, said, Ninety-three, that's 410 Walnut, past Homer. There was static. A different voice said, Right.

They pulled out, and I closed my eyes, and I could hear the car glide through traffic like a shark. Everything cleared silently away, made a path. We were underwater, we were blips on sonar.

ROGER KIAM HAD THICK GLASSES and a tattoo on his forearm. Betty, it said, with a heart and laurel. Roger Kiam had tiny scars all up and down his arms. He shot heroin between his toes, in his ankles, in the side of his neck.

He lit a Camel from Wayne Costello's cigarette. Wayne Costello didn't talk. He was Rolfe, only skinny.

Roger Kiam blew smoke at the ceiling, swallowed. He stared at the ceiling. A spot on his cheek moved.

He said, I get into any house I want. The rich pricks. Newton, Wellesley, Weston, anywhere. Any house. Any time. They're sleeping, they're away, they're screwing each other. I get in.

He said he went at night. The deep lawns, the old trees. He went at one or two. At four or five a car on the street would be noticed. At four or five people were awake, waited for birds, for gray light. At one or two they slept and didn't notice. He pulled into driveways, shut the lights off, cut the motor. He sat for five or ten minutes, looking at bushes, at windows, at porches. He listened for traffic, noticed the cars.

Then he got out, and crossed the lawn. He wore running shoes, a navy blue watch cap, dark clothes, prescription sunglasses. Even at one or two, he said, there were noises. Branches, leaves, creaking boards, insects. He said he was invisible, and it was amazing how often windows were unlocked.

He blew smoke. Rich pricks, he said. Then he looked across the dayroom. He moved his fingers. Tap. Tap. Drum.

JASMINE CAME AT NIGHT, at midnight or one. I left the back door unlocked, and she came up the stairs, tapped on the door. She kissed me, put a six-pack of beer on a chair. She said, God, and pressed my arm, and I kissed her white neck.

She wore a tee shirt, no bra, shorts and sandals. She had brown eyes, had pale, pale skin. She said, C'mere, and led me to the bed.

She pulled her tee shirt over her head. She unsnapped and unzipped her shorts, dropped them, took off her panties.

Then we were lying on top of the covers, and we handed a can of beer back and forth.

She said, Nice, and I touched her breasts.

She touched me.

Then she got on top of me, and I was inside, and she

talked as she moved up and down.

You like that, she said and I couldn't speak. Her breasts were moons, were heavy, were cool and warm. She brushed my face with her breasts.

You like this, Will Ross. You like being inside me.

We made slippery, sucking, slapping sounds. She moved one nipple, then the other, to my mouth.

Very sweet, she said. My sweet Will Ross.

Then we were lying in sweat, lying side by side, and she moved a finger from my nose to my mouth to my ear.

What're you gonna do? she asked, and I watched her face.

We pulled a blanket over us, and cracked beers, and smoked. We listened to John Coltrane and Pharoah Sanders on the radio. Then it was three, and Jasmine was asleep. She breathed slowly, and I drifted, like this was water, and we were a long way from land.

WHEN I WAS TWENTY-FOUR and skinny as thread, my hands shook when I lit cigarettes. I held them between my lips and put the heads of lit cigarettes to the unlit ends, and my hands were plugged in, wouldn't stop, wanted to dance.

Rolfe sat in his chair, and an aide whispered something in Rolfe's ear, then walked away.

Hey, I almost said.

It rained and rained. Like we would float away to some island, then sit forever. We'd sit under trees, near sand, watching water curl and foam.

When I got up late—at two or three, to go to the bathroom, and stood in the echoing tiles—I was as far away as I ever wanted to go. Down a thousand miles of road, beyond turns and forks, past trees and bushes, with eyes staring. I thought of how streets shined at night, when Roger Kiam was out, and cats moved in yards, and I'd be moving like a cat. Nobody could see me. I didn't say a word.

They walked through, and I watched, and Jasmine was

gone. She'd gone a long time ago. She was in Florida, was married to a lawyer. And people walked by, walked up and down the long hallway, past the back dayroom to the hall, then down again. They walked like they couldn't stop. Roger Kiam and his tattoo, Wayne Costello not saying anything, Lillian and her house, her kids, her job, her car.

But Rolfe sat and I sat, and Bridgewater was fifteen miles away if I did anything else. I watched and it was July, and I had come with the police, after the emergency room and the man with glasses asking questions.

How come? a woman asked all the time. Asked me, asked Rolfe and Wayne Costello, asked the small man with dark hair.

God knows, she said, and her voice rose and deepened and shook.

I don't like the sound, she said, and I pictured a skinny man like me under a sheet and a pale gray blanket. The pillow white, the bed a rectangle, and diamonds of light over everything, where it came from outside, crossed mesh, and made him pale as death, and just as quiet.

There were other times in a life. At four years old, at seventeen, at fifty-two. Dying at seventy-three, or riding a trolley somewhere. Cambridge at four a.m., and outside the window, on Quincy Street, the snow fell, and a woman in a beret and long coat walked in the middle of the street, and the light was powder at two a.m. The light made her glow.

MY FATHER WHISPERED. He said, Will, and his voice was quiet as wood, as walls, as a long night.

I said, Hey.

He was short and thin, was only five five. I was tall and thin, was six one.

Will, he whispered—when I was four, when I was seven, when I was eleven.

You okay, Will, he said. You okay?

14

I stopped breathing and my body was growing cool, was bluing, my forehead was marbled.

He moved quietly, and I heard him sobbing at night, in the kitchen, like something would never be found, and nothing—anywhere—could help.

Dad, I whispered when I was twenty-four. Dad, I said.

But the sobs made his shoulders heave, made his whole body shake, and when I was twenty-four I would whisper at four a.m., and he'd say, Will, and smile.

He had thin arms, and wore white shirts with short sleeves, and the sleeves hung on his arms, and came down to his elbows. He wore ties and baggy pants and black shoes.

I said, Dad, and he stayed at the kitchen table, his head on his folded arms, his face on the table, sobbing.

WHEN I WAS TWENTY-FOUR, they moved at night like they were invisible. They moved with their lights, and Roger Kiam slept, and the new guy named Neal slept in the room beyond Rolfe. Neal was skinny and wore glasses and smoked all the time. His index and middle fingers were yellow from nicotine. He did something to his father. Neal's father was in a hospital in Boston, and would recover. He'd be walking around.

They moved at night, and for three or four days and nights the temperatures were in the middle nineties—ninety-four and ninety-seven and ninety-five. And at night the walls were wet, and nothing could move. The beams of light were slow.

Then it rained, and windows blew and banged, and the rain streamed against the glass.

I don't know, I whispered.

I got a shot, and then the shots stopped too. A man in a suit said, A bird in hand is worth two in the bush.

He said, You can't tell a book by its cover. Then he smiled. He had a secret.

Tell me please. Do you masturbate? Do you enjoy orgasms?

15

He had a Spanish accent. He had black hair, and faint stripes in his suit.

Tell me please, he said.

His room was piled with folders and books and papers, with notebooks and looseleaf binders and paper clips.

You are a nice and attractive young man.

Then in Harvard Square, at fifteen, the man smiled and said I was nice, did I want coffee.

He wore a dungaree jacket and a brown leather tie. He said he saw me sitting on the concrete wall and he wondered.

Like I didn't know where to go or what to do. Like I'd lost my last friend in the world.

He patted my arm. His fingers were long, were white, and his fingernails were shiny.

I saw you, he said, and smiled, and his nose and ears reddened. Sitting there, and looking—well—so lost, frankly, if I knew what he meant.

He put his arm across my shoulders like a scarf. His voice grew low, grew soft, grew quiet as midnight.

His name was Dan, and he got lonely, and he noticed me, for all the world like my last best friend had gone to Patagonia, to Greenland, to the deserts of Australia.

He smelled like pine. He said he found me attractive.

THE PILLS WERE BLUE and the pills were yellow and the pills were fat and white. They came in brown containers. Some of the tablets were lime green, and some were orange and raspberry like sherbet.

The containers were in a drawer next to my bed, and I got two pills out and swallowed. Then I sat and my hands stopped shaking. Then I took two more, then another two, and it was ten or twelve, it was sixteen or eighteen.

ANGUS WAS FORTY-ONE, and his mother was in Wrentham State Hospital, and he'd been at Wrentham too. Then Met State in

Waltham, Northampton State, Danvers State, Medfield. He had a room, and he collected paper. Paper from cigarette packs, old newspapers, pages from folders, wrappers, napkins, sheets of toilet paper.

He tucked his shirts inside his underpants and cinched his belt tight.

They give me roast beef, he said. Potatoes, green beans, cake for dessert. Green icing. Coffee, sugar and cream. Anything. They tell me, Okay, Angus, that be fine with us. That be fine with you.

He looked at the ceiling, looked over his shoulder, then down at his shoes. He wore hiking boots, double knotted.

They take me to dinner, Angus said. I get hamburger, I get a pack of Camels, I get ice cream I want it. Chocolate, vanilla, they put sprinkles on it, hot fudge, butterscotch. They will, he said. They do that for me.

AT TWO OR THREE I could hear things in the walls and floors. Boards, joists, plaster. Shifting, stretching, groaning from the weight.

Before, when I walked in Newton and Watertown, in Cambridge and Boston, I saw things at two and three. Saw shadows, saw drifts of steam, saw green and red and blue lights in puddles blinking and blinking and blinking like something that couldn't stop, that couldn't help itself. Cars went by on Boylston Street, on Mass Ave., and kids stood at corners, kids in thin jackets, and they smoked and laughed. They had fights, they smoked more, they looked up and down Tremont Street, up Mount Auburn, then in the windows of stores.

In Watertown Square the river moved like silver under the bridge, and the buses were no longer running, and cars went around the rotary like pilot fish, like barn cats, like bats fleeing light. Air and earth and water.

A woman said, I don't care if that goes fast or slow. I can

sit and I don't need to tell.

She had a front tooth missing, and a black overcoat, and she said she could sit. Left to her own devices, she said.

She wiped her mouth and watched traffic circle the Square. The lights from cars flicked in her eyes.

IN THERE THE SHEETS were white and there was a light over the parking lot at the side of the building, and bats moved and it grew cool in July, in 1978. Down to forty at night, in the sixties afternoons.

Then Rolfe was gone. The chair in back, the chair in the front dayroom, were empty, and the card was gone from his door. Rolfe, Thomas J., and J stood for James or John or Joseph.

Rolfe was somewhere, Rolfe was a stone. A fly could settle, and Rolfe didn't breathe.

I sat in the back dayroom. The windows looked out over trees and hills and fields, and there were lines of road in the hills, and a car moved on the lines.

And late, when steam rose from pipes and nothing moved anymore in the streets of Boston and Newton, I'd lie on the bed and my brain went from fourteen years old to thirty-three to nothing even, and I tried to breathe slowly, and forced air through my arms and legs, but still it rushed like something trapped, like something that would die soon.

Then the footsteps were outside and bats went wildly past eaves.

My father was turning over in bed, in his white tee shirt, his boxer shorts, tissues bunched in the arm of his tee shirt.

Rolfe was in a room somewhere, with a hotplate and a water stain on the wall over his bed. Rolfe got a check every month and his pill containers were on the bureau, and there were cigarette burns in the wood on the bureau, and there was a chair from a kitchen set, its chrome flecked with rust, its plastic broken, its stuffing leaking out.

18

Rolfe sat near the window, and down the hall there was a bathroom, and no one cleaned the sink, and in the rooms along the hall there were televisions, and voices and music and laughter on the televisions.

Rolfe watched the street, and nothing moved or flicked across his face. Rolfe with his beard and size, Rolfe in his room in Waltham or Dorchester or Brighton. And I was in bed, in there, when I was twenty-four, and I was sticks and wire. I was a blip, a spot, a thing that happened at night. I was air, was darkness, was something from sleep.

two

At four years old, near Boston, I didn't know anything. I
stayed in bed and watched light move across the ceiling, light from cars that passed outside.

Eric was sleeping above me, on the top half of the bunk
bed, and I could hear him breathe deeply.

I watched darkness in the room, dark shapes, things in
the closets and under the bed. A man came to the front door
sometimes, rang the bell, wore a uniform from the Salvation
Army. He had a bucket with a slot on top, and had yellow
teeth, gray hair, red and blue eyes. I'll take her, he said, and
pointed to Martha, and laughed and Mom laughed and
Martha hid. He was under the bed. He carried a black sack,
and would take Martha away, and then he'd take me.

The air was cold outside, had icy hands, had icicles for
fingers, and found its way through cracks, through places
between shingles, boards, plaster. Thin places between the
wall and window, and the air was full of snow, and when I
breathed I could see the vapor, like icy fire, like something
from hell.

The radiator clanked and rumbled and hissed. It banged, and down in the cellar there was a furnace, and late at night, when I should have been sleeping, a man was down there. Not the Salvation Army man, but another man who wore black clothes and boots to his knees, and he smelled like the Charles River in spring. His face was sooty and his eyes were blue like winter water when there were no clouds. Just deep and clear and cold and blue.

He sat in the cellar all night, and he opened the furnace and looked in, and beads of sweat rose on his face, and his hair hung in front of his face, was vines, and he looked into the red center.

If I didn't sleep, he'd come up here, up the cellar stairs, past the door to my grandmother and grandfather's house, up the next stairs, and he'd come to the door and lift me, blankets and all. I couldn't scream. Someone had stolen my voice.

IN THE DAY IT WAS different, because everyone was gone, except for me and Seamus and Greta and Mom, and she wore glasses that lit her face like the front of a car. Seamus and Greta were lumps in blankets, only Seamus could get out of the blankets and crawl like a bug, but fat and slow, and he'd roll onto his side or back, and begin to scream so loud that I tried to put something into the hole in his face.

Greta was a blanket and a face, and Mom picked her up and poked at the blankets near her face and made noises, and Greta smiled and moved her hand like something in wind.

She gurgled, and Seamus crawled across the kitchen floor. I was under the table, and the legs of the table were bars, and Mom's legs were at the stove. Seamus tried to crawl to me, and I put a chair in his way. He tried to crawl between the rungs of the chair, and I put my foot there and wedged him between the rungs.

He squirmed and gasped. The gasps grew deeper, then he

21

began to cry. I moved my foot, and Mom squatted down, looked at me, and lifted Seamus in her arms.

Dunhdunhdunhdunh, he cried, and he was fat and blond, and was two years younger than me.

There, Mom said. There, there, she said, and his cries turned to gasps, his gasps to breathing, then he was on her shoulder, his head against the side of her neck, his legs hanging like doll's legs down her front, and his eyes blinked, looked, blinked more, looked, then closed. His eyelids fluttered, were wings, then stayed closed. I watched through the rungs of the chair.

DAD WAS TIRED. Dad needed to shave. He wore gray work pants and boots and a sweater from the Army with a hole in the elbow. He worked at a factory moving boxes and writing orders, and on Saturday and Sunday he wore a tie, and worked at an office in a hospital in Brighton.

He fell asleep in a chair in the living room, and there was an iron bed with a mattress that was a couch, and he talked in his sleep, said, Yaaaaaaa, and the sound trailed away like a train going through a tunnel.

He had to sleep because he worked so hard to put food on the table, to keep a roof over our heads. Otherwise we'd be out in the cold, and hungry, and we didn't appreciate what we had, didn't know how lucky we were, how good we had it.

You can bet on that, my grandmother said. You better believe it.

She had hands like rakes. Rakes with cables, with golf ball knuckles. Her voice was deep like a furnace. She wore glasses with steel frames, and light reflected off the glass like sun on snow.

Don't stare. Don't you dare stare, she said.

He's a wonderful man, she said, her arms folded on her chest. You don't know from Adam.

Adam was in the Bible. Someday I would know, I would

22

find out what he did if I wasn't a retard or something.

She lived on the first floor, with Bamp, our grandfather. He smoked a pipe and cigars, and he had an ashtray in the living room like a Viking ship.

They discovered America before Columbus was even born, but he was an Italian, and they stuck together, the Italians, so he got credit, not the Vikings from Sweden. Gram was a Swede, but otherwise we were Irish. Like Mrs. Murphy's pig.

We got chased out of Ireland for stealing sheep, Bamp said, and sucked flames into his pipe, his face a cloud. He smiled and Gram chuckled, and her mouth was crooked. Don't you know it, she said, and turned and winked at me.

HE SLEPT IN A CHAIR in the living room upstairs, above Gram and Bamp, his mouth open, his face sandpaper, and his eyes sunk back like he didn't get enough to eat.

Hey, Dad, we said. Hey, we said to him, and Martha sat on the arm of the chair, her legs long as broom handles.

Hey, Daddy, she whispered, and he looked up, and his eyes were black circles all the way back in his head. Eric was next to her, and leaned his side into the chair where Dad was.

Hey, Martha said, and Dad's eyes were closed.

ON THE FIRST FLOOR they had chairs with dark wood and a couch and pillows, and chairs with dark red cushions built into the seats. They had a den with a television, and chairs with stools for your feet.

We watched the fat man and the man with the hat and vest. People somewhere laughed. Bamp was in his chair, his feet up, and Gram was in her rocking chair, and Mom sat in the kitchen chair she'd brought in, and me and Eric and Martha sat on the floor.

The fat man pretended to dance, and Mom laughed, and Gram said he was fifty if he was a day. The light of the television flicked on her glasses.

Bamp's eyes were closed, and he breathed like a radiator, then Mom had to go upstairs. She said, You kids come up when this is over, and Gram said, I'll see that they do.

Then a woman came into the room on television, and outside the window there was a brick wall and a fire escape, and the woman looked at the man with the hat, then at the fat man, and said, That's right, Ralph, and everybody laughed.

The back door opened and closed, and Mom's feet went up, soft as night and far away.

Bamp breathed through his mouth, and the pipe was in the Viking ship.

You need to be careful when you go out, Gram said. She crossed and recrossed her arms, and looked at us.

They come in cars, in black cars, and they steal children.

How come? Martha asked.

They don't like questions, Gram said. They don't look highly on that.

She looked at Martha, and then she looked at me, even though I hadn't said anything.

She motioned with her big hand for Eric to sit at her feet. He moved over, and she put her hand on his head. She moved her fingers through his hair, and his eyes began to close. Bamp was snoring, and there was noise from the television.

They take children every day, Gram said. Mae Kelley lost two. Steve and Jane, she said, and looked from Martha to me, then over to Bamp. His mouth was open like Dad's.

It broke her heart. Poor Mae. Steve was four years old like you, she said. And Jane wasn't much older; a year or two.

They'll be walking along, watching the clouds in the sky.

Why, Gram? Martha asked.

They know how nasty children are. They're spoiled rotten, and they lie all the time. So the black cars come, and go up and down, just waiting.

She put her hands in her lap, and smoothed her dress on her knees.

They keep them in cellars, and give them bread and water. They don't let them out. There's water on the floor, and rats in the water, squealing.

Bamp blinked and stopped snoring. He got his pipe from the Viking ship, and stood up. He looked at us, and went to the hall. He didn't see us.

You have to watch, and you have to do what you're told, Gram said. She looked at the television, then she began to move her fingers through Eric's hair again.

God sees, Gram said.

Where? Martha said.

Everywhere, Gram said. Past the mountains and oceans. Far away, under the bed at night.

She sat back, and there was applause on television. Bamp flushed the toilet, and Gram said, Okay.

We got up, and the back hall was dark, and we could feel the cold from outside. I was behind Martha and Eric, and I ran so fast up the stairs I tripped, and my legs were on the lower stairs and someone was reaching for them.

Eric and Martha were in the upstairs hall, and the door to the kitchen opened and closed, and someone was holding my ankles.

WE WALKED A LONG long time. We walked past houses, crossed streets, waited for the lights to turn yellow and red. We passed a gas station, hedges, and then we walked more. Me, Eric, Martha and Dad.

Then we were inside, and the ceiling had pictures and was tall as the sky. The sounds echoed, and bells tinkled, and there were people, and they wore black and were giants. They stood up and kneeled and sat. They spoke together, and the whole house rumbled, then people stood in the path and walked to the front.

The front was the altar, and the men there wore gold with white and black at the neck and sleeves. They lifted their hands, and the altar was a giant birthday cake.

The people walked up and kneeled along a rail, and the man in white put things in people's mouths. Dad stood and went up the path, and in front of us there was a lady with fur around her neck and shoulders, and there were feet in the fur, and a furry head with glittery eyes, and Martha whispered that a kid was taken away, and a rat bit him, so he grew fur and died.

Dad came back, and smiled with his mouth closed, and he kneeled down and put his face in his hands. He didn't look up until the man in white spoke, and everything echoed like God in heaven, in his mercy and love.

He was crucified, died and was buried, the man said.

Crucify was when they nailed you to a cross and hung you for all the world to see, and Jesus hung there looking at the world.

He was still hanging in the front, but it wasn't him. The real Jesus was light and air, the man said. You couldn't see light, but it was there, and at night in bed, it was not there.

He was the Father, the Son and the Holy Spirit. Amen. You could talk to him with prayers.

Our Father, full of grace, the man in white said. Everyone spoke the words with him, and everything echoed and drummed and shook.

By his mercy.

In his wisdom.

With his love.

World without end, Amen.

We stood up, and Dad had his arm around Martha, and the people were tall as trees, and outside was clear and cold.

UNDER THE BED was dusty, and there were shoes. The covers hung down, and closed everything in. Nobody knew I was under the bed, because there was no room, and dust, and my mom said, Will, and looked in the closet and behind the door.

William Ross, she said, come here, and I didn't breathe.

Dad came down from the third floor, and said, Will, but I didn't move.

There was nothing for a long time. There were footsteps going down to the first floor, then a door, then nothing. The refrigerator ticked and hummed, and clocks ticked, and there were bee sounds way off in the distance.

I could stay a week or a month and nobody would find me, and then I'd die. They'd pull me out from under the bed, and I wouldn't be alive anymore. Just like I was sleeping, only I wouldn't be breathing.

They'd lie me down, and Mom would comb hair out of my eyes with her fingers and cry and tears would drop onto my face, but I wouldn't feel them.

People would come to see me lying there dead, and they'd feel bad because I was dead and had been under the bed alone so long. Gram and Bamp, and Eric and Martha and Seamus, and even Greta, in her blankets, would look at me, and Mom and Dad would be sad, and they would never be able to see me again to say how sad they felt.

And it would be for the best.

THE ROOM WAS SPINNING around and around, and I ran. I went fast toward the bathroom, and reached the hall, and my stomach came up—green and brown, with gravy over everything. On the wall and baseboard and floor, and Mom said, Will, and she took me by the shoulders and to the bathroom and held my head over the toilet.

It was white, and I saw water, saw white sides. I could feel the white against the side of my face. It was cold as nights.

Someone was turning the room around and around, slowly, and the walls tilted and I was falling over, only Mom held my head over the toilet and my face almost touched the water. I could see my face in the water, and next to my face, the ceiling—the light, and a string hanging down.

Greta was crying. Greta screamed, and the men in black cars must have been taking her. The Salvation Army man, moving quickly. He looked over his shoulder, and went down a street, then cut down a driveway. He went between bushes, over a chain-link fence, down another driveway, past a garage. He moved faster and faster, behind the backs of houses, between the boards on fences.

I lay back, and the floor was cold. There was sweat on my face and arms and back, but it was cold like wind. It was hot and cold at the same time. Then a fist clenched and unclenched in my stomach, and below my stomach, and everything kept spinning. The feet of the bathtub, the small table next to the sink, and green liquid came up, but only a little on the floor by my face.

Then I was in bed, and had a bowl at the side of my head, and three blankets on top. Eric wasn't there. Eric went someplace else. Eric wouldn't catch this.

There was a glass stick in my mouth. You're burning up, Mom said. You're a furnace. Don't bite down. Don't leave on me. Don't go.

On the other side of the wall or window there were sounds. In the cellar, and water sloshed against my feet. I heard squeaking, but there was a woman with brown eyes, and white teeth. She put her arms around me, and whispered a song. In the hills far away. In the hills beyond, there's a house in a glade of pine. Where birds do sing, where bells do ring.

I looked up and she smiled. There I'll be, there you'll find me. When I'm home, when I'm home, she sang.

A fire was burning in a fireplace, then a door opened and wind and snow came in. My stomach heaved, and something came up, and went into the bowl.

Hey, Will, Martha whispered from the door. I'm sorry.

She stood in a yellow light. I didn't mean it, Will. I won't do it again.

Martha, Mom hissed. Martha, this instant.

Fog came, and I was rocking. My back and legs were wet. There was water under my hair. I was still cold, and people would come for me.

Mom sat on the edge of the bed, and pushed hair off my forehead, and her mouth was a line. The back of her fingers moved on my face.

Mom said, Gram was asking for you. She wanted to know you were all right. I said you were. I said you'd get better.

Then I was under, and lying there without breathing, and they left me. They walked by and looked down and felt bad. They wore black, and their hair was combed, and they wished I wasn't dead. They wished I would sit up, and breathe.

But it was too late, and they were sorry.

GRAM POINTED TO A CHAIR at the kitchen table, and moved her hand for me to sit down. A tray of cookies was sitting on top of the stove and another tray was in the oven. She took a napkin, put cookies on it, then poured a glass of milk. She set them on the table.

My mother had cancer, she said. It killed her, in 1949.

She opened the oven and took out cookies. The coils were red like a furnace.

You don't know what that's like, she said. To watch your mother die. To watch her waste away to next to nothing.

She sat down. She motioned with her hand for me to eat. The cookie was warm and the oatmeal didn't taste like breakfast. There were raisins and cinnamon and brown sugar.

Go ahead, she said. She took off her glasses and there were red spots high on her nose. Her eyes were smaller and less blue without her glasses. They were sunk farther back in her head.

How would you like that, she said. See your mother waste

away, day by day, no hope for recovery?

Her eyes were wet.

Screaming out, the pain was so bad.

She wiped her glasses with a napkin. I could feel the heat from the oven. I took small bites from the cookies, sipped milk.

They doped her up, but that didn't much help. They shot her full of morphine, and she didn't know who I was, she was so far away. Whaaa, whaaa, Gram said, her hands up, her face distorted. She reached in front of her with blind hands.

Just like that, she said, and sniffed, then blew her nose. There were tears near the red spots at the side of her nose.

Screaming out for Pa.

Gram got that look on her face again. Pa, Pa, don't let them do this. Don't let them, Pa.

She looked at me, then put her glasses on.

We had the coffin closed. She was eighty-three pounds. Her hair was white, and most of it had fallen out. Her fingernails yellow, and her eyes just burning, way back there in her head. Just burned back like fire. Watching and crying, Pa, don't let them.

She called me on the phone, and said, I have cancer of the bones and won't live much longer. We had the phone in the hallway, in Newton Corner, on Emerson Street. I looked at the table, at a card from church with Jesus on the front, and a gold ring over his head.

How could you, I said to Jesus. Why do this to me?

IN THE KITCHEN on the second floor, only Mom and Dad were up, and they stayed in the kitchen, at the table, and their voices were low.

Mr. Ryan from the bank called, Dad said.

The house is all we have, Mom said, and Dad didn't say anything.

Then there was no sound. Just wind and cars going by and something drumming on the roof. Drum and drum and drum, like Indians going to war.

Then there was sniffling, and Mom said, Honey, and his voice tried to say something, but couldn't. Mom said, Honey, it's okay. We'll be okay.

I don't, he tried to say.

The rain drummed, and Eric was dreaming—of a red bicycle, a baseball glove, a dog named Elgin.

I went out to the hall and stood in the doorway to the kitchen. Dad was at the table, his head down, his hands over his head. His shoulders shook.

Mom motioned for me to go away.

Go away, her eyes said. Get out of here.

THE CAT WAS GRAY and had black stripes and he was a tiger cat. He was the same as the cats in the jungle and his name was Willie. He jumped on the chair and lifted his paw to his mouth. He licked his paw, then rubbed the paw along the back of his ear.

Willie looked at us. He had green eyes with black dots at the center. He yawned. The inside of his mouth was pink.

They were ready to kill Willie, Eric told me. If it wasn't for us, they would have put him to sleep. That's what they do to cats they can't find homes for. They kill them.

He made a gun with his thumb and finger. He pointed at Willie. Bang, he said. Bang, you dead cat. They kill you if you don't have a home. They take you out to a ditch.

MOM SAID, SHHH, and it was a whisper. It was soft like covers.

She opened the book and said, A long long time ago, in a land where the sky was always blue and the sun shined and boys and girls laughed and danced in the streets, there lived a boy who was handsome and good and sad as rain. He was sad as rain because his mother and father had passed away,

31

and he lived with his kindly grandmother and grandfather, who were very kind indeed to him. But he missed his mother and father so, and sat at the window of his playroom and watched the other boys and girls, playing and laughing and dancing in the streets.

Greta was in the crib with bars like jail, but she was watching, her eyes small plates that blinked and moved. Seamus was in Mom's lap, and Eric and Martha and me were on the floor.

He loved his grandmother and grandfather. Grandmother baked muffins and cookies and had twinkling blue eyes, and grandfather had a white beard and ruddy cheeks.

One day, in the spring, on a fine May morning, Grandmother said, What shall we do with our darling boy, for he sits all day and does not play and seems as sad as rain to me.

Grandfather stroked his long white beard and said, A dog. The boy shall have a friend at last. A great brown dog with floppy ears and white feet, and we will call him Biff.

Seamus squirmed, and Mom said, Honey, and then Seamus began to cry. First softly, then louder and louder, until Martha covered her ears. Shut up, crybaby, she said.

Mom stood up with Seamus, and handed the book to Martha. Martha turned the pages, looked at a picture, turned another page.

One day, Martha said, Biff and Jimmy were walking down the street. Cars rushed by and honked, and at the curb Biff and Jimmy stepped down and a car screamed by and almost hit them and splashed them with water from a puddle.

Martha, Eric said, and we heard Mom with Seamus in the bathroom.

Dad was at the hospital, was working until seven in the morning because someone had been fired. They used matches and wood.

They went all over, Martha said. She had freckles and a big nose and she was the tallest girl in second grade.

But it got dark and dogs barked and then they looked up and there were tall buildings, taller than houses. They went into one building and everything echoed. They were hungry and wanted for food, but there was nobody there.

Then Biff barked and barked. Jimmy thought Biff saw a squirrel or a bird, but he saw foam coming from Biff's mouth. He saw Biff's teeth and Biff made a low growly sound in his throat.

Biff, Jimmy said. Here, boy, and he patted his leg. Biff barked and snapped, and Jimmy began to run. He had new sneakers and he ran faster than a car. Then he was outside and running and there were lights blinking and winking.

I WAS SOMEWHERE ELSE. I was on the porch in front, looking through the railings, and Martha and Eric were at school.

They made you work at school. They made you sit there all day and if you made a mistake they hit you. But Mom let me sit on her lap, and said nobody would hit me, not if she could help it. When she was a girl, she had no father or mother. Down in New York City, the greatest city in the world. But no place to be alone, to be a kid, she said. No, sir.

She had a mom and dad, but they put her in an orphanage, above the city, up the Hudson River, but not in Sing Sing. Sing Sing was where you went when you got sent up the river, Mom said. Up the river without a paddle, she said, and laughed and drank from a can. Drank something sour that made her laugh more.

Here, she said, and I sipped and I almost had to spit. It had bubbles and smelled like a bathroom.

She said, In Tarrytown the nuns took care of me. They sure did. They wore black, and one of them walked around at night, Sister Mary Ruth, and she turned the lights on in the middle of the night and said if she ever caught two girls in the same bed she'd fix them, she would. A hot bath to clean the filth, and a wire brush and bleach.

There was a wall, she said, and her face was different, and there was a giant oak tree next to the wall and she sat there in the summer, with a book, and the sun came down through the leaves and made her arms and legs look like gold.

Ohhhh, she said, and sipped and tears ran down her face. She smiled and said, It's okay. Mom's happy, thinking of the wall and everything I thought back then. I'd have kids, and be a dancer and a nurse and a movie star. Every week, she said, something different.

Oh shit, she said. Oh shit, she said again. Then she said everything was gone and it didn't matter. Nothing meant anything and who was there to look out for us when she was gone.

Christ, she said. Sweet Jesus, she said, and cried, and her face was red and balled like a fist.

ERIC SAID THEY CAME at night and they moved around outside. People who walked stiffly and stared straight ahead. They walked under trees, through the bushes, on the other side of the garage, near the back porch. They walked with their arms straight out in front of them. They had white white skin and blue lips and foreheads.

They're dead people, he said, only at night, when everyone's asleep, they rise out of their graves to search the world for the ones they left behind. They want to bring them back to the graves. They moan because they miss them.

Where are youuuu, Eric moaned. Come back to me, he said, his voice low and strange.

They wander all night when the moon's out, and when the wind blows. If it's been a long long time since they've seen their loved ones, they'll grab whoever's around. If you were outside, he said, they might grab you and take you back to the graveyard.

Then he stopped, and I looked out the top half of the window and the sky was black, with pinpricks of light, with stars a billion miles away. I closed my eyes and I saw them. Cold hands and mold growing in webs on their faces. They reached and I ran, and clump clump clump they came.

Eric, I said, and there was no sound at first. Then slowly, from some deep place, there was moaning, low and faint and old as earth.

GRAM SAID IN HEAVEN there were trumpets and angels flew around in white gowns and you could have as much chocolate as you wanted and you could watch television all day. You could have a bicycle and a dog and you could eat ice cream from morning till night.

There were no bills in heaven and no disease or hunger. The sun shined most days, but there were some days set aside for rain, and some days set aside for snow, and one or two days for fog or sleet or storms. But you could push a button and change that, and everyone you loved who was dead would be there, and you could see them, and sit on couches and play the harp and sing all day.

I was in Bamp's chair, my feet on the hassock, and Gram was in her rocking chair by the window. She knitted with giant needles that clicked and scraped, and that she said could be used for other things. Mom was with Greta and Seamus at the doctor. The doctor was going to stick a big needle like Gram's in their backsides. I was lucky, she said.

Gram gave me a lemon drop from a bag in her knitting basket, and put one in her mouth. Don't chew, she said. Just let it sit in your mouth.

She clicked and scraped. I hate people who crunch them, she said, and made a face. My brother George used to crunch them and it just about drove me crazy.

She held up a black knitted patch, then set it on her lap. She breathed slowly. She pulled more yarn loose from the ball in her basket. She clicked and clicked, then looked over at me.

I've always wondered about what happens there, she said. I know about the chocolate. A priest told me that. And I know some other things from people who almost died. People who stopped breathing, who had their hearts stop on them.

Ann Murphy's father, over to Hanford Street, had that. Was having his gall bladder done, and he stopped breathing on the table, surrounded by all these people in masks. Just like a bank robbery, only instead of guns they all had knives.

She looked out the window, then brushed something off the back of one hand.

He stopped breathing and his heart stopped and the doctor just about went in his pants. Don't believe what you hear about doctors, because there's a lot more than you think.

They thumped him, and stuck him with needles and knocked him on the chest. And all the time he said there was bright bright light, like the sun was in the room, only he wasn't too hot and it didn't hurt his eyes. And there was music. The most beautiful music he'd ever heard, violins and drums and everything and little boys your age singing.

And he was rising up over the table and down below he could see himself on the table, and all the doctors and nurses were dressed in white and blue and green gowns like at an altar, and the big silver light over the table, and the trays of instruments, and the tanks for oxygen and ether and whatever, all lying down there below him.

He kept floating, and he said the light was white and warm and soft, and the music went inside him, and it was so beautiful he began to cry great big tears, running down his face, like his eyes were rivers, only they were tears of joy, of the greatest happiness he ever knew.

Then he said he was on the streets in Brighton where he grew up, and the cars were black, were Mr. Ford's cars from when he was a boy. The light was like gold, and he began to see people from years ago, kids with freckles, with knickers, with high button shoes. All of them were waving at him and smiling and saying things he couldn't hear but knew were nice things. Hi, John. Welcome back. We love you. We missed you. We hope you'll never leave us again.

His best girl was there, waving and smiling and crying, then he saw his brother Walter who died of appendix when he was nine, and Walter was smiling and his sisters Mary and Catherine and Noreen were there, then he saw the house with the skinny tree in front.

He went up the stairs, slow as fog, and the door opened and Pop was in the chair, tired after work, and Mom came out from the kitchen, wiping her hands on her apron, and they saw him.

Then he was in Wellesley, and his wife and daughters were waving and Ellen, the youngest, was calling, Daddy, Daddy, even though he couldn't hear her, just read the shape of her lips, her hands cupping her mouth.

It was just fifty seconds before they got his heart going, but he said it felt like hours. And he drifted over the most beautiful fields and hills, filled with flowers and deer and light like he'd never seen.

Then she stopped. She looked at me for the first time in a while. She looked at me like she didn't know who I was, like I was a boy who came in and sat down and started to listen.

Her hands went click and scrape, and click, scrape, click, and she said, So don't tell me there's nothing there. Don't even try.

She pulled more yarn from the basket.

Because things happen, she said. Who's anybody to know.

three

At thirty-one I moved to upstate New York to go to graduate school at Cornell. I lived in a basement apartment on a street so steep it could have been in San Francisco, in an area called Collegetown, which was full of old Victorian houses crowded together. There were carved double doorways on some houses and stained glass windows in hallways and above doors. But the houses were broken into apartments, four or five or six to a house, and fire escapes were grafted onto the front and sides of the houses, and there were old couches and chairs on front porches, and when I arrived in late August, college students hung out on the porches, tan from the summer, in shorts and polo shirts and denim skirts and sneakers and sandals and Docksiders, and someone put a stereo speaker in a window, and someone bought a keg of beer, and I heard the music and voices and laughter that first week from dinnertime until two or three in the morning.

The apartment had a living room, bedroom and tiny kitchen, and a closet of a bathroom. Pipes ran along the ceiling, and the main hallway on the floor above me was directly over my bed. There was an apartment above my living room and kitchen, and an apartment beyond the bathroom and living room. Music and voices were as clear as if they came from the next room. A man named Joe lived next door, and a woman named Aleida lived overhead. I heard them talk, heard phone calls, and one night I heard a woman tell Joe that in France that summer she'd fallen in love with a Swedish student, and she didn't know what that said about her and Joe.

Well, he said, his voice a vibration, and she said she was sorry, it didn't mean anything. There were footsteps, and five or ten minutes later the outside door opened, and two dark shapes passed the windows in the living room.

I walked around those first weeks, walked in gorges and near waterfalls that seemed like something from a rain forest in Brazil or Ecuador or Guatemala, where I almost looked for vines, for rainbows at dusk, for toucans and parrots and anacondas in the trees.

There were quads on campus, and bronze statues, and trees and buildings that looked like old English churches, with domes and columns, and down below, Cayuga Lake was forty or fifty miles long, and there were hills and farms way off in the distance, five or ten or twenty miles away. There were silos and patches of field that were brown and green, and roads snaked over the hills.

I read in my apartment, and stayed awake till three or four, nights, and went out late and walked. Walked through Collegetown, through campus, then out roads to the country, past shadowy trees, and fields of corn and hay and apple orchards that smelled like wine.

I didn't talk to people for days. I stayed home from Friday until Monday. I heard footsteps and voices from other apartments and the street, and at one or two or three, after days inside, I heard a hum, and I heard boards and plaster and linoleum, and a footstep at three a.m. was loud, was important.

SHE WAS FIVE ONE or two, and I watched her in the coffee shop in the basement of Goldwin Smith Hall. She was three tables over, and her hair was short like she'd been to boot camp. She wore dangling earrings with green glass, and had small features. She wore baggy pants, black boots, a black turtleneck, a maroon suit jacket two or three sizes too big. The sleeves of the suit jacket were rolled up on her forearms, and there was a black cat pin in the lapel.

She sipped tea, and I looked at her. She looked at a book, and I watched smoke from my cigarette rise and curl, and then she looked at me.

She gathered her things and stood up, and smiled when she passed me. Her hands were white and square, and blue veins on the backs of her hands made her skin porcelain.

Then we were outside on the front steps, and I was sitting.

She sat down four or five feet over, and we looked a minute.

Hey, she said, and moved over, and we were saying where we were from, and how long we'd been around, and how we liked Ithaca. Her name was Christina and she was from Berkeley and she was a second-year student in the MFA program in writing, only she was in poetry and I was in fiction.

She liked Ithaca very much, except for the gray weather. She was from California, and that wasn't gray. California was full of light, and red and pink and green and blue, not gray. California had palm trees and the ocean was never far away, and even when it was gray in California, which wasn't often, there was fog and surf crashing the shore, and then everything cleared. An hour later the sky was blue again.

Her voice was low, and her eyes were gray and blue at the same time, and she seemed to squint.

So, she said. What about you? What's your story?

I said I didn't have one. I'm from Boston, have only been in Ithaca a month.

You like?

I said, Sure.

She lived near downtown, had an old Saab she'd driven from California.

She put her hand on my arm. Tell me, she said. Why do you like it here?

I said, I don't know.

I was in Boston once, she said. My sister was there. I liked Boston very much. Cambridge, the river. All of it. She nodded. You miss it? she asked.

Sure.

Is there a woman?

I looked at her, and her eyes watched my eyes.

Someone I should know about, she said.

I said, No.

She said something could happen. She said she could tell.

Her hand was on my forearm.

We should be honest, she said. She had a lover, and her lover was a woman, and lived with her boyfriend, and she wanted me to know. It was important.

She said we should walk. She said she had to get home because she had to grade papers, and then have dinner with Chuck. Did I know Chuck? He was great. He was a lovely guy.

She liked teaching. Everyone taught their second year. Most of the students were wonderful kids. So tentative. So smart and unsmart at the same time. Did I know what she meant?

She looked at me. Her eyes were blue, and we were walking down the long hill to lower campus. She held my arm at the elbow. She said, Why don't you walk me home? You could see where I live. Maybe have tea. Ten minutes.

Sure, I said.

She said her parents sold their house, bought a boat, were planning to sail across the Pacific Ocean. She thought they might have left. You know, she said. Run away to sea. From California, where everything ends.

The street she lived on had big houses and old trees. Her apartment had a living room, bedroom and kitchen like mine, only this was bigger, had more wood and light. There were big windows in the living room, with a tree in front of the glass, and her couch was facing the windows. The branches touched the windows, and in summer, she said, birds and squirrels came to the screen to look in.

She went into the kitchen, and I heard water in a tea-kettle, gas puffed on the stove. I heard cups, a spoon, and when she came back she had taken her jacket off. Her sleeves were rolled to her elbows and the top buttons of her shirt were undone.

She sat on the arm of the couch. She smiled, put her hand on my shoulder. How you doing? she asked.

Good.

Is this too fast for you? This worrying you?

This is fine.

You think that maybe we should go to bed together?

I watched her.

Break the ice. Get through the barriers.

When?

Now.

Her face was even, was serious.

I shook my head.

Don't you want to?

I don't know.

There were footsteps on the stairs, a key in a lock, a door opening.

This is fast, I said.

We'll be here a while, she said. It's not a wink at a bar.

I know.

But you think this is too quick?

I nodded.

The kettle began to hum. She stood up and went through the doorway to the kitchen.

I THOUGHT OF BOSTON, late, when I tried to go to sleep. I thought of Park Street subway station and the crowds in the morning, people clutching bags and briefcases and the *Globe*, staring straight ahead, or up and down. I thought of the Charles River in Newton, and how it was fifty feet wide and brown. When the Red Line train left Park Street Station it rose at Charles Station, near the hospital and jail, and the river was there, was a half mile wide and silver, and Boston and Cambridge faced each other like stages—and there was light and air and space.

Boston at night was full of lights and cars, and later, at three or four, things stopped, and I drove along Boylston Street and Commonwealth and Massachusetts Avenues, and saw shadows and cats and parked cars gleaming under the streetlights like waiting pets, and trash spilled from bags and barrels, and on windy nights pieces of paper skittered on the pavement, slapped poles, tumbled across intersections like this was Wyoming or Montana, and paper was tumbleweed and coyotes would howl at the moon.

In Ithaca I heard footsteps outside, heard people approach, move past, the sound growing softer and softer, then disappearing in the darkness, in the distance. Then nothing. Just the buzz and hum, and small creaks, and I'd picture Boston, the steam coming from vents, snow falling in Copley Square, in the plaza next to the library, falling in Kenmore Square, past the Citgo sign, past the lights of the camera and record stores, past the blinking deli and bar signs, BUD, LADIES INVITED, and frosting the ground, then deepening, and everything was black and white and silver, and the snow took on the color of the signs and shined like the first day of creation.

I pictured the airport in Boston, and planes rising over the water, and bag ladies on the Red Line train at Broadway and Andrew Stations. And at night, Boston seemed a long way off, seemed like some other, much earlier time.

SHE THOUGHT OF BERKELEY like that, she said. She thought of it all the time. She had a brother in Oakland and a brother in Marin County.

On the phone, her voice was low and slow and relaxed. Her voice was midnight, was cigarettes and drinks.

She was busy all weekend. She had to work, and she was having dinner with Moira and Sam, but she could talk a few minutes. Could I?

Her brothers were still there, and even if the house where she grew up was gone, even if her mother and father were floating somewhere near Samoa or Pago Pago, she still considered Berkeley home. And it helped to have some family there.

She sipped wine. She said wine helped her grade papers.

When can I see you? I asked, and pictured the leaves touching her windows.

She said everything was busy, and things with Amy were kind of crazy. She had to be around, to be there, for Amy, and she didn't know. She just didn't have a lot of time.

I said, I understand.

She asked how everything was. Getting work done? Still liking Ithaca?

Sure, I said.

Had I met Bill or Stephen? Stephanie or Sue Aster? They were around; she thought I might like them. Maybe when things cleared I could meet them. Maybe we could have dinner.

She sipped more, said, So you miss Boston, and I said, Yeah, it was getting strong. The missing, the ache.

She said it was like that for her at first. She said she spent most of her first year in her apartment. Then she met Amy in the spring, and started seeing more and more people.

Paul Cody

For a while she called her old boyfriend two or three times a week. He was in Berkeley and she kept asking him to move to Ithaca.

Please, she said, but he said he wouldn't have a life. He'd be an appendage in Ithaca.

I heard a door, and Christina said hi to someone, and she told me Layla was there, had dropped by, she had to go, she'd talk to me. Be good, she said.

WORKSHOP MET AT FOUR-THIRTY. We sat at a long table, and a single arched window looked onto the Arts Quad. The light changed as we sat, the shadows grew deeper outside, and some evenings there were streaks of orange and pink at the edge of the sky.

One man was from New York City, and wrote about an old Italian grandfather who lived in Brooklyn and had a vegetable garden in the backyard, and wore a fedora and suspenders when he worked in the garden. The narrator's name was Tony in the story, and he was ashamed of the old man because he always smelled of garlic and worked as a janitor all his life, and wept when he thought of his wife Angelina, an angel, the old man thought, who died on the third rail of a subway station in Queens in 1953, before Tony was born. How could Tony mourn a woman in a photograph, an oval photograph on the bureau in the old man's bedroom? All he wanted to do was play baseball and listen to Yankees games on the radio, and hear kids on the street circle the block on their bikes and yell, Hey, Jackie, Hey, Joey, Yo, Louie, Hey, Ronnie, until nine or ten, and Mickey was lifting one in the seventh inning over the upper deck, and even there on Staten Island, miles away from the Bronx, he could hear the roar, he thought, could feel the hair rise on his back as the Mick loped around the bases, and downstairs, in the front hall, his mother was hollering, Tony, Tony. Telephone. It's Tracy, Tony, and please don't stay on half the night for a change, if you

45

don't mind, Romeo. Romeo, she called again, and he knew
Tracy heard all of it.

Tracy was blond, was the same year in school, and she
was tan all summer from her lifeguard job, and he pictured
her in her bathing suit, thinking impure thoughts.

He picked up the phone in the hall, said, Hey, and Tracy
said, Tony, and he waited for the old lady to hang up.

Romeo, his mother said, loud as a megaphone, remember what I tole you.

She had to say tole instead of told, so Tracy could hear,
and know they all came from Brooklyn. And had an old
grandfather with vino and tomatoes.

The old lady hung up, and Tracy said, Guess whose
mother and father and brat of a brother are going to Cape
May for the weekend, and did he think he could get away
overnight on Saturday. He'd have to promise again not to try
to make her do anything. She'd let him touch her, but she
swore to God if he tried to talk her into anything, with all his
bullshit baby talk and moaning, she swore, she'd call the
police, so would he promise.

He said, Absolutely. He'd say he was staying at Ed's, and
she said, Maybe they could get beer and pizza and watch an
old movie on channel nine or something.

Then it was much later, and the kids weren't riding their
bikes outside and hollering Hey to each other, and Tony was
wearing underwear and lying between the cool sheets of his
bed, and the Mick had lifted one, had banged one in the
seventh, and he could hear the low moan of boats in the
harbor, and he thought about Tracy and her bare tan arms,
and just as he was falling asleep he thought of his grandfather again, in his bedroom in Brooklyn, and the photograph
on the bureau, and for an instant, at the edge of sleep, he
wanted to cry—for his grandfather and for how quickly everything was lost.

SHE SAID SHE WAS in the middle of something, and I said I was sorry. I was just calling to say hi, and she said she hadn't been sleeping much, she'd been through things with Amy, and her old boyfriend had been calling drunk from Berkeley at three a.m., and she felt she couldn't just hang up, there was two and a half years together and that meant something.

I said, I'm sorry, I can try some other time, and she said, Okay, see you, and her line clicked, and I blew smoke at the wall.

AT NIGHT, FROM THE PATH behind Uris Library, the city and lake lay below like something you'd see from an airplane—a million spots of light that couldn't rest, and the black sides of hills with occasional lights, and on the right the lake was huge and dark, was a lead sheet in the distance.

I saw people walking in groups of two and three, carrying backpacks and briefcases, to and from Uris and Olin Libraries where the windows were yellow squares, and they talked quietly, their voices rising in the darkness.

Nights grew colder, and when people spoke, plumes of vapor burst from their mouths, and they wore long coats with tails that whipped in the wind, and gloves and hats, and at the railing behind Uris Library I thought I had never seen so much light, so much space, and this wasn't a flight into Boston or New York City, this wasn't a window or a movie or a photograph. This was my life, and the people talking, the people behind the windows in buildings, the people wearing long coats, were people like me, were there, in Ithaca, in that life.

ALEIDA, OVERHEAD, SAID she was tired, and didn't know if this was a good time, and he said, That's okay. His voice was low.

I was trembling at how clearly I could hear them.

She said she was tired of going to Micah's, and he said

Micah was okay, Micah didn't mean any harm. She said, I didn't say he meant anybody harm, I just think he's boring, and Vanessa's a witch, and I hate going over there every weekend.

It's not the weekend, Aleida, he said, and there're other places we could go.

Like where.

Like Norman's, like Carrie's. We could see movies.

I heard a zipper and fabric on skin.

He yawned, and she said she was going to brush her teeth, and there was more fabric on skin. A door opened and closed, and covers were pulled back, pillows arranged.

I went to the kitchen and got a bowl for Cheerios. There were footsteps, then she must have come back. I stayed in the kitchen, ate cereal. I washed the bowl and spoon, went back to the bedroom.

The light clicked off, and there were words I couldn't make out, whispers for five or ten minutes. Then there was nothing. Just creaks, and later, the hum in the ear.

THERE WAS A POSTCARD in my English Department mailbox Friday afternoon. Flowers by Manet.

Sorry to be so out of touch, she wrote. I've been thinking of you and missing you and wishing—at times intensely—that we were together. A powerful thing, don't you think? But there's too much stuff, and I need to run away now, am leaving for D.C. this a.m., and won't be back till Tues. or Wed. but will call then. Think of me. As ever, Christina.

She wrote with a blue fountain pen, and at the top she'd written, Friday morning. I read the card two more times in the mailroom, and checked my watch. I wondered when she'd written the card, and then I imagined her stopping in Goldwin Smith on the way out of town, walking to the mailroom, scanning the names on the boxes, then seeing my name. As ever, Christina, she'd signed, and then I thought that she wouldn't be back for four or five days, and I wondered if she'd think of me in Washington D.C., and that felt strange—to think of someone thinking of me, in a city where I'd never been.

I WROTE THAT THEY WERE having dinner together, the two women, Jane and Joan. The names weren't right, but they'd do for now; I'd go back later and change them. They were at Jane's apartment. They worked together, and Joan was married, but Joan's husband Ray was a lug. Sleeping next to him was like sleeping next to a stove—all that heat and weight, all that smell. Ray had been on a business trip to Springfield, and he'd gone to bed with a prostitute he'd met in the hotel restaurant, and he didn't think it mattered. He was wearing a white tee shirt when he told her this, and he was wearing gray sweatpants and sneakers. His stomach stretched the front of the tee shirt, and Joan noticed a yellow spot on the chest of the shirt.

And at work, late in the day, at a school for retarded teenagers, Joan began to cry, and Jane put her arm around Joan and said, What, what, tell me, and Joan began to talk, and they went for a drink and then for dinner to Joan's apartment, which was in an old house, and full of polished wood and light and plants.

So the two women were in the dining room, and Joan was having her third glass of wine, and Jane had made spaghetti and a sauce that had onions and green pepper and garlic and oregano, and she grated fresh romano and made a salad with lettuce and tomatoes and basil and oil and vinegar, and Jane lit candles, and Joan said, You made dinner for me. You made dinner, and just sat there, and she began to cry, and said, I don't know the last time someone made dinner for me, and Jane put her hand on the side of Joan's face.

Jane had short black hair that was partly spiked, and she had hoop earrings and very pale skin with freckles and green eyes that looked kind of amazing next to her paper-white skin.

Joan said, I'll do dishes, and Jane laughed, said, For once, just enjoy, for God's sake, and Joan said this felt like her birthday, and steam rose from the plates, and the wine was dry and red.

Then it was later, and they were both sitting on the couch, and the room grew darker and darker, the windows were gray, then blue, then black, only slow, only they barely noticed, and Jane had her hand on Joan's arm, she brushed Joan's hair off her face, which Joan felt moved by, felt strangely touched by, like something inside was melting, like nobody had done that since she was ten or something, and her mother called her, Joanie, Joanie, and then Jane was kissing the side of her face, was saying, You're lovely. You're a gift, she was whispering. Then Jane was kissing her hand, her fingers, then it grew in wave after wave. It was tears and liquid, and Jane wasn't a stove like Ray, Jane was light and she was slow and she smelled like shampoo, like wine, and much later Joan woke up, and she was on the couch, and there was a pillow under her head and a quilt covering her that smelled faintly of cedar.

She got up, and in deep blue light from the windows, she got dressed and let herself out. She drove through empty Boston streets—this was in Boston—and saw newspaper delivery trucks, and one or two cabs, and she reached home.

Ray was asleep on the couch, empty beer bottles on the coffee table, and she helped him to his feet. She got him up the stairs, slow as erosion, one then two then three, and he didn't know where he was. Then they were in the bedroom and she helped him off with his sneakers and pants and shirt. She got him under the covers, then she got into her nightgown and into bed. The light was turning gray in the window, and she thought, Here we are. Ray and Joan. So.

SHE WAS WEARING DANGLING silver earrings, and had dark circles under her eyes. She was near the mailroom, and she said it had been good to get away.

I said thanks for the card, it was good to hear from her, and she shrugged.

You want to walk or something, I said, and she looked at her watch.

I have an hour, she said.

She said her sister Abby was really depressed, was seeing a shrink, was taking an antidepressant. She had a three-year-old boy, and her husband worked for the State Department, and was kind of nice, but kind of a prick too, and they had this townhouse in Georgetown that was just gorgeous, and Abby was working half time. The kid's name was Jeremy, and he was amazing. He had those huge kid eyes, and he asked questions constantly, like how come her hair was so short, and how come she doesn't have any kids, and how come her car was blue and not red or green, and how come she lived so far away.

She said, My mother's not the most stable person in the world. She spent time in hospitals when I was a kid, and when she was home we didn't ever know who she'd be from day to day. Whether we had a nice-lady Mom, or someone who'd empty all the closets in the house because there was hidden dirt she had to get. And her hair would be all over the place and her eyes were burning, were bright as stars.

When I was fourteen, she said, I came home from school and heard this crying and moaning in the bathroom. I knocked on the door and you know how you have that terrible sick feeling that everything's upside down and lethal? That's what it was like. I thought maybe I should turn around and go outside or something and just walk away. Leave her there.

But I didn't, of course. I knocked again, and opened the door, and she was sitting on the floor between the toilet and the tub, and there was blood all over the place. All this red, this red on white tiles and white walls and silver fixtures. There was blood on her face and in her hair and all up and down her arms, and the amazing thing was that she didn't even lose that much blood. She opened her wrist about five minutes before I came home, and then waited.

I got a towel on the wrist, and got her to hold the arm up over her head, and then I called the emergency number. Almost as soon as I hung up I could hear the siren way off, and I listened as it got closer and closer.

I went back to the bathroom and sat on the edge of the tub and said, Mom, why'd you do this, Mom, what's wrong, what're we gonna do, and I held her hand, her other hand, and the siren got closer and closer. Finally it stopped, and the doorbell rang, and three of them came in, carrying first aid boxes, and one of them even had a little oxygen tank. They were tall and they wore blue uniforms with patches on the sleeves, and I remember thinking how amazing they were. How handsome and concerned. They had short hair and they were shaved and they knew what to do.

One had a notebook, and he asked me Mom's name and age, asked for her doctor's name, if she took any medications, if she had allergies. A second one took her blood pressure and pulse, and then took the towel away from her arm, and pressed a bandage against her wrist.

They had a stretcher, and one of them asked my name and patted my back. You okay, he asked, and I remember he had brown eyes and wore a wedding ring, and I felt sad because I thought if he was married to Mom he'd know what to do all the time, and this wouldn't happen anymore.

SAM FROM WORKSHOP called and said, We should get pizza or something. You busy? Am I interrupting work?

No, just reading, I said, and he said how about I swing by, and we go downtown, and I told him where I lived. He said, Five minutes.

He had a tape deck that boomed the Talking Heads, and he said he'd thought for a while in September of leaving the program, then he thought he'd stay, because work really sucked, having a job work, and let's be realistic, Sam, he said to himself. Even if you're thirty years old, which he was, and you don't have any money, this is not a bad place to be for a few years, then he laughed, and we went down Buffalo Street, down a long hill that went for a half mile, and he laughed. You know what I mean, he said, and I told him I did.

What about you? he asked. You doing okay? You getting along in beautiful Ithaca?

I said it was okay, I didn't think much of leaving, I was doing some work and liking that.

He went sharply left at the bottom of Buffalo, said, I called and ordered. I thought we could eat at Stewart Park. You been there?

He parked, said he'd be right back, came out with pizza, wouldn't take money.

The park was at the southern end of Cayuga Lake and had willow trees and benches and swings and picnic tables. There was a carrousel and a pavilion, and maybe a half mile that fronted the lake. There were lagoons and small suspension bridges and thousands of ducks and seagulls.

We sat at a picnic table, and Sam took napkins from one pocket and cans of Coke from another pocket. He opened the top of the box and said, Eat well, Will Ross. Eat like this is the last meal in the world.

Then he smiled. Or because you're hungry, he said.

SHE COULDN'T DO IT. Friday and Saturday were booked, and she had to work Sunday. She had a new set of first drafts from her kids, and she'd hardly looked at her own work in weeks and it was driving her crazy. That's why we all came here, to get our own work done, and she couldn't get a fucking free minute and then she was supposed to do student conferences.

How was I? Was I working hard or hardly working? Was I having fun yet?

She said she didn't know. Maybe in a few weeks. Maybe early December, even though the end of semester was always crazy and she was leaving for San Francisco on the twentieth. Where was I spending Christmas? Didn't the holidays suck?

Maybe when we got back. Maybe in January. Things would be better then.

JILL FROM DELAWARE wrote about a woman named Misty Dayes who lived in an empty house on the edge of a town, somewhere on a prairie, and how dust and wind and rain and snow blew over and through the house, and Misty watched from the windows on the second story.

Misty was probably in her late twenties, but she wasn't sure of that, and she'd lived at the house a long time, though she didn't know how long. She had pale skin and pale hair and eyes and she dreamed all the time. Dreamed about places where cats flew and dogs crowed and sad songs played from speakers in trees.

The people from town brought baskets of food and clothes and left them on the porch of Misty's house. When people came, she went to the attic and watched through a round window and didn't come down again until long after the people were gone.

Then the deepest part of winter came, and snow fell day after day, and the wind blew drifts like hills on the prairie, and nobody knew if Misty Dayes was alive or dead or ascended to heaven.

In her house at the edge of town, the snow sifted inside like powder, and ice made patterns on the windows like snowflakes and lace, and Misty Dayes dreamed of flying to a high warm place where birds carried food on open wings and water trickled over rocks warmed by the sun, and the branches of trees sagged under the weight of oranges and mangoes and bananas, and there were creatures not quite human, though they looked human. They had heads and arms and legs and hair and eyes, and they wore flowing robes and smiled, and Misty Dayes walked there, though it was more flow than walk, more drift than tread, and when they smiled it was sunlight and moonlight, was starlight and warm as a bath, and then she was floating underwater and did not need to breathe.

The people from the town used shovels and snowmobiles, and it still took the better part of a day to get to the house. They called and knocked and stamped their boots on the porch, and they finally opened the door and went inside. But there was nothing there. Just drifted snow and the sound of wind, and on the porthole window in the attic, a small clear circle in the ice, the size of a dime. Big enough to look through, to see the world out there, white and frozen and clear as air.

four

In the late winter of 1968, at fourteen, I missed school once or twice a week. Mom and Dad both worked. Dad left the house at six-thirty, Mom at nine, and on the third floor, in the big room that faced the street, I slept with the pillow over my head and the shades and curtains drawn. Mom came up every twenty minutes or so, and said, Will, it's quarter to eight, it's after eight, it's eight-thirty. I won't stand for this, Will. You missed on Tuesday, and they'll expel you, you'll end up a garbageman, and take you to court for truancy, and there'll be nothing I can do.

She turned on the light by the door and said, Goddam, and slammed the door. I heard her footsteps creaking down the stairs. There was music on the radio in Martha's room next door, and a pause for news, and a ship full of American sailors was captured by North Korea, and maybe we'd send troops, maybe we'd invade. Someone had turned out the light. A drawer opened, closed, and there were more footsteps.

The sounds faded, came from a long long way off. Then no sounds except for the street. Just a house and cars and trucks passing, and slivers of light at the edge of the windows. The dial on the clock said eleven-forty, and sometime after that I thought I heard the doorbell, but it stopped after a while.

RUSSELL FROM NINTH GRADE was kept back twice in Connecticut, was seventeen, and looked twenty. He worked weeknights at Brigham's in-town, and could buy. He had ID's, and if he couldn't buy, we stood outside Blanchard's Liquors in Newtonville and asked people going in to buy for us. We'd give them two dollars and ask for Tango, or a half pint of gin or rum or vodka, or a sixie of Colt .45 or Buddies. If it was a sixie, we hid between cars in the parking lot of the A&P next door, and broke the sixie up. We put one can down each sleeve, one down the front of our pants, one in each side pocket, and we'd open the last one, would sip as we walked to Kevin's house. We kept a thumb pressed against the opening, and we'd take hits when there was a break in the headlights of cars.

There was an old couch and bed downstairs, in the basement of Kevin's house, and a radio that played WBCN— Jethro Tull and Ten Years After and the Stones and Beatles.

Kevin said Arlene Post left a note for him Friday. She gave the note to Melissa, and asked him if he was planning to go to Kathy Keefe's house. Kathy Keefe lived near Newton Corner and her mother and father were away.

The door at the top of the stairs opened, and Kevin's brother George, who was a senior in high school, said, Kevin, and Kevin said, What, and George started down, his friend Buddy behind him. Buddy just came back from prison. He was nineteen and did pills, and sometimes he shot drugs too. He was skinny and pale, his hair dark and curly and hanging down past his collar. He talked and smoked, and George weighed three hundred pounds.

Buddy got out of Billerica. He was there thirteen months.

George and Buddy were friends a long time. Buddy's mother was an alky, lived in a room in West Newton, and sang to the television and drank wine from jelly glasses with Fred and Wilma Flintstone, with Bam Bam and Pebbles on them. Buddy's father was long gone. Buddy thought he was in the Air Force or stock car racing in Arizona or Nevada or Alaska. His mother and father never married. She's a slut, Buddy said, then said she couldn't help being a slut because she grew up in an institution, and that's how people got fucked up.

Buddy sat on the couch. He wore a brown leather jacket and sandals with black socks.

Buddy, George said, and motioned with his hand. Buddy took a tan envelope from his shirt pocket and papers. He licked the edge of one paper, attached it to a second, made a crease. He opened the envelope, tapped stuff into the crease, rolled a cigarette and licked the outside. He made two more, gave one to George.

We didn't say anything.

Buddy lit the cigarette, pulled smoke in, held his breath.

You hold it in, George said.

He took the cigarette, sucked smoke, and Buddy started to cough. His eyes were wet.

Kevin took it, and the smoke smelled thick and dense and rich. I took a puff, and Buddy said, You gotta hold it in.

I coughed, tried again. It burned. I could feel it in my lungs, then Buddy took it. The cigarette went around three times before Buddy lit another one.

It was like drinking, only slower. Buddy said the ancient Indians smoked dope, and the Stones and the Beatles smoked dope. He said everyone in Billerica smoked dope, even the guards, and he said he might try to turn his mother on to dope. Dope was better than booze. It didn't make you dizzy, and it didn't make you feel like kicking the shit out of anyone.

We watched our cigarettes awhile, watched the smoke

snake and curl and coil, and we gave beers to George and Buddy. We snapped them open at the same time, and Kevin giggled, then I started.

Sergeant Pepper was on, and the music got louder and fainter and echoed like it was coming from a window high on the wall. Buddy said in prison the Beatles were God. Like you could get stabbed for saying John Lennon was a faggot or something. In prison men fell in love with other men. They wrote love letters and gave each other presents and cried if they didn't get a letter or a present in return. He said, There's no women, so men fuck each other.

Buddy, George said, and nodded at me and Kevin.

Kevin said, How come you were there, and Buddy said because of heroin, which we shouldn't fuck around with. He said pills were okay and speed was okay, but skag was a motherfucker, skag was death.

But pot was good. The ancient Indians used it in their religion. He read about them in prison. Read how they smoked it and baked it in bread, and how the whole village sat around until the sun was going down, then went to the graveyards with their pipes to get in touch with their ancestors, their relatives who were buried there. They sat in the dark, in the graveyard, and after the sun went down it got cold as a motherfucker, cold as a fucking ice cube in January, Buddy said, and everyone started to shiver and shake with the cold, and the little kids wondered what the fuck they were doing there in the cold when they had teepees.

George said he doubted they said fuck so much, back in ancient Indian time, and Buddy said, Fuck you. You want to hear about this or not?

George said, I'm only fucking with you, and Buddy looked at him.

So it gets cold, Buddy said, like ten degrees, and they can see their breath when they breathe, and the babies and kids start crying, and the old men and ladies start moaning from the cold, but from something else too.

He looked up. He looked from George to Kevin to me. There wasn't much light in the cellar, just a bulb above the utility sink, next to the washing machine. Buddy's eyes were panes of glass and had dim light behind them. He took a hit on a cigarette and blew smoke straight ahead, so there was a cloud between us.

They were moaning from the cold, he said, but then the cold started to remind them of where they were, and the cold was like death, because when you die your body gets cold and stays cold. And then all of them knew, there in the burial ground, that they were in the presence of death, and that's what they came for—to see death and sit with it and be there with the spirits of the dead. And the moaning got louder, and the medicine man, the shaman of the village, started to chant. Ohhh—mmm—dahhh, over and over, so low that all of them began to chant together, and this loud deep vibrating sound was in all their bodies, but it seemed to come from the middle of the earth, where the spirits lived.

Buddy moved his hands, and I thought he was kidding, that he wasn't really Buddy who just got out of Billerica, and this was something from smoking dope, that people sounded like they were talking, only instead, there was a tape playing somewhere.

They chanted, and the cold got worse, Buddy said, and then the shaman stood up and lit this pile of wood and leaves and twigs that had been piled up before.

What'd he use? George asked. A Zippo?

Buddy ignored him.

The flames catch fast, and there's this weird orange light on their faces, on these beautiful Indian faces—the copper skin and high cheekbones, those black eyes shining in the orange light. And with the fire and light and flames and heat, it's like they're not so much returned to life, because everything surrounding them is still black and cold, but the spirits have risen and they've come up and brought the heat and life with them. And that heat and light is supposed to be the years they lived, and the knowledge and experience they had when they died.

So the people sitting in the graveyard freezing their asses off, they know what you lose when a person dies, and they know that it's cold and scary to die, like sitting in the graveyard, but that if you sit long enough, you'll see you're surrounded with the spirits that bring fire, that bring warmth and light.

And then they break out the dope, after the shaman does some holy chants, and they fill one pipe—because everyone has to have the same source, the single source—and they sit and take hits of this premium dope and pretty soon they're all wasted, and they stay around the fire and they watch little sparks and embers lift into the sky, which is completely black except for the stars. And the sparks are supposed to go all the way up and become stars, and the stars get to stay there thirty days, until the next moon. Each spark is a dead person who's been released from under the earth, because his descendants came to the graveyard and remembered.

And they couldn't do it, Buddy said, without dope.

He looked at the forty-watt bulb. He licked his lips and sipped from his can, and closed his eyes.

I closed my eyes. I could see spots of light in the darkness.

THE HELICOPTER BLADES went whup whup whup whup, and guns went pop pop, but softer than popcorn or firecrackers, and the elephant grass was waving and moved like water in wind, and everything was black and white, but so densely green, the man with the microphone said, that you felt as though there were thirty-seven shades of green.

There was a truck with a canopy over the back, and skinny short people wearing pajamas and wide straw hats like umbrellas. Some rode bicycles, but most walked, and some carried babies and kids walked and carried bundles and bags. There were animals the size of cows, only they had horns and were water buffaloes.

There were huts with thatched roofs and kids without clothes and people squatting over bowls of rice and fires, in huts that were open on one side. There was a broad field and men and water buffaloes waded in paddies that reached the men's waists.

There was another helicopter, more whup whup sounds and pops. Men were pulling a body onto the helicopter and a big gun in the door was firing, was going pop pop, and puffs of smoke rose from the door. The feet of the body were sticking out as the helicopter lurched and swayed and rose, and there was dust, and grass that waved again like water.

MY FATHER WORE a short-sleeve shirt and sat on the side of his bed. He undid his tie and took his shoes off.

He said he was tired, he wished he didn't have to work so much.

He had two jobs at the same hospital in Brighton. One on weekends, one weekdays.

He said he couldn't remember anything, couldn't remember his name almost, and felt tired all the time. He felt like sleeping sometimes at his desk at work, his eyes closing and voices coming from a distance, like from the other side of a veil or curtain or something. He didn't know. Maybe he was losing his mind.

He pushed hair off his forehead. He lay down on his side on the bed. There were piles of notebooks and papers on the desk near the door and a bookcase full of books and pamphlets and three-ring binders.

He said he worried about us all the time. He woke up at night and thought how we were ruining our lives. Not going to school, and he said he could never sleep. He worried about money, because even with Mom working, there wasn't enough, there was never anything left at the end of the week.

He breathed deeply and looked at me. What am I supposed to do? he asked. He knew he wasn't a very good father. He wasn't smart, but he tried, and sometimes everything seemed hopeless, seemed like nothing would ever come out right.

HE WAS DEAD on a balcony in Memphis. Men in suits pointed, and he was lying on the balcony. The shots came from a window or the street. One or two or three shots.

I AM A MAN, the signs said. On walls and on placards and attached to fences. I AM A MAN.

He said, I might not get there with you, and they said, Amen. They said, Yes.

There were long pealing sirens as the sun went down, and pop sounds and fires and cars tipped over.

The police had shields for their faces and white helmets, and they had rifles and cars were on fire. People were running through broken store windows with clothes and TV sets and stereo speakers. A man ran down a street with a tire and his shirt was open and waving behind him like a sail.

There were more sirens and a block of stores was burning, in Watts, in Detroit, in Atlanta, in Chicago. The police were dragging a man along the street to a police car. The bubble on top was circling around and around and around like a lighthouse.

A woman had tears running down her face. They killing us, she said, and the camera lurched sideways, went to the pavement. There were pops and a siren and the camera got up and there was a single fire a half mile or a mile down the street and an overturned car and the street was gray and shadowy and drained.

Then he was in a casket, and his widow wore a black veil and a choir sang, Lift me Jesus, to that high far place.

The choir was in Atlanta, was in Boston, was in Roxbury. The station moved to Washington, D.C., and Richard Nixon and Robert Kennedy were in church in Atlanta and wore black, and the widow had wet eyes behind her veil and looked like she wouldn't be able to walk again.

THE MAN IN HARVARD SQUARE said he'd like to buy me lunch. He said I looked like I could use a friend and he wasn't doing anything special. He wore a suitcoat and a thin dark tie that shined and loafers and white socks.

He asked why I wasn't in school.

He said, You gonna let me buy you lunch?

He said, You like burgers?

Inside there was noise—voices and hamburgers frying, chairs scraping, silverware, dishes.

He said he noticed me sitting there and thought, There's a kid who looks lost, and a good-looking kid too, so what the hell. Do something, I said to myself. Introduce yourself, and here we are.

He touched his mouth with a napkin after every bite. He sipped Coke and told me he was still in school, believe it or not. Twenty-nine years old and still in school.

Graduate school. Literary theory, getting what's called an advanced degree, he said.

He was from Chicago, and had been there four years already and would you believe it, he still got lonely, he still lay awake at night, in bed, and stared at the ceiling.

He liked to sleep naked at night, he said, because he liked the feel of the sheets on his skin. He hoped that didn't shock me.

He talked softly.

I lie there and think of how I'm by myself in this nice big bed and how it would be to have somebody, he said.

What do you wear? he asked. To bed at night?

He had brown eyes. He watched my face.

Boxers or briefs?

I stood up, and he said, Wait, but I went quickly between two people near the cash register by the front door. Wait, he said, but I began to run.

RUSSELL SAID BACK in Connecticut he had married women chasing after him. He said they had the experience and knew how to keep a man happy, and were sugar in bed, were ripe and firm and hungry.

Kevin said, You're so full of shit your eyes are brown, and Russell said, Fuck you.

He stood up and went to the utility sink, turned on the water and started to pee.

Russell finished, turned off the water and said, Down in Connecticut, Burt and me used to visit the ladies when the men were off working. Sitting there in negligees, their tits showing, and he and Burt would pretend to be looking for the husband, would go in. They'd have a beer, would watch a little TV, Russell said, and then he'd see the nipples get hard and he'd know they wanted it. Wanted it from a man, wanted all ten throbbing inches.

How bout a foot and a half, Kevin said. How bout a yard.

Russell cracked a beer. He said he wanted to rob the Star Market in Newtonville Square, over the Mass Pike. He said on weekends they had all the money from the week, had over a hundred thousand dollars. He said you'd arrange to leave someone inside the store after it closed. He'd knock over the night watchman with a billy club or a set of brass knuckles and then he'd have a car pick him up—not in Newtonville Square where the fucking cops would be looking—but down on the Pike. He said there were vents from the Star that went directly onto the eastbound lane of the Pike. Five, ten minutes, and he'd be in downtown Boston with a hundred grand.

Just to make sure the cops didn't know where to look,

he'd get someone else, a third guy—and he looked at me—to throw a boulder through a jewelry store window in Newtonville Square. The alarms would go off and the cops would be totally confused.

We don't have driver's licenses, Kevin said, and Russell said we were spineless cowards. He said we were penny ante, and that Onassis started small, but Onassis thought big.

He looked disgusted. He had a long nose and short hair. He was over six feet tall, and had big shoulders and arms and bow legs. He wore tan laced boots, and his jeans came to the top of his boots. Kevin said they were flood pants.

Russell worked at Brigham's Ice Cream and made a hundred dollars a week. He gave forty to his mother. He lived with her and two sisters in a second-floor apartment near Newtonville Square. His mother was a secretary for a lawyer, and they moved to Newton the year before, and left the father behind. His sister Marty worked, and the other sister was fat and shy and in the seventh grade.

Russell said his father drank and fell asleep on the couch or chair, and sometimes pissed his pants, and his mother was always trying to keep the furniture covered with plastic. His father hit his mother and his sisters, and he said he used to beat the shit out of him too, but he got older, and the old man didn't dare touch him.

He was all fucked up on wine and shit, one night. Hadn't shaved and smelled like a sewer and started screaming at his mother. Calling her a liar and a fucking useless old cunt, and he took his belt off and he could hear his mother crying and sniffling and trying to breathe. Then the belt was making a cracking sound, and he said he started to moan and growl, and he went to the kitchen and swung two or three times, and the old man went down.

He said it wasn't even that he hit him so hard, just that he was drunk as fuck, and nobody ever laid a hand on him, and his father was on the floor near the stove and his mother on the floor near the hall, and his heart was so loud he thought it'd explode.

Russell was looking at the can that rested on his knee. He blinked.

THE HUTS IN THE VILLAGE went up fast and the smoke was black. The people jabbered and cried and a helicopter was on its side in a rice paddy.

No VC, no VC, a woman cried, and an old man said he was old and would die soon and would be happy.

There was smoke and the whup whup of blades beating the air.

THERE WAS RAIN and wind chimes and someone was laughing. Someone else was laughing, and someone said, Hey, and "Beggar's Banquet" was on the stereo. On the back porch the rain didn't come through the screens and Stacy and I were on a sleeping bag we spread out on the floor. It was sixty degrees and after midnight. The house was surrounded in back by trees and bushes and the wind chimes were ice and crystals, they bonged and pinged.

Stacy said she didn't feel cold, she felt like she could lie there forever. She said she liked beer better than wine. Wine made her tired, made her feel like going to bed, and she didn't want to do that.

She said, You okay? You're so quiet. Are you being shy?

I said, I'm listening to the rain, and we were both quiet. We could hear drops slap the leaves and grass and roof and we could hear music and people inside.

She sipped from a beer and her eyes were sleepy in the darkness, her eyes were soft.

I put my hand on the side of her face and told her I liked her, told her she was pretty, and even as I said it I couldn't believe I was saying it. I sipped beer and said, I can't believe I'm saying this, and she smiled.

Her hair was near my face and I could feel her body pressed against me, and it was like being somewhere I'd never been. She smelled like clean clothes and beer and perfume. She was warm and her hair tickled my face.

I put my arms around her, and the wind chimes pinged and the rain kept falling. She said at camp in Maine, when she was a kid, she loved when it rained because that meant they'd have to go inside, and everyone sat on their cots with blankets over them like capes, and pine trees surrounded the cabins, and they could see the rain on the screens and on spider webs. And they'd tell stories. They'd tell about where they were from, and what grade they'd be in in school the coming year, and how many brothers and sisters they had, and which boys they liked and thought were cute.

What animal would you be if you were an animal? What kind of day? What kind of woods? Or weather? Or body of water?

What was your worst day? Your best? How far had you gone with a boy? Did you let him touch you? Did you touch him?

Then they stopped and sat under the blankets, in Maine, and listened to rain. Camp was deep in the woods, near a lake, and one summer she saw a moose in the woods, and she couldn't move and couldn't speak and stood and watched the moose sniffing a tree. Then it looked at her, and turned and walked into the woods.

She didn't tell anybody. She wondered if she had really seen it, then she thought nobody would believe her, and started to think if she said anything, seeing the moose would somehow change. Like it might not be sniffing a tree, or maybe it didn't look at her and maybe she was dreaming that day.

She said I was the first person she'd ever told, and she supposed it didn't matter much anyway. It was years ago and way up in Maine and nobody else had been there anyway.

HE WAS SHOT in the kitchen in California and didn't die right away. Lying on the floor, his eyes staring, and if he lived he would be a vegetable. He would be in a home, and a machine would breathe for him, and nurses would feed him baby food, spoonful by spoonful.

When he died later, it was a little better, or not as bad, because the idea of him with a straw hat on his head, staring like a doll, was enough to make people pray for mercy, for God to take him, my grandmother said.

She said there was a curse on the family. She said they had money and were handsome, but they wanted too much and God punished them. First the one in the airplane, the older one, and then the sister in the airplane, the sister married to the duke or count or somebody. A royalty, she said. Someone fancy. There was another sister who was funny, if I knew what she meant to say, a little off in the head, and she was in a home someplace with the sisters, the nun sisters, like penguins.

She said the next one was the worst because he was leader of our nation, and she said maybe it had to do with them being Irish and Catholic. A lot of people hated the Irish, and with the Catholics they thought the Pope in Rome was running things, that he had a special phone that ran from the Vatican to the White House, but she thought that was a lot of baloney, that was bull pucky, if I knew what she was trying to say.

But she said maybe this latest one, who she thought was a good man, a good husband and father, and had a house full of kids to prove it, maybe he shouldn't have tried to become president.

His body came back on a train like Abraham Lincoln, and people stood on the sides of the track, and they cried like their friend died. There were tears falling out of the eyes on TV, and at Saint Patrick's Cathedral, his brother said he saw wrong and tried to right it, and then his voice broke, and he almost began to cry, but then he caught himself.

Gram's needles clicked, and she said you couldn't tell these days, everything was so crazy, but she thought the moon was moving too close to the earth maybe, and it was like Friday the thirteenth and a full moon and black cats all rolled into one.

She said it wasn't like years ago. People didn't go around killing each other for no reason. People killed each other, but you used to know why. Now she said it was crazy, these weirdos running around. You didn't need a reason anymore.

AT THREE A.M. there were almost no cars out and Kevin and I ducked behind bushes and fences when we saw headlights. Stacy and Kathy were supposed to be sleeping on the back porch at Kathy's, and when we got there they were wearing nightgowns that made them look like ghosts in the moonlight and they spoke in whispers. They said they'd just heard Kathy's mother go to the bathroom and then go back to bed, and they let us in, and I got into the sleeping bag with Stacy and she whispered that it was colder outside at three a.m. than at any other time, just about, and there was dew on the lawn.

Kevin was lying down with Kathy, was whispering things I couldn't make out. Stacy wanted to know if we'd seen any cop cars on the way over, and she said she and Kathy had been talking, and she guessed she'd sleep all morning Sunday, and her breath was warm and smelled like Crest.

She wasn't going to camp that summer and she felt sad about that. She'd work in her father's office in Boston, and her mother would go to the Cape, so it'd mostly be her and her father in the house because her brother Stanley went to camp, and Patty, her older sister, had a job near her college in Boulder, Colorado.

She whispered that Kathy was in love with Kevin, and they almost went all the way and Kathy worried that she'd get pregnant. The crickets were making sounds in the grass. Air moved through the screens and there was no sound from where Kevin and Kathy were lying down.

Stacy said we were the only people awake in the world, and she said it was like that at camp too. She was always the last one to go to sleep, she whispered, and she liked that. It was as though she was protecting everyone who slept, and she motioned to the lawn.

Look, she whispered, and there was fog on the grass, a gray hush over everything.

I closed my eyes and I could feel her there in the dark. I was drifting like water, I was a cloud at night. I felt her hand on my head, and I was four again.

five

They called from Boston, from Newton and Winchester and Manchester in late March and April and May. Martha called, and Greta and my mother called, and I spoke to Seamus and Eric as well. He was very very sick, they said. The doctors had tried everything. They tried to wean him from the vent, but he couldn't breathe on his own for more than a minute or two. They had a feeding tube to his stomach, but there were infections. He aspirated fluids and most of the time he wasn't there at all.

The phone lines from Boston to Ithaca, when I was thirty-five, sounded like long echoing tubes. There were blips and waves of sound, and in our apartment in Ithaca, I could see students crossing a bridge on their way to school.

It doesn't end, Greta said. It's been weeks.

Mom went to the hospital every day, and Gram was ninety-two, turned ninety-three in early May, and she could barely walk anymore. She said she wanted to see her son. She said she didn't think they were doing all they could. Doctors were only interested in money, and her big hands moved in her lap, and her glasses had lenses thicker than aquarium glass. Her eyes swam, were blue and wavering.

Mom said he didn't seem to be in pain. Kasakawa, his doctor, didn't want to give up, but a social worker said a best-case scenario was a chronic care facility, where the vent would breathe for him, and where he'd be fed with tubes. Kasakawa folded his arms in the hall outside the room, and shook his head.

In Ithaca, in March and April and early May, I was teaching my final semester. My students were writing stories and essays. They were writing about sisters who were retarded or who had anorexia, or about grandfathers who died. At the funeral of a grandfather, in Chicago, the family of one student put a Cubs cap in the casket at the funeral home because the old man was a Cubs fan for seventy years, and his granddaughter thought she'd remember that forever.

In April the days were lengthening into the evenings, and trees and bushes in the Arts Quad were blooming. Forsythia and Japanese maple, and trees with pink and white petals, and the students said, Yo, said, Hey, and lingered after class, and wanted to talk of what they planned to write about— Little League baseball, or a friend in Hong Kong who moved to West Africa and it was like the friend had fallen off the side of the earth.

They came to the third floor of Goldwin Smith, sat on the other side of the desk, under the slanted ceiling, and said they were tired, this was a crazy time of the semester, they couldn't wait for summer. Some were taking courses with me for the second time. I had them as freshmen or sophomores, then as juniors or seniors. One was graduating and moving to New York City to do something with stocks, and he said he'd send postcards, he'd remember the class because it was the last time in his life he'd be able to use the left side of his brain, and on the subways in New York he'd think, What would happen if there was a massive power failure and the city stopped and everyone started walking toward the Jersey Shore. What would people do? How would they act? Would they roll the cuffs of their pants and sleeves up? Take their shoes off? Look at the sun as though they had never seen it?

ANN, AT NIGHT, in bed, said we should go, said we'd waited too long already. She said we hadn't been there since December. Then Greta called from the kitchen of the house in Newton. Mom was in the background, was boiling water for coffee. I was in the living room, and could see trees outside and the bridge.

Greta said they'd just come home from the hospital, and she paused.

Kasakawa said the problem was in the brain, was not well understood; the brain didn't tell the body when to breathe. He'd never be able to breathe on his own, and there was probably brain damage because of oxygen deprivation.

Kasakawa said they could keep him comfortable, could keep him out of pain, could give him Ativan so he wouldn't be agitated.

They'd give the DNR order to the staff. Do not resuscitate, Greta said. She was a nurse, and she said it was awful to see them with the paddles, saying, Stand back, and pressing the paddles to the chest and the body jumping.

ANN WAS FROM TENNESSEE, had been in the MFA program in poetry. She was thin, and had short hair halfway between brown and blond. She had blue eyes and wore contact lenses. At night she wore glasses around the apartment that made her eyes more blue.

She taught at a rural girls' school in Kenya for a year, after college, and lived in Manhattan after that. She ran four times a week, in the morning, in the hills above Cayuga Lake, and when she returned her skin was flushed and the freckles on her nose and cheeks were suddenly and briefly visible.

In Kenya, she said, the colors of things were deeper and brighter. The earth was red clay the same as Tennessee. Mountains were high and distant and rose from plains so flat that from twenty miles away they looked like places where gods lived. Rising from nowhere and rings of cloud and snow at the top, even when the weather was ninety degrees down below.

Reds and blues and browns and greens were so bright, she said, that at first she had to blink her eyes all the time and started to wear sunglasses. On the plains, she said, you could look in the distance, on a clear and dry and sunny day, and see a storm that looked as wide around as a dime, ten or twenty miles off, and the children in the village would stand outside laughing and pointing and chattering, waiting for the circle of storm to arrive.

Then it was twenty minutes of wind and dust, and rain poured, then the storm moved away like a truck that passed through the village, and everyone stood outside again and watched the storm grow smaller and smaller, until it was the size of a dime, and then it was nothing and already the ground was dry, the dust was back, and the sky was blue and cloudless as an ocean.

Ann put her hand on my arm and said, Tomorrow. It'll be okay. We'll get through it. And in Kenya, I thought, it's midday. The sun was out and birds were moving in the cloudless sky.

THE ROOM WAS on the sixth floor, and he was bone and skin, and his eyes were closed and sunk back in his head. His lips were dry and faintly blue and his hands seemed huge and dangled at the ends of stringy arms. His ears were big like his hands, and a blue tube was attached to the tracheotomy in his throat, and the machine went hiss and click, and I saw his chest rise and fall, heard the air go in.

Mom said he opened his eyes every few hours, but mostly he slept. She said he opened his eyes less and less. Eric and Martha and Seamus and Greta came in every day, or every other day. The nurses came in every few hours to move him in the bed, and Kasakawa or one of the residents came in and stood and asked how we were doing. They spoke softly, and nodded much of the time. Kasakawa went to the bed and lifted my father's wrist, held it in his hands, felt for a pulse with his index and middle fingers. He looked at his watch, counted, then put my father's arm down by his side. He patted his hand and felt at the side of his neck.

He patted my mother's arm and asked if there was anything he could do. He said he'd stop by later, before he left for home.

THEY PUT TWO COTS in the room, one under the curtained windows that faced the hall and nurses' station and one near the outside window. Most of the time the door was closed and the lights were low. Ann drove back to Ithaca on Sunday.

Eric came from work at six and said the traffic hadn't been bad. He leaned over the bed, kissed Dad's forehead, then he took his hand and sat on the vent side of the bed. I could see waves of tiny nerves in Dad's face move.

Greta came at eight with magazines and soda, and sat on the other side. She said he looked pretty well, his color wasn't bad, and she took his blood pressure. It was one thirty-six over ninety-eight, which was elevated, but not too much. She said his heart was having to work hard to get oxygen to his extremities, but he was okay.

IT RAINED IN BRIGHTON and Newton, at one a.m., and there were almost no cars out. The streets, the houses and trees, the signs and traffic lights, were wet and shining. Mom said this had been coming for years, but she almost became numb to it or used to it or something.

We passed Oak Square, the fire station, and a small fenced park in the middle of the rotary, and she said it must be more of a surprise, of a shock, to me. She said I hadn't seen him since when? Since Christmas? And he was okay then. There was the breathing, but he was taking his medications and he was doing okay.

At Christmas the house was cold, and the windows rattled and he sat at the kitchen table and turned the channels on the small television on the table. He spoke in a whispery voice, sounded like paper in a dry room.

The radiators clanked and hissed at Christmas, and on the third floor there was dust on everything, and he sat at a desk on the second floor, in the back bedroom, and books and papers and magazines and pamphlets were piled on the desk and on a bookcase and on an old coffee table. He said he couldn't remember anything, he was losing his mind.

Gram, in late May, said he was a wonderful man, a beautiful man, and she was upset his own kids didn't see that until he was lying there in his hospital bed. He was the cleanest man there was. He took a bath or shower every day, and kept his shirt tucked in and never swore or said a bad word against anyone.

She opened a drawer in the small table next to her chair and took out photographs. His high school yearbook picture, one in the backyard, wearing a white shirt and baggy pants, and holding a baby wrapped in a blanket.

That's you, she said. The face at the top of the blanket was white, and the eyes were closed, and there was a small nose and mouth, but nothing I recognized.

There were pictures of when he was a kid, on a lawn in sunlight, at three or four, squinting. His hair was straight and fair, and he wore a sailor suit in one picture and an Indian headdress in one—a band of paper, with feathers taped to the forehead.

He never gave trouble, Gram said.

She asked, Is he all bones?

No, I said. He doesn't look bad. He's thinner, but not much. Mostly he looks like he's sleeping, and he's not in any pain or anything. It's like a deep sleep, and he's probably dreaming. Dreaming about you or being a kid.

She didn't think she should go see him. She knew she'd remember him that way. That's how she remembered her mother, from the end, from when she was ninety pounds, was no more than a skeleton. No hair. Just a wisp and a skull.

I said, Would you like to call him? He has a phone in the room and Greta's there. She could put the phone to his ear. You could talk to him.

She said she wanted to do that.

I dialed and Greta answered, and I told her, and Greta said he was way out there, she was sure he couldn't hear.

I know, I said, but put the phone next to his ear, and she said, One sec.

Okay, Gram, I said, and she took the phone, and I tried not to listen.

Buzz, she said. Buzz, this is Mom. Buzz, I love you, she said, and she was crying and talking.

Get better, she said. I love you and I miss you. Come home. Please come home, Buzz.

Then she kissed the phone. I love you. This is Mom.

She kissed the phone again. Please get well, Buzz. This is Mom.

She handed the phone to me, and Greta said she held the phone to his ear. Greta said she thought it was getting closer and closer, and thought we should be there all the time. She didn't want him to be alone.

Okay, I told her. Thanks, I said, and she said, Maybe he could hear her. Who knows, and we hung up.

Gram, I said. Greta said he smiled. She wasn't sure, because he's in such a deep sleep, but she thought he smiled, like he heard your voice.

She nodded. She said she wouldn't be surprised.

She said, Maybe it will help him. She said, I had him longer than any of you, and he knows my voice better. Maybe it will help him.

THE HOSPITAL AT NIGHT was blips and pale light on waxed corridors, and the windows were dark and reflected the inside, reflected the walls or rooms, or whoever stood in front of them. But when you were close to the window it was like walking through a mirror, and then there was an outside, a dark field that had millions of tiny lights.

We could see the Charles River and a good part of Cambridge. We could see Brighton Center, and beyond that, lights in Newton and Watertown. We could see downtown Boston, the Prudential and Hancock Towers, and the buildings near the financial district, near South Station. A car moved on the street and I wondered where anybody could be driving at that hour.

The nurses were quiet at three a.m., they spoke in whispers. They went in and out of rooms and smiled. The doctors who came to the floor were young, were residents with dark half moons under their eyes, wore sneakers and hadn't slept in a long time. They sat at the nurses' station and looked through charts, and talked quietly to the nurses and to the security men in blue uniforms who passed through, who paused and said hello, how you doing.

His hands were blotched, were nearly purple. Martha said blood wasn't circulating as well as it should, but we didn't have to worry. Mom was half asleep, was all the way asleep, in a chair on the far side of the bed.

Martha was a nurse and Seamus was a nurse. They knew about heart failure and blood pressure and respiration and arterial blood gases, and they'd seen people die. Martha said that it wouldn't be horrible, I shouldn't worry. He wouldn't thrash around or turn blue or vomit blood. His eyes wouldn't bulge out and he wouldn't scream.

She said, It'll be okay. It'll be a release.

We walked past the nurses' station and into a lounge that was dark. It was three-twenty a.m.

Martha hugged me, and her arms were powerful. She went to the window. She said it could be a matter of hours or it could be days.

A week? I asked.

I don't think so. He's had almost no fluids and the body can't sustain itself that long. She said it would be quiet. The vent would keep breathing, but his heart or kidneys or liver would stop functioning.

The vent couldn't be turned off until a doctor came in to pronounce him, and that only took a few minutes. They'd listen to hear that his heart stopped and that would be it.

What do they do? I asked.

She said after the family was gone, two or three of the nurses would come in, would close the door. She said they detached tubes or wires like IV tubes or feeding tubes or the vent. Then they detached the bottom sheet from the bed, and wrapped it around the body. There were gurneys with something like flat tent frames at each end, so they'd shift the body to the gurney and tent it over, so you wouldn't have what looked like a corpse in a winding sheet. You'd have a tent, and it could be towels or supplies, and when you moved the body into the halls and down the elevators, people wouldn't know.

She said two nurses brought the gurney down, and the attendants there helped them put the body into the drawer. She said they used toe tags for identification.

HE MUST HAVE DREAMED of something, of other places and times, because his brain wasn't dead, and his eyes, under his eyelids, seemed to twitch and ripple in small waves.

He was a boy again, in 1924, was three years old and wore knickers, and it was April or May, but warm like summer, like high summer. It was Sunday and his mother or father's family, a brother or sister, a grandmother or uncle, had come to visit, for dinner, and they were sitting in the backyard, on the stairs, on a few kitchen chairs they'd brought out.

The neighborhood people were strolling past. The women wore long dark skirts to their ankles and white blouses with high necks and small flat hats pinned to the top of their heads, and the men wore dark pants and dark vests and suitcoats and high shoes. They walked slowly, after a morning of church, an afternoon of dinner and family.

The grass smelled rich and dense, and when he pressed his face to the earth he could see pale roots, brown earth, and Uncle Charlie laughed, and he looked over, and Uncle Charlie, his father's older brother, had strong white teeth, like the teeth of the horse that pulled the milk wagon. Uncle Charlie looked at him, then looked at Momma, and he was older suddenly, was twenty years old and on a train moving through Arkansas and Mississippi going to Fort Hood in Texas in 1942, and the fellows were singing "I Dream of Jeanie with the Light Brown Hair" because they were going a long way from home. They weren't bad fellows, though they kidded him, made him sleep in the bunk by the door where the cold air came in, and one of them stole his Waltham watch while he was in the shower and that was TS for him. That was tough shit.

Outside was flat and brown and bare forever, except in towns where the train slowed, and the wheels clacked less quickly, and there were a few houses, a water tower and a few brick buildings, then nothing again, then poles with wires for telegraphs, to tell that someone had been killed, but mostly just flatness and barrenness, an ocean of dust and moaning wind.

He was rising and floating, and we were on the other side of thick glass. Mom's lined face, and Eric with his beard, and me in glasses, the lenses catching light like his mother's glasses. Then Ohio when he was thirty-one or -two, and he painted houses, he stood on a ladder, and the paintbrush felt like it weighed twenty-five pounds and it was ninety-three degrees out and he was in church in Ohio, and Martha and Eric were already there, and he and Margaret stood, and Margaret held Eric, who was three months old, and Martha was able to stand and hold his hand even though she wasn't two yet, and she'd grow up to be a strong little lady, and have children of her own and pray in church with them, would provide them with a strong family life centered on the Catholic Liturgy.

At night he didn't move, because things were in the house, his mother told him. They came after the lights were out, so unless he had to go to the bathroom, and he better go because if he wet the bed anymore she'd take him to the doctor and the doctor would use a knife and cut it off because he wouldn't go to the bathroom like he was supposed to. He better stay in bed, because two or three of them came in, and wore black and wore chains that clanked when they walked, and they made moaning sounds, and their eyes were green and they had cold fingers like ice from the ice truck.

They were chanting in the monastery in Wisconsin, sometime after Texas and the Army, and the ceiling of the chapel had dark beams, and everyone wore brown robes with hoods, and the light was dim at five a.m., and no one spoke except to chant, to respond in Latin, and God was great and God was good, and if you prayed hard, prayed with your hands tightly together and your eyes squeezed shut, He might hear, might know, if your thoughts and deeds were pure, were clean as snow, and you might hear His voice, His calling. His head would be shaved and he'd take the oath of poverty and chastity and obedience, and not see his mother or father for years and years, like he had died, but he was on the train again, and women had hair as fine and light as silk, and their lips were red and they smiled and swelled at the hips and on their fronts, and he prayed, Lord Jesus, in Your Grace and Wisdom and Love for us, please let me know Your Will for me.

His hands were long and full of bone, were no longer purple, were white and blue at the fingertips, and he was at work, or home after work, and they would never leave him alone, the five of them, and Margaret, God Bless Her, and his mother and father downstairs. Seamus needed glasses and there was the dentist, and shoes, and the price of milk was up two cents a gallon, and they'd use powdered milk, and Will was wetting his bed and Greta had nightmares and Martha got A's in everything. Sister Marian said Martha was a splendid child, and wished she had a class full of children like Martha.

At night he woke up four or five times, and thought he smelled burning, and thought one of them had stopped breathing, and he heard things in the house—down to the furnace, which was boiling, and had flames to keep everything warm, but it wasn't flames that killed people, it was smoke that crept along the floor and walls like poison. And he couldn't believe he was awake, and Margaret lying there as warm as July, and he didn't know how he could keep this up without losing the house, and the kids going hungry and their teeth rotting and falling out. It was supposed to be different. It wasn't supposed to be this hard, this unrelenting.

IT RAINED FOR NEARLY a week, in early June, in 1989, when I was thirty-five. By Monday and Tuesday and Wednesday we thought it would never end. The machine would breathe on and on, and his heart would never stop, and we would never sleep again, never for more than an hour or two, and only the sleep where there was a thin curtain between waking and sleep, and we'd turn over, would see the clock, would think, We'd better get back there.

Two or three of us were always in his room, at all hours. We sat and lay on the cots and talked quietly, but mostly we sat at the side of his bed and held his hand and whispered to him. That we were there, that we'd be there all the time, that we were sorry, that we hoped he wasn't afraid, didn't feel alone, didn't feel pain.

Greta leaned forward, and rested her head on the pillow next to his head. Mom said, Go with God, honey.

Rain dripped down the window, and at rush hour I watched the traffic creep by down on Cambridge Street, and all of it glistened, all of it shined.

Seamus and I both sat on the cot, our backs against the wall, our shoulders touching, and he said he was amazed, he didn't understand how Dad could still be alive, he'd never seen anything like it. He blinked his eyes and put his hand on his cheek. He said, I don't know. I don't get it.

THERE WERE DARK SPOTS and white spots, and they moved past his eyes, and when he reached they seemed to rush away, like balloons in slow motion. He waved and smiled and then it was sunny and there was a field with yellow and red flowers, and he thought he'd glide from flower to flower. But he was back and awake again, and all five of them were there, and it was Newton in Massachusetts, just outside Boston, and not Ohio anymore.

Martha and Eric were born in Ohio, and they were pink and small, and he worried all the time. When they coughed he thought he saw blood, and it sounded like the insides of their throats and lungs were raw like they'd been skinned, and scarlet fever could kill them, and rheumatic fever could damage their hearts, their brains, their lungs. Temperatures over a hundred and five could damage their brains too, and they'd go to the bathroom in their pants and drool and not know how to tie their own shoes.

Outside the wind moved and he heard leaves on pavement and the apartment was two rooms and they all slept in one room. Then they were back in Newton, and they bought the house for sixteen thousand dollars, and Mom and Dad would live downstairs and pay some rent and he'd work two jobs. He wasn't afraid to work, was glad to work, and Margaret was big again, there was another one on the way.

Will was born, in late December, two days before Christmas, and then Seamus and Greta, and in seven years there were five of them, and at night he woke up, and the men might be in the house, there would be smoke as silent as breath, and all of them would die.

He just wanted to sleep. He wanted to lie down and be left alone and pull the covers over his head. But Seamus needed glasses, and Will ran away from the dentist's office, and Martha was nearly as tall as him, and her friends wore makeup already.

How could it happen so fast? when all he wanted was sleep? to go away and be left alone?

She said it was quiet. His mom said nobody would hurt him if he was quiet, and if he let them do their work, and then he'd be able to eat as much ice cream as he wanted.

The room was tall and white and there were lights outside, on the side of the building, that burned all through the night, and she kissed him and went out, and women in white came in and held his arm for a minute and wrote something down, and then two men with glasses came in and they patted his head and said not to worry.

People were standing all around, and he wasn't sure. Maybe it was back with his tonsils, or even earlier. Maybe 1920 and everyone staring at him through glass. The fat lady with the big nose and the man with the mustache and the other two, one with his collar up, the other with a scarf. They waved and made faces. So many times, like Wisconsin with his appendix, and he stopped breathing and the priest came and made crosses with oil on his forehead and hands and feet.

But they were always there, the five of them, and Margaret and Mom and Dad. When he went to sleep in the chair, they said, Dad, wake up, Dad. They pulled at the sleeves of his sweater and said, Hey. Wake up. You're sleeping.

Will needed a pill at three a.m., and Seamus had asthma and he could hear the air trying to get into Seamus' lungs, but there was no room.

Nobody talked to him, and he would have liked so much to talk. To say, Hello, my name is Henry or Walter or Dan. My name is not what it is, and then he'd be able to talk. There were things he thought, and items in the paper, and he wished he could talk with someone. But they were sneering, were sulking, would barely say hello. Even when he was hardly big enough to walk. When he fell in the grass, in summer, and did not cry.

The lawn dense, the clouds far up in the sky, and he thought he could rise there. Thought that colors could change if he went far enough through the clouds, would go from blue to silver to a black that was nearly blue. Then streaks of orange, then it would explode into purple. The air thin, but bright as a giant flower, and nothing anywhere. Just silence and rest and peace. That's all he wanted, all he hoped for.

They were walking after him, the five of them, and Margaret, and he had a lead on them, a half mile or a quarter mile, and the fields were clear. He saw Martha put her hands to her mouth and call to him, but he didn't know what she called.

Hey, they'd say, and he was in the back room, and they were gone, except for Margaret, and Mom downstairs, but Mom couldn't walk anymore, she was older than God. He sat at the desk and there were piles of things, of papers and books and pamphlets about healing, about prayer.

Late in the afternoon, in winter, when Margaret was out shopping or walking, or at choir practice, he'd look out and see the roof of the garage and bare trees. And he didn't know what it was, or where it came from, but it came over him so powerfully and deeply that he'd feel tears rolling down his face. That all of it was lost and there was no one to tell. That branches without leaves made him feel like the last person on earth, and his shoulders shook and he put his face down on the desk.

They were there, then, at the end, at six, Sunday morning. Standing around the bed and crying and saying, Goodbye.

And he was bones and skull and skin, and his mouth was slightly open and his eyes stared. As though there were some other words left and something else to see.

six

It was dark in there, in 1953, before anything. It was darker than sleep or night or death, and darker than ebony and darker than the deepest cave in the world.

But how could he know? How could he have any sense of dark? Nothing had begun, and there had been nothing like light, so it was dark the way an absolute, the way a void, was dark.

Everything floated, was warm, and there was a thump every second, more than every second even, seventy or eighty times each minute, though time was also something that hadn't begun yet, something he couldn't know about. Time moved, was out there, but hadn't started yet for him.

The brain had already begun, the heart had started, or would soon start, its long work, and the electricity in the brain and heart were firing. The brainstem had formed but the rest was like a fish, was armless and legless, and had a diaphanous, veiny film over closed and bulging eyes.

It was like space, because of the cord, and because of floating and the vast darkness and maybe the tiny electrical exchanges, the earliest synapses, caused visual sparks, caused something like inner specks of brightness—and they were the suns and moons and planets and stars.

Surely there was movement and sound other than the steady thump. There were cries, and voices must have been like vibrations, must have been weirdly distorted, like a record at slow speed, but there was nothing to compare sound with. Nothing more or less or like, and no ears to hear, but sound would be waves, would be vibrations on the skin, in the sea.

And walking, standing, sitting, breathing, yawning, would all be sensed too, and the blood and food and fluids nourished them—though one wasn't quite a one yet, wasn't even a half, was beginning—slowly—to emerge, but was nonetheless the size of a fingernail, and that large only lately.

IT MUST HAVE BEEN MARCH, late March, and it was probably at night—at nine or ten or eleven.

Ten or eleven was late for them. They had two young kids, jobs. They worried and did not sleep well and woke at five or six in the morning.

They had only been in Newton in Massachusetts a few months, less than a few months, in fact. She had come with the two kids, with Martha and Eric, in September of 1952, when Eric was a month old. She stayed with her husband's mother and father, with Gram and Bamp, in their big apartment in Newton Corner, where he—her husband, the father of Martha and Eric—had grown up.

The furniture was old and dark and heavily upholstered. There were standing lamps with tasselled lampshades, and an upright radio, and a heavy chair in a corner of the living room where Bamp read the newspaper after work each evening.

She came on the train in September, from Ohio, in 1952, when Martha was fifteen months and Eric one month, and the three of them slept in a bedroom on the second floor,

Eric in a crib that Bamp had brought up from the cellar, and she and Martha on the double bed—Martha near the wall, where she couldn't fall out.

Martha, at night, slept so deeply those first months in Newton, that she, Martha's mother, worried the child was ill, was slow, had stopped breathing. She sometimes reached over in the bed, late, very late—after the church bell had bonged two times on the far side of the train tracks in Newton Corner—and she felt Martha's head and arms and chest, felt if she was still warm, was still breathing, and she'd hear Eric moving his arms and legs in the crib, the way he seemed to do for much of the night, and then she'd roll over, and later there was light at the edge of the windows and Martha was pulling on the sheets, was pulling at her mother's nightgown.

He stayed in Ohio, stayed in a room he rented from a German woman named Mrs. Schmidt for three dollars a week, on the third floor of her house outside Cincinnati. He worked as a housepainter, and he worked helping the brother of one of the painters on weekends, moving furniture, and he saved most of the money he made and sent postal money orders to Margaret, his wife, in Newton.

He wrote her letters at night, lying on his bed, and said how much he missed her, how much he missed the babies, but how he would see her soon, see her before Christmas, and he worried that the children were not getting enough to eat, were maybe not being kept warm enough.

Did they have fevers? Temperatures? A cough?

And then in December, with his duffel bag from the Army, he arrived at North Station in Boston, on the twenty-third, a year to the day before the new baby would be born. He rode the trolley all the way from Scollay Square to Newton Corner, and there were shouts when he came in.

Margaret, Gram called, and Bamp called him Buzz, his nickname.

When she came downstairs holding Eric in her arms, he said, Honey, and she put Eric in his arms and kissed his cheek, and thought he had grown thin, grown pale, though it could have been from the train, from the rocking and clacking, from the endless towns and miles, the endless sight of bridges and crossings and water towers.

So three months later, in Newton by then, working two jobs and living in two bedrooms now at his mother and father's apartment, they were alone together.

Eric and Martha were asleep in the room next door and they could almost hear the babies breathe.

Gram and Bamp were asleep in the big front bedroom, but the two of them—Eric and Martha's mother and father— had stayed downstairs, on that Saturday night, and listened to music, live, from a ballroom in New York, and then the news—about President Eisenhower, about the ailing Red strongman, Stalin, about Tito in Yugoslavia and a general in Egypt.

A car went by outside and a clock in the dining room ticked, but mostly there was silence.

She was thirty-one years old and wore glasses and was barely five feet tall. He was thirty-two years old, but looked much younger, looked twenty, or twenty-two. He was still thin and pale and his eyes were dark brown, and in the light from the tasselled lamp, her eyes were so blue, were so dark they were almost black.

He said maybe they should go upstairs, and from the strain in his voice, from the tight shaky sound to it, she could tell what he meant.

It's late, she said, and they stood up and they shut the lights off and he checked the locks on the doors.

Then they were in the room and they didn't say anything. The lights were off, and they moved almost silently, touched almost without feeling.

It couldn't have taken too long. They were tired and tense

and even after three years of marriage, nervous, and they were glad of the dark and the silence, and glad too that the next day was Sunday, and they would be able to sleep until seven or eight. Then church, of course, then breakfast—eggs and bacon and toast and juice and coffee—and they drifted in the still bed, then, and seemed at peace at that moment.

And the baby was there, was possible.

HOW LONG A WAY was it? How far to swim?

Was it like swimming across an ocean? A lake? A pond?
Did it drift? Float? Feel movement?
And then the meeting. Was it stars exploding? Clashing?
Was there light? Sound?
Then what?
Silence, warmth, rocking and swaying?

He lay there, floated there, a long long time, though he didn't know about time, of course, and didn't even know what floating was either. It was all he'd ever known or done, and it was silent and utterly dark, and there was nothing else—no memory, no sense of any other life.

But could there have been something in the genes, in the double twisting ladders of the DNA? Something on the rungs, on the sides, in the places where the ladders twisted and touched?

Some sea of memory? A sense of something? A speck where everything was, where memory was kept, and was present during the sleep, but died during the journey out, at the explosion into light and cold?

How much did the speck hold? What was on it?

Could it go back to geologic time? To hundreds of thousands of years ago? To millions of years?

Did planets explode and stars fade to red and dying circles in the sky?

Was there darkness on earth? A vast blanket and water over everything? Silent water? Unmoving water? Water as

92

dark and lightless as the earth?

And dense clouds of dust and particles over the water—as dense as forests, as canopies of leaf—though there was no such thing as forest or leaves then.

And the dark and water and clouds of particle and dust would last a million years, a hundred million years, and outside, in space, there was cold and darkness and specks of light on the darkness, and trillions of miles of stars and galaxies—and clusters of light, and yellow and white and blue and red stars and moons and planets, and it went on forever, could go all the years of the world and still be just beginning.

Could it happen that way?

There were molecules, were atoms that began to mix and bond, and elements fused, became other elements. There was hydrogen and carbon and oxygen and nitrogen, and in ten million years the canopy was less dense, less full of dust and particles, and in spots there were crags of earth, of stone, emerging from the water.

There was something like light, only it wasn't really light, just darkness that was less absolute, and nothing else for millions of years. Then elements and chemical exchanges, and there was something in the water, something like mold, only smaller. Millions of years more and the mold was larger, was more complex, and the memory of it—the place on the ladder, the place where it might be stored—would take millions of years still.

Water evaporated, became other elements, and there were things creeping on land, things that should have been in the water. Things with gills, with flippers, with webbed feet. And there were plants everywhere, green plants with huge leaves, and then time would slow, would have to slow, because so much happened so quickly. Instead of hundreds of millions of years, it was millions, and then hundreds of thousands of years.

There were flying creatures the size of houses, only houses

wouldn't exist, of course, and lizards taller than trees, and creatures with scales and fangs and great webbed wings that flew and no longer swam.

There was fire everywhere, or there was ice over everything, but the ice would come before the fire. Great masses of ice, bigger than a thousand mountains, heaved and cracked and groaned over the surface of the earth, and then in a hundred thousand years there was fire.

And small creatures with warm blood, with fur. Creatures that did not lay eggs, that lived in trees.

MARTHA HAD A COAT with a hood and fur around the inside of the hood, rabbit fur or maybe cat fur, Gram said, and Margaret said she was tired, she was feeling tired all the time, and she said, Gram, we're grateful you let us stay with you, and Gram looked at her and didn't say anything.

At night, when her husband Bill came home from work, they rode the buses and trolleys and walked, and saw houses that were for sale. Houses that needed paint, houses with three bedrooms, houses that had dim bulbs in ceiling lamps, and men in gray tee shirts sat at dining room tables, while Mr. Barber, the real estate man, showed them where the bathroom was on the second floor and what the furnace looked like, and how nice everything could be with a little plaster and a little paint.

Gram watched the kids while they went, and when they returned, she said Eric knocked his food to the floor and Martha had gone to the corner store with Bamp for ice cream, and in April the trees were blooming and the veterans would guarantee their loan for as much as twenty thousand dollars, just as long as they inspected the house and thought it was a good investment.

She said she was tired, she said she'd like to go upstairs for a while, and Gram said okay, she didn't mind looking after the kids. They were good kids, most of the time, and she smiled and gestured for Martha to come over for a hug.

Martha looked from her mother to Gram, and her mother said, Go ahead, and Martha went to Gram, leaned her head against Gram's side and Gram held Martha's head against her apron, against her stomach.

Gram said, You go up, dear, and Margaret thanked her. Gram was so nice sometimes, and as she climbed the stairs she heard Gram tell Martha that they should watch Eric, because Eric was a boy and you could never tell what boys were up to, they were always into something, even if they were only six or eight months old.

She lay on the bed and she knew she was pregnant again. She knew from not getting her period, and she knew because of how tired she felt and the faintly sick feeling, like she'd had too much to eat or she'd had too much coffee and was nervous and scared and full at the same time.

The room was big and had a high ceiling, and had a molded thing the size of a plate in the center of the ceiling. That was from the old gas jets that were gone now.

She pulled the spread over her legs and stomach and lay back, and she could hear cars and dogs way off and a door slamming.

She prayed for ten minutes. She said five Our Fathers and ten Hail Marys and ten Acts of Contrition. The prayers made everything slow down, and the sounds were even farther away, and she was aware of her stomach, of her insides, of her legs and breasts, and she was almost sick, but she was full too, was warm, was strong.

She heard footsteps downstairs, and then she thought of Bill in the morning, getting into his underwear and socks, and how white his skin was, how thin his arms and legs were. She wished he'd eat more, wished that he could find something better than work in a warehouse, than a filing job on weekends. He said he couldn't remember and that he'd lose his head if it wasn't attached, but she told him that wasn't so.

She heard a thump downstairs and she closed her eyes, and could see darkness and streaks of light on the darkness.

How long? she wondered. Another six or seven months? Then there'd be three kids, and still they didn't have enough money to buy a crib, to have a couch or a chair or a rug.

Like when she was three or four in New York City, and the Depression hadn't even started yet, the long lines, the men with gray skin, with rips in their dark overcoats. Rips at the pockets and at the underarms and twine for shoelaces.

There wasn't a father that she could tell. Just her mother, who was thin, and had gray hair and dark eyes sunk back in her head.

She didn't say much. She sat on the side of the bed, and there were water stains on the walls from pipes overhead. There were sounds, voices—doors and drawers and windows slamming, brakes and footsteps, even crows from over by the park and seagulls from the rivers, from Staten Island.

Every month, every six months, they went to another room, and sometimes she stood with her mother in lines, on Eighty-ninth Street, on Second Avenue near the el downtown, and she'd see rich people in black cars that shined like they were wet and drivers in black uniforms stood near the cars.

Her mother coughed. She sat on the bed and coughed, and she held a cloth, she held a piece of newspaper to her mouth and she coughed more. She coughed like it was hard to breathe, like the inside of her chest would come up, and she saw white bubbly liquid on the newspaper and red specks in the bubbles, and she coughed again.

Was that Eighth Avenue, on the second floor? Or One Hundred and Fifth Street? The room on the sixth or seventh floor, in back? And bricks out the window and voices in the airshaft, voices from the stairs and hallways, from the cellar.

Was she nine? Or four?

Had her mother gone yet?

Which time?

She went to the hospital on Welfare Island, to the unit, her mother called it, and she had to be careful not to infect anyone, to give it to other people, especially to her, because she was just a girl, a child, and she had to grow up strong.

She coughed.

Maybe someday she would have little girls and boys of her own. Maybe that would happen and maybe it wouldn't.

Did she know how much her mother loved her?

It wasn't a sin to be poor. It was not wrong in God's eyes.

The engine chugged and brown waves slapped the sides of the boat. Paper floated by, and the brown water churned up, and the gulls squawked like they wanted to say hello, to have something to eat. They fluttered and squawked and beat their gray wings.

Then the buildings were smaller and smaller. They were taller than trees and clouds, but the boat went farther away, and the buildings were the size of blocks, and the docks were shelves on stilts, and they could have been on a rug.

There were low moans, like a giant in the clouds. Low, long, vibrating moans. Moans like hunger, and her mother said they were foghorns, and the blasts were tugboats, like when you pulled on somebody's sleeve. Only the tugboats were small and low in the water, and they had tires nailed on the sides, all the way around, like a necklace of old tires, and that was to push the big boats, the ocean liners in and out of the harbor.

Ocean liners were bigger than buildings, were the size of whole city blocks, and ten or twenty stories high, and she said, Like Grimm? Like the princess and the frog? And her mother said, Not that kind of story. A kind like the layers of a cake, one on top of another, like dishes stacked up.

She said they had pools and dining rooms and ballrooms, and orchestras played and beautiful women in long white dresses danced with handsome men in black coats.

The boats went to Europe, on the other side of the ocean.

97

The ocean was as big as the sky, and Europe was where France and England and Germany and Spain were. And Ireland too. They had kings and queens there, who sat on thrones and wore crowns and lived in palaces. They ate on tables that were long as telephone poles, only flat and shiny, and the knives and forks were silver.

There was an island, and there were long gray buildings, and there were people in white walking near the buildings.

Her mother coughed, and the chugging became slower, became lower.

She said in Europe the kings and queens ruled everything, and when they had babies the babies were princes and princesses and dukes and duchesses and earls. They rode horses, and sometimes they went sailing in boats, and they had hundreds of people in jewels to dinner and they laughed and music played, and her mother said it was grand.

A man on the boat threw a rope to a man on the dock.

Inside there were windows all the way to the ceiling and smells like the bathroom after her mother cleaned it. Women in white wore things in their hair that looked like wings and they talked in whispers.

Her mother kissed her, told her to be a good girl, to behave, to remember her prayers. She kissed the top of her head and she went down a hall and through doors.

A woman said, You be a good girl. You be a lady. She could hear seagulls, like they'd had no food in years.

Then it was late, and she was wearing a stiff white nightgown, and there were nineteen other beds—ten down one side of the room, ten down the other side. There was a picture on the wall of the Governor of New York, and a picture of Calvin Coolidge next to the Governor. Calvin Coolidge was the President of the United States, the woman told her. She had a white uniform, and her arms were so big they wobbled.

The President was like the King of England. His job was

to rule over everybody.

Off with their heads, the woman said, and laughed.

Then the lights were off, and it was dim, blue light from outside, and five girls on the other side of the room, and the Governor and the President watched over her. By then even the seagulls were quiet too.

BY JUNE AND JULY the windows were open and there were more smells. There was tar from the repair crew on the street out front and the smell of paint from two houses down, where men climbed over the house like insects, and late in the day, when they were cleaning their brushes, the smell of turpentine drifted over.

At night the windows stayed open and the curtains puffed out like sails, and Martha began to cry and thought the curtains were ghosts that had come out for the night.

There were earth smells at night, too—trees and bushes and grass and the loamy smell of soil and flowers. Lilac and forsythia and hydrangea.

Inside was a lake, was a drift, and slower even than a few months before. There were arms and legs by then and fingers, and maybe memory. Some sense of smoky plains, of great fields of ice, of lumbering creatures eating great leafy plants, and breathing fire or smoke, or sleeping on rocks that overlooked mountains.

Anything was possible. Wasn't it? Earthquakes and volcanoes? Birds?

Thunder and lightning? Hailstones the size of oranges? Electrical storms that split the sky like a melon and rain that fell for three moons, and made creatures scramble for high ground and cling to crags of rock, trembling with cold, fur sleek with rain, eyes dark and staring?

Then the air would be clear, and maybe creatures with arms and legs, with a heavy ridge of bone over the eyes, would hide and watch, and thousands of years later would lean back, would stand for an instant on two legs, would see over the grass.

The arms and legs could move inside, but slowly, because they were underwater, and the muscles were involuntary, were mostly spasm and electricity and instinct. Something moved behind the veiny eyelids. But it was electricity, was dream, was memory.

Groups were squatting around fires and there were sticks and pieces of stone and bits of bone and fur. Thunder at night was terrifying, and death was constant, but they piled rocks on top of corpses to protect them from dogs and wolves, from birds and rats, and sometimes they put beads, put sticks, in the dead hands, would cover the faces with fur.

Maybe they thought of something that would come later, something for after, on the other side. Something to do with the place where thunder came from.

SHE WENT AT TEN to the sisters in Tarrytown, above New York City, on the Hudson River. Her mother's skin was gray, and she coughed all day and night, and stayed on the island with the women who wore white, who moved silently, even though they were not sisters, were not the brides of Jesus.

She went first to the building on Ninety-seventh Street, where they prevented cruelty to children.

Cruelty was where they locked boys and girls in closets or in basements and hit them with belts, with hands, with the handles of mops and brooms, with coat hangers. Cruelty was when there was no food, or when the food had small white things like tiny worms in it, that moved, and you could almost feel them in your stomach.

Cruelty was cold all the time. On your back and sides and legs when you tried to sleep, and the wind whistled like a teakettle through the cracks in the window, through the patch where the cardboard was. Only it was not steamy like a teakettle. It was ice all up and down and especially where the coat didn't cover, and her hands were stiff and swollen and thick with the cold.

The lady said she would be given a dress, a beautiful nice dress like she'd never had before, and she'd be grateful she had such a nice dress. Many little girls didn't have such things.

Did she know the word *gratitude*? Did she understand?

The woman had blond hair, had hair like sunshine and smelled like a chocolate.

They wore bows in their hair on Sunday after church and they could go outside to play on the lawn, and then she had to go inside to Mother Superior's office, and Mother Superior's face was long the way the night was long.

She said she had news, she had sad news, news she would probably not understand and news that was difficult. But God did not place burdens on us we were unable to bear, and she felt it was best to tell her.

Sit down, Mother Superior said, and pointed with her long hand to a chair, and she was only sitting for five or ten seconds when Mother Superior said, Your mother passed on last night.

I'm sorry. I'm very sorry, Mother Superior said, like she had done something wrong, like she had lied or cheated or stolen something and she would have to tell Father in confession.

She is at rest, Mother Superior said. She is with God.

God had a white beard and a circle of gold that floated over his head. He had a deep deep voice like the foghorn in the harbor, and when he smiled his teeth were white and his face was happy and sad at the same time.

Mother Superior said she should pray to God the Father for her mother. For the repose of her soul in heaven.

Repose was like sleep, like dreams, was like when the sandman came very late and you didn't know till later, till you had woken up. Repose was when there was no sound anywhere in heaven and earth. Just silence for a million miles and a million years.

SHE WAS AS BIG as a house, big as a barn, as big as God even.

Not really. She shouldn't have thought that, but it was funny what it did to her, in October, with all the leaves as bright as sunshine and fire, and the wind at night blowing and the leaves sounded like a graveyard then—dry as death, rustling like whispers in a funeral home.

She felt kicks and she felt huge and slow, and she felt quiet too, and sometimes dreamy and feverish. The way she thought sometimes, it made her wonder. Funny and strange, like someone had slipped her a mickey.

Mickey Finn was it? From Dick Tracy or Steve Roper or Terry and the Pirates? Men with square jaws, with blue guns called gats.

Swell, Dick Tracy, someone said, and there was a drink on a table and a man with shifty eyes poured something in the drink. Powder or pills or something, without anyone seeing.

And Terry or Dick or Steve picked the drink up and thought it tasted funny, tasted bitter, but maybe not. Maybe it was imagination.

So he finished, and there were stars and exclamation points all in a row.

What!?!?!? And then he went down and it was all a giant spiral, with weird voices and fat ladies with jewels and rouge asking if he wanted a drink, and laughing loud and high, like witches.

Then houses spun by, and lampposts and roulette wheels and hours or days later he woke up in a room, and there was a beautiful red-headed woman holding a cool facecloth to his forehead.

Some drink, Steve or Terry or Dick, she'd say.

They'd always know his name.

Spinning like that? Seeing the girl who slept in the next

bed over, the man in the uniform on the corner of Fifth and Twenty-third?

Bill came in, and he was thinner than before, and he said there was a house, the house they'd seen on California Street, in Newtonville, the two-family. Mom and Dad could move into the first floor and help with rent, and they could move in December. That was possible. Right when the baby was due and they'd have their own house, even though the bank would own it.

WOULD IT BE QUIET inside by then? Quiet and solemn and peaceful as anything could ever be?

Like floating on a lake in summer, in silence. Maybe in Vermont or Maine or upstate New York. A small lake surrounded by trees, a hot hot day in July, and only the buzz of insects and the blue sheet of sky. The lake lapped and jostled, but slower than anything, and way off in the sky, so far away it could be in another state, a puff of cloud.

But nothing else. Just floating and drifting. Just soft movement.

Only darker, of course. Vastly dark and warm. Shy and quiet as something at night.

And maybe some memory of people on floes of ice, and tilling the earth with sticks. Pyramids and Pickett's Charge would all swirl by, would be so close together it would be hard to tell, hard to know. Aristotle and the Birdman of Alcatraz, Jesus and Babe Ruth and Myrna Loy and Charles Dickens and Tom Thumb. Those people and others. They happened so fast.

Bill came home at night, and they moved December 9, 1953, to the old house with three floors, and someone had painted the hall on the second floor red, a deep blood red, and Bill said they could paint it eventually, but for now there were other things.

The first floor was empty at first, till the following summer, and the third floor would be closed too. There were three bedrooms up there, two with slanted ceilings, and the air felt so cold on her skin that she shuddered from the feel of it.

Bill said she shouldn't have gone up there, not in her condition, and she said she wanted to see. The halls and the walls and the worn wood floors—she kept touching them, kept running her fingers over their surfaces, and there was cracked linoleum on the bathroom floor and the bathtub was enormous, and had feet like the paws of a cat, and out front, on California Street, there was a tree, and traffic moved past and the Charles River was only a few hundred yards away.

There were four carloads. Mr. Levernz from Pearl Street drove them back and forth, and Bill gave him twenty dollars, but Mr. Levernz gave it back.

There was a bed and a table for the kitchen, and the crib Gram and Bamp gave them. There were chairs for the table and two big chairs that smelled like a cellar, and for two nights there was no heat because Bill forgot to call Edison and have it turned on.

Martha pounded around on the bare floors, and her footsteps sounded like the inside of a church, echoing and echoing. And Eric looked at the slats of the crib and looked at his mother and father with dark eyes like his mother's. He stared so long they had to blink.

Why so serious? she wondered, then everything slowed again, and she lay on the bed and there was a slip of paper with the number of the cab company. Veteran's Cab.

She could hardly move. It was a bowling ball or a barrel of beer or a ton of bricks. Her legs ached and she felt pains down below, but at first she wasn't sure.

They were strong, were deep, and there were lights on the houses and Bill had bought a skinny Christmas tree for the front room, and they put some bulbs and tinsel on the tree.

Gram came over. Gram said the radio mentioned snow, and she didn't know if that was good or bad.

She winced, she almost cried out at the pain. She knew about this. There was nothing for her to do.

Then Bill was there from work, and they called Veteran's, and the pains were every nine minutes or every thirteen minutes or maybe five minutes apart.

Was that possible? Would she have a Christmas baby?

The driver was worried, and she saw the lights on the front of houses and wreaths on the front of the police station and courthouse in West Newton Square.

Then it was fast—down corridors and that funny smell like ammonia and blood—and loudspeakers everywhere. Dr. Heath saying it would be fine, everything was fine, and Bill hadn't shaved for a long time. He said he was sorry, and she gasped at the way it felt, like her insides were splitting.

And all of it was like a boat sinking, the sea rushing in and out and everything in turmoil. Then out, and all of them yelling, and cold like the middle of space. And brightness, in the eyes—so that even though his eyes were closed the light was like needles, and they held his ankles, and slapped and slapped, and he screamed like his lungs were exploding.

And even though his eyes were closed and the room was warm, he was drifting with giants, in ice and sunlight, and sounds like thunder. And it wouldn't be over for a long long time.

seven

In 1976, in the bicentennial year, there were people out there doing things. I read the newspapers and I read magazines and books, and I knew what they did, usually at night, when people were sleeping. I was twenty-two, and I had prescriptions from a half dozen doctors, I was a customer at four pharmacies, and I knew what happened.

They crept around at night, in dark clothes, in old cars, and they brought their tools with them. Rope and handcuffs, guns and knives with tape on the handles, lengths of wire, duct tape. Some used hammers and pliers, sometimes rocks or their hands.

They didn't look strange or funny, didn't twitch when other people were around. In Washington State and Oregon and Utah and Colorado he had blond hair, was friendly, handsome, talked well, had a smile, had nice teeth.

In California he wasn't much more than five feet tall and played the guitar. In Chicago he was tall, had blue eyes, and in Texas he was blond, had been a Marine, had been a marksman.

He was The Measuring Man in Boston before he became The Strangler, and he was probably still alive, was in the Bridgewater State Hospital for the Criminally Insane.

He was a compact man, had dark hair, and could talk. A killer couldn't talk that well, like he'd gone to college and majored in English or Speech or something. Outside the door, smiling, looking shy.

I represent a modeling agency and I'd like to talk to you, and if it's not too embarrassing—and I know some ladies would be too shy—I'd like, if I may, to take your measurements. To keep on file, for when assignments come up. I'm sure you understand.

The landlord asked him to check faucets, radiators, the paint on the bedroom ceiling. The gas company worried about a leak, the power company about electrical sockets, the fire department about smoke. There was a mayor's commission taking a survey for the elderly, there was a poll for a nationally known concern, and people willing to participate were eligible for the grand drawing, a trip to South America or Paris, for a dinette set, for a washer and dryer.

I WORE CHINOS to the doctor's office. I wore loafers and black socks and glasses. I had terrible headaches, headaches that brought tears and nausea. I was working too hard, unable to relax or sleep. I had to put ice packs on my head, had to lie down in the dark, had to lie still as a blanket.

Was I allergic to anything? they asked.

How much did I smoke?

Did I drink alcohol? Coffee? Soft drinks?

Did I eat cheese? Chocolate? Berries?

Did I get exercise?

Was I under pressure? Stress?

Any unusual changes? Any deaths? Partings? Major moves?

They wore glasses and white coats. They took my blood

pressure, pulse, tapped my chest. They took urine and blood, and tapped my elbows and knees with a rubber-headed hammer, felt with their cool fingers at the side of my neck, at the base of my skull.

They said, You have to be careful with this, and filled out the pad. You have to avoid driving, avoid alcohol, be careful not to mix them.

One was Q.I.D., one T.I.D. Fifty tablets each, with four refills.

They said, Call in six months.

Q.I.D. meant four times a day, T.I.D. three times.

At home, I took two tablets, and then two more, and then two after that.

There was a strand, a web, on my face, and I brushed it away. I went downstairs. Mom and Dad were trying to relax.

They worried about me just painting houses sometimes and not eating enough, and sleeping half the day and reading stuff.

How could I read about those people? What was wrong with me?

Wasn't it kind of morbid? Mom asked. Kind of sick? Didn't it keep me awake nights?

She said, Will, and looked at me, and Dad said the junk on television was sick. Singing chimps and dancing dogs. Why couldn't they leave the poor animals alone?

I said, What was it like when you were growing up?

Dad said all the cars were black, and there was no such thing as television. Mail was delivered twice a day and a postcard cost a penny.

There wasn't much noise, Mom said. People were friendly. Everyone didn't lock their doors all the time.

I could feel the pills. Loose and warm and sweet as music and food. Like floating through a cloud. Like a warm day. Like ice cream. Like the softest bed in the world. Like sleep.

Mom said, We were nicer to each other. Even in New

York City, even in Manhattan.

THEY WENT OUT AT NIGHT and drove to the neighborhoods in the hills, above the city, and down below they could see millions of lights. The houses were enormous and dark, were set a thousand feet apart, and had bushes all around them. There were smooth lawns and patios and pools that were sky blue, and lawn furniture.

This was in the summer, and doors were unlocked, and screens were down, and the air was so still they could hear a car a mile away, down in the canyon, on the road built into the side of a hill. Noise came from the other side of the bushes, but was farther away than it seemed. They knew how tricky things could be at two or three in the morning. How shadows were things, light made skin glow, eyes were large and shiny, and from the lawns they were sure they could hear people breathing inside, could hear them murmur in sleep, could hear them turn over and press a hand to the side of their faces.

Sleeping people lying there, surrounded by warmth, their eyes closed, their breathing deep and regular, dreaming of horses that flew and drifting trees and a sky as red as roses.

There were four of them. Three women and the tall man, and they checked the front door and it was unlocked. Maybe because this was California, and warm and sunny all the time and oranges grew in trees, and it felt like being a kid again.

The living room had beams in the ceiling, a huge fireplace, three or four couches. The breathing was louder in there, and the blond woman from Iowa or Nebraska or somewhere began to giggle, and he had to shush her, though he knew the feeling. Like he wanted to laugh, and in there they slept like they were four years old, were cowboys and movie stars and pilots in the sky.

His heart was a drum in a band, and he had no idea how many were sleeping behind doors that probably weren't even closed. He didn't know what would happen, the four of them standing next to the couches and polished tables and lamps that looked like balloons in the light from the moon outside.

The blond woman started to move, crouched over, in a sideways sliding motion. She moved between the couches, in front of the fireplace, past the big window, past the shiny tables and the lamps, and she began to hiss as she moved, hiss so softly that they wouldn't have been able to hear her, her tongue and teeth and lips, and all the esses like a radiator, like something in the grass, if it wasn't so late and so still. Then the other two women started moving and hissing, and the man joined them, and all four were gliding sideways, were hissing so low it was only air, and they crouched as they moved, and any minute, any second, someone might hear, might sense in sleep, might open their eyes, stand up, pause at the door, peek toward the living room. Someone with matted hair, with sleep-puffed eyes and cheeks. Someone in a nightgown, in pajamas, in shorts, in underwear. Someone naked, his flesh ghostly in the weird light.

What then?

The blond woman stopped and picked a glass ball off an end table. The ball was clear and had a starfish embedded in the glass, and she held it up—there in the moonlight and named for the sky.

Ssss, she said softly, and pressed the glass to her cheek, to her throat, to her breast. Then she went to the front door and they glided out, crouched over, and the lawn was moon-lit. The pool was blue, the pool was moving.

I SLEPT FOURTEEN HOURS, and when I woke up my head was stone and my mouth was dry. I lit a cigarette and blew smoke at the ceiling. The house was empty. When I moved my head it took me a second to catch up with the movement. There was an echo to everything. My lips were sloppy on the end of the cigarette, they couldn't grip.

Paul Cody

I FLIPPED THE PAGES of the paper. The nude body of a woman had been found Sunday by hikers in the Blue Hills Reservation. There was a sock on one foot and a thin gold chain around one wrist. There were ligature marks on her neck.

There was a body in a Dumpster in Saugus and a body in the trunk of a car, in the parking lot of a bowling alley on Route One, shot twice in the head at close range. There were powder burns. In Utah two young women were reported missing. One was twenty, the other twenty-three. One was last seen hitchhiking near a bar. The other lived in a basement apartment, and her bed was made. There was a spot of blood on the pillowcase. In Nebraska, near Lincoln, he worked as a garbageman, had red hair, was barely over five feet tall. Starkweather. Little Red.

He said, The more I looked at people the more I hated them because I knowed they wasn't any place for me with the kind of people I knowed. I used to wonder why they was here anyhow. A bunch of goddamned sons of bitches looking for somebody to make fun of, some poor fellow who ain't done nothing but feed chickens.

His girlfriend was fourteen, he was nineteen. He said, They said they were tired of me hanging around. I told the old lady off and she got so mad that she slapped me. When I hit her back her husband started to come at me, so I had to let both of them have it.

He went to the bedroom and killed the two-year-old girl, the half sister. They made sandwiches, turned on the television. The house was quiet.

He said, Don't know why it was, but being alone with her was like owning a little world all our own. Lying there with our arms around each other and not talking much, just kind of tightening up and listening to the wind blow or looking at the same star and moving our hands over each other's face. I forgot about my bow legs when we was having excitement. When I'd hold her in my arms and do the things we done together, I didn't think about being a red-headed peckerwood then. We knowed that the world had give us to each other. We was going to make it leave us alone. If we'd been let alone we wouldn't hurt nobody.

They went on the road. They killed a farmer, killed a sixteen-year-old girl and her seventeen-year-old boyfriend. He said, I began to wonder what kind of life I did live in this world, and even to this day I'm wondering about it. But it don't matter how much I used to think about it. I don't believe I ever would have found a personal world or live in a worthwhile world maybe, because I don't know life, or for what it was. They say this is a wonderful world to live in, but I don't believe I ever did really live in a wonderful world.

They stopped at the house of a businessman, killed him, his wife, the maid who worked for them.

He said, Nobody knowed better than to say nothing to me when I was aheaving their goddamn garbage.

In Wyoming, on the side of the road, they killed a shoe salesman taking a nap.

He said, I had hated and been hated. I had my little world to keep alive as long as possible, and my gun. That was my answer.

AT NIGHT I WALKED, after drinking coffee, after pills. I went up the streets to West Newton Hill, where the houses were enormous, and there were three or four cars in driveways and statues on lawns.

At dinner time the windows were orange and yellow, and people stood at kitchen counters and sinks, sat on couches and rocking chairs in dens and living rooms. They wore glasses and had gray hair. They were thin.

When it was dark, I walked down driveways and sat on swings in backyards, on benches under oak or elm or maple trees. I saw people and heard traffic and saw airplanes winking across the sky. I took more pills, then stood up and cut through bushes or climbed a fence into another yard. I sat in the grass behind a stucco house that had dormers on the roof on the third floor, that had a giant screen porch on the back of the house. The lights were off, and after watching, I tried the door to the porch, went in and looked around, and there was wrought iron furniture, chairs and a couch, a table with a glass top.

The French doors to the living room were locked. I punched the pane of glass next to the door handle, reached in, unlocked the door.

The house smelled like nobody had been there in a while. There was a giant blue couch, a glass case of porcelain figures and a tall grandfather clock near the door to the dining room.

I walked through the living room and den, crossed a hall, went through the dining room to the kitchen. I took a juice glass from a cabinet, ran water. The faucet sputtered for a moment and I could smell rust. I let it run for two or three minutes, then filled the glass, took two more pills.

The stairway was broad and carpeted, and the hall on the second floor had a bay of windows with a window seat that looked out to the backyard. There were six bedrooms on the second floor, and the biggest one was over the living room. It had its own bathroom and fireplace and another bay window looked out on the front yard.

The bed was enormous, was made of dark wood, and might have been in a castle. There was a white bedspread and a folded afghan at the foot of the bed.

Something moved, but it was a mirror. It was me.

I took my boots off, and set them at the side of the bed, and unfolded the afghan. I lay down, got the afghan around me, tucked under my feet and legs, my back, around my shoulders. The house was quiet as dawn, but darker. I could feel the size of the house around me.

I closed my eyes and I was somewhere else, was with people I didn't know.

HE HAD HEADACHES so powerful they made tears run down his face. He typed a note. I don't quite understand what is compelling me to type. I have been to a psychiatrist. I have been having fears and violent impulses. I've had some tremendous headaches in the past. I am prepared to die. After my death I wish an autopsy be performed to see if there's any mental disorder.

He wrote, I've decided to kill my wife Kathy tonight. I love her very much. I don't want her to have to face the embarrassment my actions will surely cause her.

He went to his mother's apartment and killed her. He wrote, I love my mother with all my heart. He wrote, 12:00 a.m.—Mother already dead. Three o'clock—both dead. He wrote, Life is not worth living.

He went to the observation deck of a tower with two pistols and a Remington rifle, and began to shoot. He shot forty-six people, and killed sixteen. He was blond, had blue eyes.

In Chicago, in Boston, in Los Angeles and Houston and Seattle, he walked quietly, walked quickly, walked like he had somewhere to go. He wore one arm in a sling, or used crutches, and seemed to have trouble carrying his books. He dropped them, and a young woman outside the library helped him pick them up, and he thanked her, said she was very kind, she was thoughtful, was pretty, if she didn't mind his saying so.

He had a black wallet with a badge pinned to it and he had handcuffs. He went to the bus station, to a coffee shop that was open all night, and a bar where there were drugs, were women out front, women down the block, under streetlights, in doorways of empty stores.

He told the kid he was with the Drug Abuse Administration and he spoke loudly. He barked.

Get against the car, you little motherfucker. Hug the car. Hands on the roof, he said, his voice deep.

The boy was skinny, wore a tee shirt and jean jacket, was

from Michigan or California or Maine. The man ran his hands over the boy's arms and chest and back. Then down his legs, over his ass, his crotch. He wasn't wearing underwear.

The lights from cars crossed the kid's face and his eyes were large. He had a small nose, small teeth, pale skin.

The man said he'd book him for vagrancy, truancy, for prostitution and possession. For being a runaway, a minor, for having no means of support.

He said, Where you from? And the kid said, Baton Rouge, sir, and spoke softly, with a trace of the South.

He was fifteen, and left home in December, before Christmas, and he didn't think they even knew he was gone.

It doesn't matter, the kid said, and the man said, You hungry? You need something to eat?

The kid looked down, and the traffic moved past, and it was midnight by then, it was one or two.

C'mon, the man said.

The kid thought of a room with a bed and a dresser, and a peephole in the door. Green paint, and the baloney sandwiches for lunch and dinner, and soup, and the kid two doors down with bad skin and teeth, with the tattoo on his hand. The one in the shower with the hard-on, saying, Hey, and his hand full of soap. You, he said. I mean you.

The man pointed and told him to move. He wore a heavy gray overcoat and black gloves and he wasn't tall. Maybe five eight or nine. But thick. At least two hundred pounds.

They drove a long time. They went on an expressway and through neighborhoods where trash cans and cars lined the curbs, and TV aerials were on top of all the houses. They went on a road that ran next to a river, and the man drove fast around curves. The kid was pressed against the car door, and could see trees and bushes rushing past and he imagined the pavement.

Then they doubled around, and the man asked him if he did drugs.

He handed the kid a joint and a lighter and said, Go ahead. And the kid smoked, and he was very tired, was hungry. As hungry as he'd ever been.

They stopped in front of a small ranch house, and parked between a car and a van. Everything was quiet and it was colder than before.

There was an aquarium inside, and pictures on the wall of clowns, and a twenty-one-inch television. There were hand-cuffs on the counter in the kitchen.

Sit down, he said, pointed to a chair at the table and opened the refrigerator. He took out bread and mayonnaise, ham, Swiss cheese, lettuce and tomato, a jar of dill spears. He made a sandwich, took out a plate, got chips from a bag in a cabinet.

Go ahead, he said to the kid, and pointed.

He set a napkin next to the plate, and the sandwich was gone as though the kid had inhaled it, like a seagull or some-thing.

Then he stood up, and the man took the handcuffs and said, Lemme show you something, and the kid hesitated. They looked heavy, looked real, not something from a joke shop.

C'mon, he said. I'll show you how to get out of them.

The kid put his arms behind his back and heard the snap. Metal against metal. The man took a dish towel from next to the sink and said, Open your mouth.

GRAM SAID THAT SHE didn't believe Howard Hughes was really dead. In some hotel—a whole floor of a hotel—in Las Vegas or Reno.

She said he was crazy as a loon. Didn't have both oars in the water. The lights were on but nobody was home.

Fingernails as long as knitting needles, and he weighed a hundred and ten pounds. And this was a tall man, a hand-some man too. Years ago he could have been in the movies. Going with Jane Russell and that crowd. Flying around the world like Charles Lindbergh. Lucky Lindy, who flew to Paris, France, and then his little baby got kidnapped and murdered.

She said, Get yourself a piece of cake. Out in the kitchen. Orange cake, with frosting. She said it was delicious if she did say so herself.

She said she'd read he was worth a billion dollars. Imagine, she said. A billion dollars. And for what. So he could stay in hotels and eat grapefruit and bananas. And pick everything up with tissues so he didn't catch any germs. Wouldn't go outside, had hair and a beard down to his shoes like he thought he was Jesus himself come back, and staying on the top floor of a hotel in Las Vegas.

She said he was doing the whole thing, saying he was dead and such, so he'd be left alone, would be left in a little peace and quiet for a change. They were always after him for pictures and interviews and money money money. She said she didn't believe he was the man behind the CIA, and owned three quarters of the silver in the world and most of the airplanes too.

The things people would say, she said. Just to get in the newspapers, to get on television. People were supposed to believe about the grapefruit and tissues.

And that thing in Philadelphia, that hotel. All those legionnaires dying like flies. Now that's one hotel, she said, where they'd never see Howard Hughes. Those long carpeted hallways, the doors to rooms, the men downstairs in the dining rooms and bars. Big guys with stomachs sagging over their belts, with red faces and watery eyes. Cigars and cigarettes and stories. In Georgia, they'd say. In Germany or Paris or coastal England. In the Pacific, where the sky was so blue you needed sunglasses, where the water was infinite like the heavens.

Later, in their rooms, the pain was extraordinary, was powerful as appendicitis, that cold shaky feeling like the flu, pain and heat and cold—all at the same time.

How many died? Gram asked. Twenty? Thirty? Forty?

Everything was strange, she said. Not like before, when she was a girl. When things were normal.

AT TWO A.M. I could blink, and say things softly, lying in bed in my room. Say things out loud, but quiet as clouds.

Quiet, I whispered.

Soft.

Hey, I said.

Hey.

Hey.

And I could see sound waves leave my mouth and rise to the flat gray ceiling, and the candle flickered, and the waves reached the ceiling and rippled like a pebble in water, and lapped and lapped for a long time.

I knew how dark the streets were at four a.m., how quiet and calm.

I hummed songs and heard voices that said the weather was cool, was dropping down overnight into the low thirties.

Someone on the radio called from Landover, Maryland, said she couldn't sleep, and the man said, Why not, and she said her husband was overseas in the Navy and would be away three more months.

She had a son and a daughter, nine and fourteen.

A man in Chicago was drunk, and said Boston was a good town if you were a fish or a bean, but was no place for a human bean.

A girl in a town in Missouri disappeared, was walking home from school, and never reached home. An eight-year-old girl with dark hair, with black hair and white ribbons in her hair, with blue corduroy pants, a light blue coat. Imagine the poor mother, a woman said. No body, no nothing. Like a spaceship on a lawn, its lights blinking, and a ramp came down and there was soft bright light inside.

Come to me. Come inside to me, a voice said, and there was music so beautiful a child couldn't keep from listening.

Don't talk to strangers. Don't accept candy. Don't get close to cars that stop, where the driver rolls down the window and tries to talk to you.

Someone with quick eyes, with wet lips, who said, Your mom was hurt, and had to go to the hospital and wanted me to pick you up.

Mom and Dad moved away, they forgot you, they died in a car wreck. You'll be okay. I'll look after you. I'm a friend.

IN JUNE, ON GAINSBOROUGH STREET, on Commonwealth Avenue, on a street in Lynn, north of Boston, he strangled women. On Grove Street and Columbia Road and Huntington Avenue and Park Drive. In Cambridge and Salem and Lawrence, and the women were found with stockings, with cords, around their necks and tied into bows, and they were naked from the waist down.

Out there at night, moving quiet as air, soft as sleep.

From the landlord, from a survey, from a plumbing contractor.

He wasn't tall and he spoke well and was just standing, his hands in the pockets of his raincoat, and maybe he was nice.

A boy in western Massachusetts was missing. From a supermarket, in a town in the Berkshires. Leafy streets and white houses with black or gray trim. He was with his mother and went two aisles over to get peanut butter and didn't come back, and she thought he wandered away, wandered out into the fall afternoon, into the leaves, to kick a football, to feel the season, the last scent of summer.

He was eleven, a boy who went for long bike rides, and there were flyers with his picture, with his height and weight. He was wearing jeans and a white tee shirt and white sneakers. He was wearing a Red Sox jacket, he liked bicycles.

I BOUGHT A SODA from a machine at a gas station and sat on a bench.

There were kids moving past, on their way from junior high, from football or band or choir practice. They carried books and walked in groups of two or three or four.

I took two pills, crossed my legs and sipped soda.

The sky was dark, the traffic dense. I waited.

A kid crossed the intersection, his hair still wet from the shower, and he didn't see me.

Two benches down, a man was sitting and waiting. He wore a dark overcoat, an alpine hat, and I could feel the pills. Spreading and growing warm.

The man stared at his feet, his lap, and I watched him.

Three girls approached the intersection. Their hair was long, was tied behind their heads. They wore skirts and their legs were thin.

I watched the man and he didn't look up.

Then they were past, and I sipped and lit a cigarette and watched traffic. Five minutes later I looked again.

The bench was empty and everything was dark, was shadow, was night. Things were out there, were waiting. Kids from Missouri and western Massachusetts. People in bed in California or Houston or Seattle, breathing quietly, or standing under streetlights in Chicago—like all of this was made up, was happening to someone else, was something from a book or a movie or a dream.

eight

The nuns, when I was seven, dressed in black, with starched white parts around the neck and face and a white bib in front, and they could have been penguins, or they could have been men in ballrooms—only their rosary beads clacked all the time, and they wore glasses with steel frames, and they didn't dance—not ever, not even for a moment.

They were the brides of Christ, and they moved up and down the aisles of the classroom like great black ships in sea lanes, and Sister Mary Boniface stopped at Joseph Marinozzi's desk and asked where his pencils were, where his homework was, where his lunchbox was, and he didn't look up. His hair was so short there were white nicks from shears all over his head.

Sister said, Are you deaf, young man? And Joseph Marinozzi said, No, and Sister said, No what? And Joseph said, No, Sister Mary Boniface.

She said, So? And he said he forgot.

Forgot what?

Everything.

Sister said she supposed he'd have to go without a lunch, and he would be hungry all afternoon, and he might begin to know what it was like to be a starving orphan in Africa or India.

She said, Joseph, and she put her hand on the top of his head, where the nicks were—Joseph, do you feel you would be able to remember your head if it wasn't attached to you? Would you remember that, do you think? And Ann Whitmore and Ginny McNamee began to giggle, even though their hands were in front of their faces trying to stop. Then everyone began to laugh.

Sister Mary Boniface taught second grade in the morning, and Sister Mary Rose taught in the afternoon. Sister Mary Boniface was old and had a wart on the side of her face, and she was bald under the wimple, which was the part of the habit that went over the head.

A habit was not like biting your nails or picking your nose, or even a good habit like brushing your teeth and being nice to your brothers and sisters. A habit was black robes and the white bib and the wimple on the head, and being bald underneath. To protect from vanity, and to be a bride of our Lord and Savior, Jesus Christ. Amen.

And bow your head when you say the name Jesus Christ, not like some heathen or atheist.

Sister Mary Boniface said there was no such thing as an atheist in a foxhole, and Melinda Coleman asked what Sister meant by that, and everyone almost smiled because the trick was to get Sister Mary Boniface to talk about heathens and savages and atheists and Godless Communists, and to talk about hell and sins and harlots.

She said foxholes were trenches, were like holes people dug in the ground during wars, and David Turque asked if they were like graves, where people were buried, and Sister's face brightened and she said, Well yes, David. I guess they are.

She said men crouched down, and there were bullets and bombs and shells whistling overhead, and she made a low whistling sound and her hand was flat, was chest high, and as she whistled she moved her hand fast from side to side, like a bullet from a German or a Communist, and she said when you were about to die, when you didn't know if any one bullet had your name on it—and she didn't mean your name in pen and ink, but your name from the Divine Engraver—she said every man, especially the atheists, got down on his knees in the mud and the slime and the muck, and prayed for grace, prayed for His protection and guidance.

Cecelia Grady, who everyone called Cici, asked if Sister had ever knelt down to pray in the muck of a foxhole, and Sister said, No. Only in the foxholes of life. At the end of a day, in Confession, and each morning when she got out of bed.

She said life was a war between God and the Devil, and we must be armed like soldiers for the battle.

Bradley Hager, who was really a girl, although she had a boy's name, asked Sister about Kansas, where Sister Mary Boniface had been a girl a long long time ago.

Sister sat down on the edge of her desk and looked at the windows. There were five giant windows along one wall, and they were so tall that Sister had to use a huge pole to open and close them.

It was gray outside and raining, and the bare branches in the trees looked like the legs of a spider.

Sister said, Okay. Because it's Friday, and because it's raining, we can put our studies aside.

Peter Nordland said, Yeah, Sister, and Sister said, Quietly, and everyone put their books and pencils and papers inside their desks.

Sister shut off the lights, and there was just the gray light in the giant windows. She said, Put your heads down, and we folded our arms on top of the desks and laid our heads against the cool wood, and Sister began to walk slowly up and down the long aisles, the leather of her shoes squeaking, the boards in the floor making slow groaning sounds.

Sister held her rosary beads so they wouldn't clack, and she said, Back in Kansas, when I was your age, when I was seven and eight years old, and I was, believe it or not. I was a girl with pigtails who got mud all over her shoes and hated to sit in class all day, just the way you hate it now.

Her shoes kept squeaking, and the rain fell outside with a billion feet, and Sister Mary Boniface was in the corner near the coat closets and she was turning at the bottom of the second aisle, and I could see Kathryn Parker's legs and shoes and red stockings, then Sister was walking slowly up the aisle near the blackboard, which was washed every Friday afternoon by Joseph Marinozzi, even though he forgot everything else and didn't have too much upstairs.

Kathryn Parker's father owned a funeral home and wore black and never smiled. Mark Edrich, who was two grades ahead of us, said there were coffins and dead bodies in Kathryn's cellar, and he said if Kathryn or her sisters were bad, if they lied or stole or cheated or swore, they had to spend the night in the cellar, sleeping in one of the coffins, and one night the lid fell down and Kathryn couldn't get out, and she screamed for hours, but nobody heard her.

Sister Mary Boniface said she was just a girl once too, hard as that was to imagine, and she said you blinked your eyes and looked in the mirror, and suddenly you were wrinkled and your skin dried up and your hair turned gray and you needed glasses to see your own hand. She said it was like a burglar came at night and stole your time away, because when she was a girl in Kansas she never thought it would happen so fast, like going to sleep one night a girl, and waking up an old lady.

She said one of the tragedies in life was getting older and learning things, and losing your loved ones. Losing your mother and father, your grandparents, losing your brothers and sisters.

But when you died you came face to face with our Lord, Jesus Christ, and Jesus took out a piece of paper that listed your sins, venial sins and cardinal sins, and Sister said that Jesus knew things, like Santa knew who got coal in their stockings, only with Jesus the coal was lit, was hot and fiery, and the screams of agony in hell fell on deaf ears.

Walter McManus looked up and refolded his arms and his face was puffy, like he had really fallen asleep, and the rain kept falling, and leaves and sticks and gum wrappers and paper cups were rushing in the gutters and everything outside shined like your skin after swimming.

Sister Mary Boniface said Kansas was very big, that you could fit five or ten states the size of Massachusetts into Kansas, and that it was mostly flat, flat as the top of a desk, and there were hardly any trees. She said people were farmers in Kansas, and farmers worked very hard growing the wheat and hay and corn and oats so we could have bread and so cattle could eat and then we could eat the cattle.

That was the food chain, she said.

She sat on the side of her desk and her eyes moved over us.

There was wind and the winters were like something from a story. Ten-foot snowdrifts and cattle frozen to death, standing like statues in the middle of a field. And sometimes, she said, she and her brother Willie had to stay inside for two or three weeks, and the windows were covered with blankets and her mother began to talk to herself.

Her mother would start to talk to *her* mother, even though her mother had been dead eleven years, and she'd talk to her brothers and sisters who still lived in Johnstown in Pennsylvania, where the great flood had been.

Sister's father went out in snowshoes and with fur all around him like he was a bear, and he took two horses, one to ride and the other to carry supplies. He was gone four or five days to check the livestock and to sleep in shelters way off, on the far side of the farm. Farms were a two- or three-day ride across. They were huge.

She said her mother hadn't gone to the hospital yet, and her brother Willie hadn't died from the tractor accident, but her mother talked in great explosions of words, like the Johnstown Flood rushing down twelve or fourteen miles of canyon, with trees and cows and a wall of mud a hundred feet high.

Her mother talked about Jesus, and she said that Jesus knew the hearts of men and women, and her mother's brother Jason crawled under the bed at night because Lucifer with his horns and tail was outside. Jason shook from the cold, and Johnstown was never sunny, and the mountains were on almost every side, and the mouth of the canyon was still there, with the creek winding softly down the canyon.

The rich men from Pittsburgh had the club in the mountains. The hunting and fishing club, and they had the huge earth dam so they could have a lake in the mountains, and the dam was fifty years old and was not high enough or thick or strong enough to hold a million tons of water.

The mayor of Johnstown said it was unsafe, and the people all worked in the Iron Works in the side of the mountains, and down in the bowl of Johnstown they had wood frame houses.

Then it began to rain and rain, Sister's mother said. Rain like the flood in the Bible. Rain like outside, Sister said, only far far harder and far longer, and all the rich men from Pittsburgh had houses around the lake in the mountains, twelve or fourteen miles above Johnstown. Frick and Carnegie, who owned steel mills and railroads, and who had houses like palaces, with fifty rooms and enough servants to run a hospital.

Sister said she and Willie stayed under the covers, and

126

her mother put more wood in the stove, and her voice was high and cracked when she said the rich men in their houses did not get wet, did not lose anything, did not die.

The snow began to fall in Kansas, outside the house where Sister Mary Boniface and her brother Willie and her mother were, and it fell almost sideways because the wind was blowing so hard.

Sister's brother died when a tractor tipped and fell, but that was in Kansas. And Sister's mother, from Johnstown in Pennsylvania, had a brother too, but his name was Jason and he stayed under the bed at night. A winged thing with dark eyes was after him, and they laughed. Sister Mary Boniface's aunts and uncles laughed, but that was before Jason had to go to the special hospital, and that was years before Willie died, and before Sister's mother went to the special hospital in Kansas, and her mother's skin was pale and her eyes, as she talked of the flood, burned.

JOSEPH MARINOZZI WENT on the ice on the Charles River near Watertown Square, and his older brothers didn't watch him the way they were supposed to. They were trying to build a fire from sticks and they were going to cut a hole in the ice next to the bank of the river, and the fish would be very hungry, they hadn't eaten in so long.

They were looking for sticks, and the ice got thinner and thinner toward the middle of the river, and the brothers didn't hear him or see him.

There was just a hole in the middle, and Larry, the oldest brother, ran home, and the police came with rowboats and hooks and went slowly up and down and up and down, and there were fire trucks too, and bursts of smoke came from the mouths of the men watching from the side of the river. Men in rubber coats and boots that went to their knees, and they were dragging the bottom of the river with hooks, above the dam in Watertown Square, because his body wouldn't float past the dam, and with the ice he wouldn't float up to the top either.

They found him near the edge, Gram said, under the thickest part of the ice, and his eyes were still open, and she said she thought Joseph was looking at what he had done to his poor mother, who would never be the same the rest of her life, and he was looking at Jesus too, on the other side, and she said Joseph wouldn't close his eyes ever again, and would never sleep or be at peace, even though he was dead.

SISTER MARY ROSE WAS FAST like a squirrel, and she was the same age as Peter Nordland's big brother, who was twenty-three, and she'd been a nun one year, and had hair under her wimple.

Sister Mary Rose sang a song about a bonny boat on a wave, and the song was sad and happy at the same time, and even Sister Mary Boniface said Sister Mary Rose had a beautiful and God-given talent, and if our Lord and Savior, Jesus Christ, hadn't called her, she might have been a movie star in Hollywood, California, or on Broadway, a street full of stages in New York City.

Sister Mary Rose had five sisters and four brothers for a total of ten, and they grew up in a house in Cambridge, and went to Saint Patrick's in Watertown. Her sister Bridget was named after Saint Bridget, and was in Africa feeding the hungry orphans, and her brother Matthew—for the Apostle— was a policeman in Cambridge.

She had brothers named John and James and Mark, and sisters named Maureen and Ann and Catherine. Catherine wasn't much older than us, Sister Mary Rose said, and might one day grow up to be a teacher or a nun or a nurse.

She said her mother was very tired, from having ten children, and raising them, and she said we must always be obedient and respectful to our mothers and fathers. She said if Joseph had listened to his mother and had stayed off the ice, he might be with us today. She said God had called him to be with Our Lord in heaven, but maybe if Joseph had not been on the ice, God would not have needed to call him.

She said God worked in mysterious ways. Jesus wanted the suffering little children to come unto him, and that's what Joseph had done. So maybe it was okay for Joseph to be called. God knew when your time was up and he wanted Joseph to be with him in heaven, next to his golden throne.

It was the same as wearing clean underwear. You never knew when you might get hit by a bus or a car, and if you had to be taken to the emergency room and they had to undress you, and if you weren't wearing clean underwear, then what would they think, and how do you imagine your mother would feel. Her brother James fell out of a tree and broke his leg in three places. At the emergency room they had to cut his clothes off with a giant pair of scissors, just like peeling an onion.

Thank God, she said her mother said, that James was wearing clean underwear.

MY BROTHER ERIC was on the top bunk and I was on the bottom, and Dad came in and shut the light off, and said, Be quiet now, and, Goodnight, sweet dreams, and I said, Dad, would you stay, and he said, I'm tired, and I said, Just for a few minutes? and he said, Okay.

He lay down on top of the covers, and I moved over next to the wall, and up top already Eric was breathing like a radiator, and I said, Will you die?

He didn't say anything.

Dad, I said.

Everyone dies.

Then what?

Your soul leaves your body and goes to heaven.

How?

He said, Enough. Go to sleep.

He lay facing away from me, and I was on my back, my hands folded on my stomach, the way I'd be in my coffin.

I moved my arms, put one at my side and one over my head, so if they came during the night while I was sleeping, they'd see I wasn't ready.

Then I moved to my side and I could hear Dad's breathing and Eric's breathing, and the house was quiet. There were squeaks and faint hums, and later I woke up and Dad was gone, and Eric was still breathing.

I got up to go to the bathroom, and down the long hallway there were panels of light on the floor like ghosts, and everything else was dark.

The wind blew outside and leaves scraped on the street and sidewalk out front, dead leaves, and someone was down the cellar, and someone in a dark raincoat was standing outside on the corner, holding Joseph's hand, and they stood and waited.

THE PARK HAD a baseball diamond and jungle gyms and a slide, and an open space, and then the pit where steam shovels had come and dug out a space, and then just left. Weeds and grass grew in the pit, and there were steep smooth sides like a bathtub.

The leaves were gone, and soon there would be a turkey to eat, and Mom said it was okay to play in the backyard, only don't even think of leaving the yard, because she had enough to worry about as it was.

It was getting dark earlier and earlier. The sun was falling into the tops of the bare trees, and the sidewalk out front was empty and smooth, and big cars went by. Some had yellow eyes and went fast and made a whoosh sound as they passed.

Lawn Avenue was two houses down and was a dead end. Kenny D'Agastino lived on one corner of Lawn and California, and Walter Allen Prendergast lived on the other corner.

Then there was just the giant gray house—the haunted house—past Walter Allen's and then Nevada Street.

The gray house was a hundred years old, Gram said, and had seventeen rooms, and had a tall skinny part like a lookout, with windows all around. Gram said a prince might be locked away in one of those rooms, and bats flew there at night and late in the day. Bats were blind and squeaked, and they turned into vampires and drank your blood. When you slept, and if you weren't careful. They bit your neck, and then you had to die or become a vampire.

The park was wide and almost completely dark, and the trees in the far corner hid the swings and the jungle gyms.

There were lights on in houses, past the fences and bushes, but nothing else. Over on California Street the cars whooshed by, but the whoosh sounded like a hum from the park, and all the cars had eyes.

I stood at home plate, on the baseball diamond, and there was a pitcher on the mound, and he wound up and threw, and I swung, and the crowd stood up and roared, and I ran to first base, and then to second, then third, and just as I rounded third and started home, I saw the man next to the backstop, wearing a dark sweater and dark pants, and he said, Nice hit, and I stopped.

He said, I saw you and I stopped to watch.

The park was dark as night, and the lights of the cars and houses were a mile or five miles away.

The air was cold, and I was breathing hard, and he was as tall as the backstop behind home plate.

My name is Charles, he said. What's yours?

Joseph, I lied.

That's a nice name, he said.

He squatted down. He said, Don't be afraid. There's nothing to be afraid of.

He had dark eyes, and he pushed his hair off his forehead. He wore glasses, and I could see lights from houses on the lenses.

You in school? he asked. Second grade? Third grade? Big fellow like you, he said. Must be third grade.

First, I said.

He said, You must have brothers and sisters. Lots of brothers and sisters. I bet they're as big and strong as you.

I didn't move.

They as sweet as you? he asked. Sweet as a lollypop?

He made a slurping sound.

What's your favorite subject in school? he wanted to know. Did I like arithmetic or reading or sports?

He could tell, he said. Big strong fellow like you. Must be sports.

Did I play baseball and football? Basketball? Kickball?

He bet I was good. Strong little kid. Running around, getting sweaty. Sweaty all over.

He stood up.

Had to take a shower after, he said. Down in the locker room. All the guys sweating and dusty from practice, and taking off their uniforms, and crowding into the shower together. All that water and soap.

I said, I have to go, and he said, No one's gonna hurt you.

He said, No one knows you're here.

He said, You must get kind of excited sometimes.

He said he could understand that. He got kind of excited.

Did I want to see?

I know how that can be, he said.

I ran fast, ran like my legs wouldn't carry me, and my heart was louder than cars. I ran down the pit and then up the other side and through the parking lot. I ran across Nevada and behind the haunted house and past a garage. I went over a fence and through Walter Allen Prendergast's, past shovels and rakes and lawn furniture. There were lights on in houses, and someone might have heard my footsteps and my heart the drum, but I crossed Lawn Avenue, under the streetlight where he could see me, and then through D'Agastino's, through hedges, and over the chain-link fence and a dog somewhere was barking and I went behind Moreau's garage and tripped on a hose and fell.

The ground was wet, and I scrambled and he was maybe chasing me, and then I was behind the garage to our house.

My heart was a drum and a hammer and a trapped bird, and my hands trembled, and I looked around the corner, toward the street.

Cars went by and the lights in the house were on. Upstairs and downstairs, and I could stay there a long time.

I stood for five minutes and a half hour and an hour. I heard cars starting up, and doors slamming, and a plane went overhead.

Then my heart would slow, and I'd go inside and up the stairs.

Mom would turn, would see me, but she wouldn't know.

It was our secret. It was me and the man. And it was Joseph in heaven, knowing everything now.

nine

The sky was always black in 1979, when I was twenty-five. At five a.m. I was waking up and the radio said it was eleven degrees out, and I'd had three or four hours of sleep.

I was thin and rigid as glass. In the mirror my eyes were blue and blinked often, and I walked with careful steps, and heard my father at the kitchen table, eating cereal, flipping the channels on television.

He was wearing a white tee shirt and blue pajama bottoms, and there was a crumpled Kleenex in the sleeve of his tee shirt. He looked from me to the television and said it was cold, the temperatures weren't going to get any higher, and he didn't like the winter.

I drank coffee, and walked the mile to Watertown Square. The snow and ice squeaked underfoot and there were no other people walking in the half-light. Just cars, their tailpipes smoking from the cold, and the sky in the east, toward downtown, was gray, and the stars were growing dim overhead.

Near Watertown Square I walked along the river and there

134

was ice all the way across, and I went left over the bridge, and a sign said the river was named by early explorers for King Charles of England, back before the witches or the Minutemen, and the lights in the trees from Christmas, in the park in the middle of Watertown Square, were still up and lit, and there were three or four people standing at the bus stop. A woman with a Channel Two bag, and a man in a furry hat that looked like Moscow—and they looked at me, and I stood, and the sky was changing and something went through me, something so sweet and powerful and brief that my hands didn't move and my stomach settled. Because they didn't know to look at me. I could be there, in the morning in Watertown Square, like anyone else.

In Harvard Square, at seven-fifteen, there were hundreds and thousands of people. People with briefcases and backpacks and handbags, in scarves and coats and hats and gloves, in boots and sneakers and shoes, and everyone moved fast. I went down the stairs, through the turnstyle, then down the long cold ramps of cement, onto the platform. There were ads for banks and cigarettes and technical schools and beer. A man on a mountainside, a woman on a beach, a cat with sunglasses.

The train came in, silver cars with red trim, and the steel wheels screeched on the track, and it was an Ashmont train, would go to Columbia Station, and the doors slid open and I got a seat by a window. It rocked and clacked, and it was suddenly black out the window, like a tomb, and there were solitary light bulbs, and the train would go for miles under the streets, snaking past pipes and sewer lines, and rats would squeak and blink when the train roared past.

A voice said, Central, and there was another platform, with light and ads and people, and a woman next to me wore a long black coat with a red beret, had pink skin and black eyes, and she opened her copy of the Boston *Globe* to the sports page, and began to read about the Celtics, and I could smell soap or shampoo or perfume, and her hair was still wet from the shower.

Past Kendall Station we rose to cross the river and people lifted their heads and looked out, and there were miles of light and air, and cars with yellow headlights crept along Memorial Drive and Storrow Drive, and there suddenly was Beacon Hill and the gold dome of the Statehouse and the Esplanade, the Hatch Memorial Shell, the Prudential and Hancock Towers.

Then we pulled into Charles Station, next to the Charles Street jail, and razor wire was coiled on top of the high black wall and in the courtyard there were windows with bars.

THE SKY WAS ALWAYS DARK back then, and the door of the jail was heavy, was oak and had iron brackets and studs and nails, and they wore dark clothes, there in Boston, a long time ago, the man said.

The classroom was cinder block, was painted yellow and white and had no windows. Just rows of fluorescent tubes on the ceiling, and the man in the coat and tie stood up front. He wore glasses and had curly black hair, and he talked slowly, his voice circling in and around, and he walked up and down and from side to side, and I stayed in the back row, the cinder block wall behind me.

He said, Picture him at twenty-three. Picture him there in Salem, in the first half of the 1800s, just out of college, living in an attic room in a house with his mother and sisters.

He reads all the books he can get his hands on night after night, and he stares out the window. He can see Salem Harbor, the ships from all over the world. Spice ships from the Indian Ocean, ships from England and Italy and China and Africa, and he watches and then goes back to his desk.

At night, in the dark, he goes out for long walks. To the harbor, past the alehouses, past the house with the gables, and then out roads that take him inland, past marshes and reeds and tributaries, and he goes by farms and sees a light in a farmhouse and hears a dog bark somewhere.

Picture this, he says, for year after year. For six years, eight years, ten years, twelve years.

He stops near the door, and looks at us. His eyes behind the glasses go up and down the rows, pausing, moving on.

And imagine, too, if you will, this man, brooding on a crime that took place in this same town generations earlier. A crime that has since become famous, that has become almost a caricature, has become a parody of Halloween.

But to him, in Salem, with the Puritan tradition very much alive, the crime is no caricature, no Halloween parody. To him it's a guilty presence—is in every shadow, every street corner, in every house in the city.

Not just because it's there, but because his ancestor, his great-grandfather, or great-great-grandfather, was one of the principal judges at the trials.

And if you doubt what that meant to him, and the extent he brooded upon it, look at the spelling of his last name, and how he changed the spelling so that it would be different from the way his great-grandfather, the judge, spelled his name.

He wrote the name twice on the blackboard.

I don't want to dwell on this, he said, but it's crucial. It's crucial to this opening. The door of a jail, sad-colored garments, steeple-shaped hats, the talk of the townspeople. All of that—the grimness and sadness, the heaviness and severity of the door, the steeple-like hats which echo church, the gathering people, the talk—all in the first paragraph.

JASMINE'S APARTMENT was on the third floor, was enormous and rent-controlled and was in Brookline, less than ten feet from the Boston line, a hundred feet from Commonwealth Avenue and the trolleys that clacked past.

Jasmine said we should live together, said we should think

about getting married, and kissed my neck and said she was in love with me despite everything, and always would be, and knew I felt the same way, so what the fuck were we waiting for.

She kissed my mouth, her tongue going lightly over my lips, and she said, You taste good, Will, and her arms were on my back and she said, You don't know how much I miss you when you're gone, and how much I think of you, and how I want to fuck you.

She stepped out of her shoes, and was pulling my shirt-tails from my jeans, and unbuttoning and unsnapping, and she was white and smooth as glass, and warm, and her mouth was liquid and she whispered that sometimes she thought she'd go crazy, and we lay down on the bed, and had our socks on, and her tongue was on my stomach, and she said, You make me a crazy lady, and her breasts and ass, her long curved sides, were smooth and pink and soft.

She said, What do you do all week? What do you do when I'm not there?

She moved my hand to her middle, and it was wet, and she said, See what you do. See how wet you make me.

She moved her hand up and down, and she said, I do this to you, and she licked the edge of my ear.

We were each on our sides, and her breasts were full, and my tongue went along the sides, then around the nipples.

Outside was gray, and the lights were out and the curtains open, and I could see the tree and the building across the street.

She said, Will, we should slow down, and everything was urgent. She said, I miss you, and she said, You're lovely, Will Ross, and it was years and years we'd known each other, since after high school, and her eyes were brown and shining, and she said I was lovely.

LATE AT NIGHT, at Jasmine's, there were people in the streets, and with the squares of light from the streetlamps on the ceiling and walls, I heard bottles smash, and voices shout, Hey, shout, Fuck you, and the *you* was long as night, was a song echoing between the trees and cars and buildings.

Then there were no voices, and car doors slammed, and a woman somewhere was laughing.

Jasmine slept for hours, and I watched her face—the closed eyes, the mouth loose and dark and partway open.

She blinked her eyes, seemed to look at me a second, closed her eyes and breathed deeply again.

Ten minutes, an hour, three hours later, I was drifting. There were veils passing over my face, and wind from somewhere, and I was rising up, was floating on air or water or breath and everything was so bright that I couldn't see much, just faint shadows on smoke.

Shit, someone shouted, and squares of smoky light were on the ceiling, were on the closet door. There were scarves hanging on a hook on the door and they were dark, were blurred.

Jasmine's, I thought. At Jasmine's.

A car started up, and I was behind a screen or a curtain, then I was much younger, was wearing shorts and brown shoes and yellow socks. The socks had red bears on them, and there was a scab on my knee. I'd fallen down the day before, two days before, and the blood ran down my shin and into my sock, and it burned and burned and burned and wouldn't stop.

Two days? Twelve years? On California Street, and Gram was inside, was wearing glasses with thick lenses, and she had never in all her years seen such rotten, spoiled children?

Or Vermont, only later.

Vermont? With Kirsten, who smiled the way sunlight came from behind the clouds?

Climbing the Green Mountains in November, and no

leaves left in the trees, and ice in pools between rocks. The sky a deep blue like Colorado in August. A feathering of cloud way far off by the horizon.

Someone turned over. Jasmine was shifting, was making a sound like bubbles in her throat.

But no Chapstick for three days, and the air as cold as January, and wind all the time, and my lips were cracked and sore. Was Jasmine there? Kirsten?

Kirsten wore brown hiking boots. Long legs in jeans and the wind pressing against us in our sleeping bags.

In the city they asked, Can we get you a drink? They smiled, and were wearing white, their hair combed back like Elvis, only lighter. Brown, almost blond.

The glass was beaded, the head of foam was white, and the rest was yellow, was gold, and outside was hot.

One of them sipped, and the white foam was on his lips, and he laughed. Boy, he said, and sipped again.

Boy oh boy, he said.

Then in Brighton, late, the whole bar long and dark, the lights low, the line of bottles shining, and people standing or sitting on stools and sitting in the booths along the side wall, not making a sound, moving like slow motion, and looking as I walked to the bar and said, Gin and tonic, please.

Speaking quietly.

The bartender was bald and wore a bright shirt—red and green and orange—a parrot shirt, and he washed a glass at a small sink and he wiped the glass with a white towel. The towel was on his shoulder, and he turned away.

Gin and tonic, I said, and my voice was small. My voice was seven or nine years old. He turned away and everyone heard me.

I could taste the gin and tonic. The ice cubes, the weight of the glass in my hand. A slice of lime. The warm feeling, then warmer. Swimming.

Sir, I said, and they were saying things, but no sound.

Just lips and tongues and hands moving.

The bartender leaned down, and had a baseball bat in his hand and his teeth were bared like a cat's. He swung, and I fell backwards, crashed into the side of a booth, my head slamming the table.

My teeth were broken, and I was crawling and they were laughing, were pointing, and my head couldn't stay up. On my hands and knees, and he swung the bat at my ankles, at my arms, my feet, my head.

His arms were hairy, were thick, and he had a barrel of a stomach. He grabbed my hair, and dragged me to the door, and outside was busy. There were cars and people and neon. Ten o'clock, Saturday night. And there was a bottle on the curb. Dark brown, and I crawled to the bottle, and it was full, and I was happy, was trying to break the seal and get the cap off.

There was an elbow in my side.

Will, Jasmine said. Will, she said. Will. You okay? Will. You're thrashing around.

The squares had moved to the door to the hall. Scarves were on the closet door.

Will, she said.

Then it was much later, was four or five, and there was a car engine and more curtains and veils and scarves, and a fat lady, a three-hundred-pound lady said, That's what I said. That's right, she said. That's exactly what I meant.

GRAM SAID THAT THE SHOWS used to be good. They used to be nice shows about interesting people, and you could watch them and enjoy them.

People with problems. Amnesia and car accidents and a woman regaining her sight after two years of blindness. Looking down and seeing her son for the first time. Her baby boy.

She moved her hands in the air in front of her face.

Or maybe a man losing his memory in a car accident, out

141

on the highway somewhere. Maybe an ice patch, or a stranger in the middle of the road, a tall stranger in black, standing in the middle of the road at two or three a.m. And the driver—Keith or Malcolm or Ian—had to swerve suddenly, and the tires screeched and the whole world reeled sharply away and over.

Then sirens, and bits of glass like grains of salt sprinkled over everything, and Keith in a coma, and nobody knew about the stranger, except for Nadine, the night duty nurse, who heard Keith whispering before dawn—the road, black clothes, middle of nowhere.

Maybe it happened, Gram said. But sometimes she thought it was crazy.

Dylan and Max, Ruthann and Layla. Kim spying on Josh, and discovering the secret of him and Felicia, and Felicia was married to Kent, and the baby was due any day, any hour.

Nina had a multiple personality, and Clarke could never be sure which Nina was the one he'd fallen in love with. And then Antonia, from Rome, arrived, and had a strange claim on Nina. Something happened in Rome, years ago. Moonlight, candles, wine, promises.

Maybe it was Keith's accident. Keith knew Nina in the old days, before she inherited the company from her father. If Keith woke from the coma, he'd be able to say.

Gram smiled. She said, These days you can't tell what to believe.

She said they had people on the shows who were homos, and she didn't think that was right, didn't think it was normal. Why couldn't they be like everyone else? Why'd they do things like that? Like what they did?

She looked at the television, then asked me if I'd adjust the curtain. The light was bothering her eyes. She said she was too lazy to get up herself. Too lazy and old.

When you're thirty-nine like me, she said, there are things

you can't do.

She said there were cookies in the pantry. Get yourself some. Bring me a few. They're oatmeal. They're pretty good, if I say so.

She made them yesterday.

The cookie jar was shaped like a house. It had brown doors and windows, a red roof.

She said there was no such thing as being a homo when she was young. She said it was crazy. Never heard of such a thing.

She said, People didn't act like pansies in my day.

What do homos do when they're together? she asked.

What do they see in each other? Do they want to get married?

She said, Can you imagine their poor mothers?

HIS NAME WAS JOHN, and he'd been sober seven years, three months, twenty-one days. He was the luckiest man in the world, and he said all he used to think about was wanting to die.

Behind the podium a sign said, Keep It Simple.

John was in his forties, was bald, wore a black sweater. His face was red and he was missing a tooth on the bottom, in front. He said each night he got down on his knees, at the side of his bed, and thanked God for helping him stay sober one more day. He said he told God how grateful he was.

Dear God, he said he prayed, let me not pick up one drink today. Give me the strength and courage and wisdom. Help me through the doubts.

In the basement of the church, there were pillars holding the ceiling up and windows were high on the wall. There was a piano and stacks of chairs against a wall, and thirty or forty chairs in front of the podium. Half were full.

He said, I was one of those people you see downtown. One of those guys who look like they crawled from the swamp. One of those people who lie on the sidewalk, who you step around. The matted hair, the urine and vomit, and two weeks of sweat, and no bath for a year.

He said, I know about Boston State and Met State. I know about Pine Street and Harbor Light. I know what they pay for a pint of blood downtown. I know the grates that're warm, and I know where to go when it's five degrees out and you have to be out of the wind.

You crawl into a Dumpster when it's full and surround yourself with garbage, and you're insulated. It's not goose down, but it's not dying either.

He said, I know the tunnels under the streets. The heating tunnels, and the ones for power lines. The tunnels for the trolleys. I know how dark they are and how water drips down the walls and from pipes.

He said, The rats live down there, whole families and colonies and nations of rats. Big rats, rats the size of small dogs.

He said the old Scollay Square subway station was still down there, under the streets of Boston, even though it hadn't been used in twenty or thirty years. He said the tracks were there and the old platform where people stood, and even some benches built into the walls. He said there were still billboards on the walls, hanging in the darkness. Torn and moldy, but you could read them by the light of a match.

He said, Think of it. Living there, with the rats and the dripping water. Me and a pint of wine.

Year after year, he said. For so long he thought it was almost normal.

FROM THE SIXTH FLOOR of the library at school, I could see ten or twenty miles in every direction. I could see the airport and the great silver planes rising over the water. I could see most of Boston Harbor and most of downtown. The cluster of tall buildings at the financial district, and to the west, the Hancock and Prudential towers. Farther west I could see trees and hills and roads and houses, and Morrissey Boulevard directly below—the *Boston Globe* building, and the streams of cars going past.

The harbor was blue or green or gray or almost white, and the harbor islands looked close enough to swim to. Pirates used to hide in the islands years and years ago, and the Puritans sometimes hung pirates from trees on the outer islands to warn other pirates away.

There had been a prison on George's Island during the Civil War, and a Confederate wife disguised herself, had been captured, and died on the island, trying to find her husband. Her ghost haunted George's Island, was supposed to moan and echo and clank along the stone hallways, in the heavy damp walls, the rusting bars. The men died in the Boston winters, men from Virginia and Mississippi and South Carolina, were buried in unmarked graves on the islands. The men who were barely men. Who were seventeen and nineteen and twenty-two.

Thompson's Island had been a boys' reform school, and Long Island had an asylum for tuberculosis patients and the mentally ill and the poor.

The sixth floor had enormous windows, and couches and carrels, and few people. I took my shoes off and pulled two sections of couch together, put my feet up, began to read.

In Africa, in the rain forest, the people lived by hunting and gathering. They used bows and arrows and blow darts, and they knew about poisons, about putting a substance on the end of the arrow that would paralyze a monkey or bird.

They prayed to the gods of the forest, and they knew thousands of different trees and vines and plants, and which ones could be eaten and which ones could kill. People from the outside seemed huge and gangling to them, seemed like barbarians.

The people who lived on the plains were terrified of the

rain forest. It was dark and confining and dangerous. It was snakes and poison plants, was a maze that could swallow a man and never let him see the sky again.

When the small people went to the edge of the forest they saw the plains as a vast desert, as a place without shade or food or cover. As a place that could not sustain life.

The man lived with the people for months and months. He ate their food and slept in the forest. He learned the language, participated in the rituals.

A woman sat down at a carrel twenty feet away. She had black hair and she wore glasses with pale frames. She was twenty-five or thirty. She was reading, and paused every few minutes to underline a passage, to take notes. She pushed her hair off her face and twined strands of hair around the pen. She wore a red turtleneck and silver earrings that dangled an inch below her earlobes.

The sky was overcast. A plane crossed the rectangle of window and headed east—toward Paris, Brussels, London.

In the rain forest there were initiation rites for the young men. Dreams of snakes and birds, creatures with iridescent skin. A boy had marks cut and burned into the skin of his arms and chest and face. Then he went into the forest, two days' walk away. He went where nobody would see him or find him, and he waited until a dream came.

A dream of broad wings and light filtering through the leaves and everything so dark and green and wavering that this could have been underwater, could have been at the bottom of a sea somewhere, and he was swimming or flying, and he was leaving something, and there were blood and screams. It was agony to go.

There was a sharp trill from a bird, and yakyakyak, whoooo, in the forest, and he thought he could return.

The woman in the carrel was gone, and the sky was vast and blank and white.

MY FATHER CRIED—when he sat alone in the back room, or lying down in his bedroom or sitting late at night at the kitchen table, the lights off, the house as silent as a ship at sea.

I heard the sobs, the uneven breath, the sniffling. Saw him from the hallway, his shoulders hunched over, his face in his hands and the sounds that were quiet but that seemed to come from a deep deep part of him.

He cried for twenty minutes or a half hour, and my mother knew about it, she had talked to him. He made her promise not to say anything to anybody.

It happened when he was alone in the house, late at night, or at the end of the afternoon and the light was gray, was turning blue and black.

And it came over him. As he sat there. And he didn't know why. Just that it was powerful for a while. Was something he couldn't help. There in Newton, when I was twenty-five.

ten

At fifty-two I will be slower, and my hair will be gray. Probably things will be more or less the same, only ten or fifteen years later and ten or fifteen years different. Different cars and clothes and a different president, and different people will be movie stars, people nobody knew about in 1991.

Maybe I will be with Ann, and she will be lovely still, in 2003. She will be forty-nine, and her hair will be gray, but she will run each morning when I am sleeping, will run when the day is beginning to fill with light, and birds will whistle and caw.

We will live in upstate New York, will look out the window and across the road, and see fields and hills and flowers—for miles and miles. We might see deer bounding across the fields, white tails bobbing, and for a moment at the window, we won't say anything.

Or I will be in Tempe, Arizona, living in an apartment complex, and Ann will have left me years earlier. She will send me postcards once or twice a year from New York City or Durham or Palm Beach. She will be married to a stock-broker or an optometrist or a veterinarian, and she will be a lawyer. She'll miss me and think well of me, and will feel sad—for a few minutes each month—at how she and I spent the best years of our lives together, and how it didn't work out the way it was supposed to.

She'll write from the terrace of her house, say, in Palm Beach, overlooking a formal garden, and beyond the line of bushes she'll see the ocean, the shifting colors and lights on its surface, the occasional boat drifting beautifully by.

The sun will be bright in Palm Beach, but a breeze will cool things off by dinnertime. Ann will look up, and will see Nibs, her black cat, stalking something on the lawn. A fly, a moth, a butterfly, a mosquito. Nibs will have gold eyes, will be sleek as silk. And she will watch Nibs absently until a bird squawks, and she will blink, and come to, and will sign the postcard, Love, Ann.

In Tempe I will have a two-bedroom apartment on the second floor. There will be a small kitchen, a combined dining room and living room, and a sliding double door behind the couch that leads to a small balcony that overlooks the pool.

The pool is always vividly blue, and almost hard to look at, it's so bright. I will wear sunglasses much of the time, and will be used to seeing lizards and cactus and sand everywhere, and I will like the sun and the heat.

I'll have a job at the local community college, teaching English, and even though I'll teach four courses a semester, and won't make much money, I'll like the students, will like their youth, their suntans, the way they'll wear shorts and sandals and sneakers to class each day, and they'll all have part-time jobs. As a cashier, a waiter, a cabdriver. As an aerobics instructor, a groundskeeper at the golf course. At a clothes store, a beauty salon, a bar.

I'll try to teach them Henry James and Melville and Mark

Twain. I'll talk about Thoreau calling himself a self-appointed inspector of snowstorms and rainstorms, and I'll look out the window, past the parking lot, to a long treeless strip of banks and fast food places and signs and utility poles—all wavering in the noonday heat, and I'll suddenly think how strange and wonderful this is. Thoreau in the desert, Walden overlooking the strip, and my students with their painted toenails and earrings and tee shirts will look at me and smile, will say, Cool.

At night I'll spend time in the second bedroom, my study, grading papers, and looking through the anthology for future assignments, Kafka and James Joyce and Borges. I'll hear the traffic outside and I'll see the strange desert light fading, sitting on the horizon like some last row of neon someone forgot to turn off. And the lights of the strip, the streetlamps and signs, will be glowing on the near edge of the night.

Maybe the phone will ring, or people will be splashing in the pool. David Mendez, from downstairs, swimming his nightly laps, or Mrs. Emerson taking her post-dinner walk. She's old and has a bad heart, and her kids don't call, she'll say if you see her. What's wrong with them? she'll ask.

If I answer the phone it might be Wendy Lee, my friend from the English Department. Wendy will be thirty-four years old, too young for me, I've told her, but she'll laugh and say, Says who.

Wendy has a son and a daughter, and lives in a subdivision with curving streets and bicycles on lawns and small anemic trees held up by wires and stakes. Her ex-husband's a policeman, and is seeing another woman, who also has kids, and the other woman's daughter is in Wendy's daughter's class, and they—the two girls—don't like each other, and Wendy's daughter wants to go to private school.

We'll talk about Bill Herrin, the chair of the department, who looks like the Marlboro man, and whom everyone likes, or Wendy will tell me she thinks she has a kid, a student, who copied his paper from somewhere, but she doesn't know where.

Carrie, her daughter, is thirteen, and says she wants to live with her father, and her son, whose name is John or Glenn or Charlie, has a serious case of asthma. He almost stops breathing at night, his breathing becomes so labored and raspy and sad, she'll say, that she hasn't slept well in ten years, in all the time he's been alive.

I'll be barefoot in the living room, will be wearing olive green shorts that I'll have had since Ann and I were together. My legs will be skinny and tan, and my feet will be enormous. I'll be wearing a black tee shirt, and I'll smile, listening to Wendy talk. She will have blond hair and a long face, or she'll have brown hair and strong shoulders. We'll have gone to bed together once, at the end of a long night, a night of dinner, a movie, a walk in the desert, then an hour of sitting carefully in the living room and talking, our hands touching, a knee brushing a thigh, an arm against a side, and the strange and lovely smell, the hiss of breath—all of this while her kids slept noiselessly in their rooms, and later, we barely spoke of it, called it an accident, a mistake that probably—maybe—shouldn't happen again.

Or at fifty-two I'll live in Boston, in a rented room with a hot plate and electrical cords plugged into the light fixture overhead. Sirens will wail outside, and the smell of cooking, of boiled vegetables and animal fat, will cling to the fading wallpaper, the blistered paint, to the worn green carpet in the hall.

I'll work the midnight shift somewhere, will make seven or eight or nine dollars an hour. As a watchman in a department store, walking from floor to floor, in Filene's or Jordan Marsh. I'll walk past the Housewares and Men's and Lingerie Departments. Past Sporting Goods and Luggage, and racks and racks of coats. And the mannequins will stare, and at night, at three or four, I'll almost talk to them, there in the dim light, there in the dark with the clean soft smells.

Or I'll work overnight in a home for former mental patients, an old brownstone somewhere on Commonwealth Avenue, that has ten or twelve bedrooms, and the patients, the men, will be two or five or nine years out of the hospital, and they will all take lithium, or one of the major tranquilizers—Thorazine or Mellaril or Haldol or Prolixin, or something new, that didn't exist in the nineties.

They'll be guys who dress funny and talk to themselves. Once in a while they'll break into laughter, and they won't shave well. They'll miss spots under their noses or at the chin or on the neck, and they'll need to be reminded to take showers.

One will have a long and obsessive routine each night, before he goes to bed. His name will be Roger or Ed or Thurston. He'll be small and extremely neat. He'll tuck his shirttails inside his underpants, and he'll take fifteen minutes to brush his teeth and three minutes to pee—carefully zipping and unzipping, and watching the water in the toilet, and he'll shave at night because he takes too long in the morning; in the hospital, where he lived for twenty-six years, they always shaved him at night, before he went to bed.

Another man will tell about his sister, who doesn't exist, or about his father the sea captain, though his father is long dead, and was—in life—a prominent Boston attorney.

I'll live in a room, will work the overnight in the house. My job will involve light cleaning—washing the towels, maybe making notes in the log about unusual occurrences, and talking to the residents for whatever brief time I see them before they go to bed, or if they get up for the bathroom during the night.

If someone has a seizure, has particularly bad dreams or tremors or hallucinations during the night, I'll be there to talk to them or to call an ambulance.

But mostly it will be quiet, will be shadowy, will be silent as sleep. Just cars or sirens, or the small city noises. Raccoons snuffling through trash barrels in the alley, footsteps somewhere, a high whirring sound. I'll listen to the radio often, will listen to the talk shows, people calling about UFOs and conspiracies and the assassination of President Kennedy and the depletion of the world's water supply.

Hey, a caller will say. He'll tell about a friend who started to act funny, to do strange things.

What kind of strange things? the host of the show, a man named Norman, will ask.

There'll be silence for a few seconds, and I'll think, What? What'd he do?

He started talking in these strange languages that didn't make any sense. Not French or Chinese or Italian or anything. Nothing that sounded like anything he'd ever heard, and he started to stare in this amazing, intense way. This incredibly hateful way.

One time, the caller will say, he looked up from watching baseball at his friend's house, and his friend was standing in the doorway, holding a butcher knife and staring at him, at the caller.

The caller asked him what he was doing with the knife, and he said he didn't know, it was just there, in his hand. He didn't remember picking it up.

What else? Norman will ask. What other things?

He'll say, He has all the things, the four things the Catholic Church says you should have before an exorcism can be considered.

What're those?

Unusual strength. Like strength far beyond what that person could be expected to have.

I'll turn the volume up and lean closer to the radio.

Uh huh, Norman will say.

Then they're supposed to have clairvoyance. Like they can read minds. Can tell you things about yourself, about your family, your history, your thoughts or fears, that they'd have no way of knowing.

Like my friend asked me if I still thought of my mother, and he had no way of knowing she died when I was a kid. But I did. I thought about her all the time.

He asked me if I still felt sad and if I missed her, and if I wouldn't like to be able to talk to her somehow.

Norman will whistle. What else? What's the third thing?

Languages. The ability to speak languages you never studied, that you had no way of knowing. And sometimes really strange or obscure languages. Like Turkish or Sumerian or something.

Not a couple of lines of French, Norman will say, and the caller will say, No. Not hardly.

The thing is, he'll say, is that this is extremely rare these days. They just don't do exorcisms very often. They have these people checked out by doctors, by neurologists and psychiatrists, and after ruling out medical causes, they'll bring the evidence before a board.

So the fourth one? The fourth thing?

Levitation.

Levitation?

That's right.

You mean floating in the air?

That's right.

Norman will whistle, and I'll hear a sound somewhere, possibly upstairs, on the second floor. A creak or a grunt, or maybe a humming sound. A sound like someone chanting quickly, chanting in a voice I don't know, chanting in a whisper. Or the sound will come from downstairs in the basement, where I have never been. The door to downstairs will be in the hallway. There will be a small door, and I'll walk to the hall, stand next to the door, will press my ear to the varnished wood.

And I won't be able to hear anything. It will be quiet as

three a.m., quiet as dust.

I'll listen closely, will press my ear more tightly to the wood, and I'll see shadows at the other end of the hall, near the front door. Then I'll hear something again. I'll hear what sounds like quick and repeated whispering, high and soft and quavering.

A yu yu yu yu yu, it'll say. A yu yu yu yu yu yu.

Oooma oooma oooma, and then something that I'll think is saying Will Will Will Will, but so quickly the words run together, and I'll have to go down to check the sounds out.

Then I won't know. I won't be sure if there's any sound at all. Maybe it's air or a pipe or boards and molecules, and I'll listen so closely that I won't see shadows behind me, won't know what year it is or where I am or what I'm trying to listen for.

AT FIFTY-TWO I WILL LIVE in Cleveland or Akron or Gary or South Boston. I will wear baggy pants and cardigan sweaters that are worn at the elbows, and shirts that were once white but will be yellowing or gray, and will have small blue ink stains at the bottom of the breast pocket. I will wear canvas sneakers, or black shoes with rubber soles and a blue watch cap. My teeth will be gone, and my eyes will be red at the edges, and I will have white skin with liver spots—on the backs of my hands and on my forehead and neck.

I will have a room at the end of a long hall on the second floor, and I will have a portable radio on the table next to the bed. The table will be painted orange and will have a small drawer where I'll keep my pints of wine. A single pint will last me a day or two. It will take very little to keep me drunk. A single sip every hour or so.

I'll dream about prison cells, and televisions playing all the time. The game shows blasting, the announcers, the laughter and applause, the ads for cars and beer and soap and toothpaste.

Or the cell will have concrete walls and no windows. The door will be steel and will have a single glass peephole at eye level. There will be a light bulb overhead, a two- or three-hundred-watt bulb that will burn all the time, and every few days the door will open a few inches and an arm will reach through the crack and leave bread and a plastic container of water.

Every sixth or tenth or fifteenth day a fat man in a blue uniform will come into the cell and will kick and punch me. He'll call me feces, will call me vermin, ugly, depraved. He'll kick me in the back, in the thighs, in the neck and face and arms.

And when I am on the floor and no longer moving, he'll say, You must be thirsty, and will unzip his trousers and will urinate on me.

Then I will wake up, and outside the window I'll see the kids on bicycles, will see delivery trucks, and will realize that I have wet the bed again, something I do more and more frequently.

AT FIFTY-TWO I WILL STAY HOME with our two children, Rachel and Bill. I will have a job that keeps me at home. I'll be a photographer or a furniture maker or a technical writer. I'll have a small workshop or studio in the backyard, beyond the garage.

We'll live in Manchester-by-the-Sea, in Massachusetts, on the North Shore of Boston. Ann will be a lawyer and she'll take the train into Boston two or three days a week to work for a law firm. It will be a firm made up mostly of women lawyers who specialize in class-action or first amendment or antitrust work. She'll wear dark suits, and I'll make breakfasts in the morning, and I'll drive Ann to the train station and Rachel and Bill to school.

Rachel will be nine, and will have dark hair like I once had. Bill will be seven, will wear glasses, will be fair and pale like Ann, will be in special classes for gifted children. He will have his mother's intelligence, will wear red sneakers, and Rachel will be embarrassed by him.

She'll say, I wish he was normal. I wish he wasn't my brother.

But Rachel will be getting to the age where everything embarrasses her. That her parents are so old, that she's tall for her age, that she has dark hair, that her mother works in Boston and her father at home.

We will live in a big wood house, a ten-minute walk from downtown Manchester, five minutes from the beach. The house will have a yard with plenty of trees and no neighbors in sight. The house will have five bedrooms, a den, a study, a finished basement. There will be a deck on the back of the house. There will be hardwood floors, two fireplaces, a three-car garage. We will have a bull mastiff named Bubba, a cat named Queen.

My sister and her husband and their two daughters will live on the other side of downtown, and my brother and his wife and three kids will live nearby, five minutes past my sister. There will be lots of stopping by each other's houses. To say hello, to pick up or drop off kids, tools, a record, a book, a tape.

We will get together for Chinese food at Martha and John's house, at Eric and Michele's, at our place. Martha and John's girls will be in college, but they will be home for summers and vacations, will stop by, will call and write. They will have long hair, will be tall, will walk the beach with Ann and Bill and Rachel and me.

In the summer, doors and windows will be left open, and we'll wear sandals and shorts, and we'll cook out at each other's houses. Hamburgers and chicken and sausages, and we'll sit on the deck as it grows dark, and Seamus and Greta will be there too, with their families, with their kids.

AT FIFTY-TWO I WILL WALK around my dark apartment, will pause at windows, will press my face to the cold glass, will look out at the street. At one or two a.m.

There will be parked cars and trash cans and skinny, dying trees. There will be shards of glass and scraps of newspaper, and beer and soft drink cans, lying in the gutter, on the sidewalk, under the pale streetlamp that bleeds light onto the middle of the street.

Sometimes groups of teenagers will walk by, thin kids in leather, in boots, in tight black jeans. They will have long unwashed hair. They will have bad skin and teeth, and one will have a tattoo of tears falling from the side of an eye. Blue dots dripping from a tear duct.

They will carry baseball bats and knives, and will have guns. They will swing at the hoods of parked cars with chains. One will pick up a trash can and will smash the windshield of a car.

I will hear them laugh, swear, will hear them call each other cunts and fucks and assholes.

One night I will see them catch a dog, and I will watch them beat and cut the dog. Its screams will be with me for days. I will hear the yelps when I try to go to sleep, and I will see the skinny one with the tattoo swinging the dog around by its tail, the blood spraying out in wide circles on the cars and street and the other kids will be laughing, and I will think for a second that one of them sees me standing at the window, but it is too dark and there is a grate on the window, and four locked doors, and the streetlight doesn't reach this corner of the building.

Or I will look out and there will be trees in April, pale green in the streetlight like ten thousand flowers, or like something underwater, and I will have a friend, a woman, with me.

Maybe not Ann, and maybe not Wendy from Tempe, Arizona. Maybe someone called Mandy or Sara or Jill. Someone I've known for years, and love. Someone who's forty-seven, who used to have a husband, who loves ballroom dancing.

Someone named Trixie or Trudy or Tyne.

Maybe we're married and love each other still, after twelve or fourteen years together. She'll turn to me, and the lamplight will catch the side of her face—the thin nose, the lips, the bones in her jaw and cheek and brow, and she'll smile so slowly and with such warmth and distance that I'll know she sees me the same way she did twelve years ago when we first met, on a cruise in the Caribbean, with music playing and the strange electric phosphorescence on the water, in the wake of the ship.

Or maybe at fifty-two, she and I will be on a sheep ranch in Australia. Trudy and I. Me and Tracy.

There will be dust and huge expanses of land. A hundred thousand acres. Two hundred thousand. There will be fierce months of drought, and our eyes and mouths and ears and throats will be coated with dust.

At night, at two a.m., the moon will be so bright the outside will look like milky daylight, and Trudy will be sleeping, her dark red hair fanning over the pillow. A bird will call. A cockateel or a macaw, or something else. A strange and beautiful bird with bright red or green or blue patches on its face and wings. Its call will be loud, will be almost human in the moonlight.

I'll go quietly downstairs and out to the porch that nearly circles the house. I'll see clusters of trees and bushes, and I'll see fence and garden. The garage, the sheds, and then I'll hear a howling sound far off. A wild dog maybe, and a bird will call, and I'll look up and the stars will be enormous and bright, and I will walk down the steps and past the trees.

I'll think of the size of everything, will think of how far and how long I could walk without seeing a car or a road or a person. I could walk all night, in the strange air, in the milky light, and I'll want to go inside and wake Trudy up, and say, C'mon. Out there. The sky and the light. The size.

AT FIFTY-TWO I WILL HAVE ARTHRITIS, and my knees and hips will be stiff, will ache, and I won't move much. I'll have a chair near a window, in Minneapolis, near the Mississippi River, near Knoxville on the Holston River, and I'll have drugs for the pain and swelling. Codeine or Demerol or maybe something new.

I'll live in a subsidized apartment, on the first floor, and a home health aide will come in for three hours each day to help me bathe, to cook meals, to clean up. His name will be Carney, and he will be forty years old and he will be a former Merchant Marine and will have a tattoo on his forearm that will say, Rose.

Carney will say things aren't the same since he retired—after nineteen years, and he'll tell about the ships and the guys he knew and the places in the world he's been.

He will sit in front of the television with me, our two chairs, our two little tables in front of us, and eat lunch. Tuna sandwiches and tomato soup and Pepsi and pretzels. Carney will wear a white tee shirt. He'll be bald and will wear aviator glasses tinted a rust color, and he'll say that Melina, the blond on the soap opera, is quite a dish, and reminds him of a woman he knew in San Francisco, years back.

Had a place on Telegraph Hill, he'll say, and I'll sip my soup and reach out and take a codeine from the container. I'll watch Melina, but I'll listen, and Carney will tell me she was the sweetest, warmest woman he ever knew, in all his years on God's good earth.

But there was one thing, he'll say. Just one thing.

I'll pause, and Carney will wait for me.

What was that, I'll say.

She was a married woman, he'll say. Married to an FBI

agent, no less. A man who was very high up in the Bureau. Very well connected in the Bay Area, if I knew what he was trying to say.

He'll be watching the TV like me, and he'll take a bite of his sandwich.

You might say I was playing with fire, he'll say. Burning the candle at both ends. Holding a tiger by the tail.

He'll look over and wink at me. He'll shake his head.

She was a beautiful, beautiful woman, he'll say. And I told her she was the one, as far as I was concerned. I told her I had plenty of money in the bank, and I was willing to marry her and even have kids if that was what she wanted.

He'll nod and swallow and watch the television screen.

But you know something, he'll say. You know something I found out back there in San Francisco?

He'll pause and wait for me. I'll be feeling the codeine, will feel like scratching a place on my arm, my face, my leg. There will be wisps of fog.

What's that, Carney, I'll say. What'd you find out?

I found out that a woman will hold on to what she has, even if something better comes along.

He'll look at me for a moment, then back at the screen.

And that's a fact, he'll say.

I'll blink my eyes. Voices will seem a long way off, will seem to come from the other side of a veil.

AT FIFTY-TWO I WILL DIAL phone numbers from my apartment and I will ask for people. For Carl, for Lane, for Price, for Simon or Tully.

Kids will answer, or old men.

Sorry, they'll say. You have the wrong number. What number you trying to reach?

I'll tell them the number, but will change one digit, and they'll laugh. Close, they'll say. Try again.

Then most of them will hang up. But some of them will

pause. They'll pause after I tell them the number, or they pause when I ask for Mike or Patrick or Lisa.

They know someone by that name, or they think they know my voice, or they hear something else. Maybe it's a young woman, a woman who's twenty-three and overweight. A woman who would be very attractive if she'd just lose some weight, if she'd try using makeup, who would look so much better if she'd just stop wearing those slacks that are two sizes too small.

Or a woman in her thirties whose husband is away in Denver for a week, whose kids are in school, or asleep, or visiting grandparents.

A woman who eats cookies, who eats ham and cheese sandwiches on bagels, with lots of spicy mustard, with pretzels and dill spears on the side. Or sips wine, a white table wine, with a dry aftertaste, and listens to Edith Piaf records.

She'll say, No, there's no Mike here. No Patrick, no Lisa.

I'm sorry, I'll say. Maybe the number's wrong. Lisa's an old friend from college, from law school, from graduate school. I haven't seen her in twenty years. I came across her number, in pencil, in the back of a book.

There will be silence.

Twenty years, she'll finally say.

I'll chuckle.

That's a long time, she'll say.

She was wonderful, I'll say. She got me through college. I wouldn't have made it without her.

She'll laugh.

That's sweet, she'll say. That's so romantic. After all these years.

And the number was in pencil, inside the back cover of a Russian novel. Imagine, I'll say.

She'll say, I love it.

There will be another long pause, and I'll hear tiny clicks on the line.

I'll say, What about you? What are you doing?

She'll say, Oh Jesus. One of those.

What?

Next thing you'll ask me what I'm wearing, if I have on red panties.

No, I'll say. No.

She'll laugh. She'll say, You stay home all day, you start having weird thoughts. Funny thoughts.

She'll breathe.

It's scary, she'll say. Scary what the mind can do. All this time, walking from room to room.

She'll say, I don't know sometimes. Maybe there's something wrong with me.

I'll look at the white phone. I'll see magazines and newspapers stacked under the window. I'll see a box of crackers on the table. I'll see crumbs and rusted water stains in the sink. The faucet dripping.

AT FIFTY-TWO I WILL BE LEAN and tan and fit. I'll wear tee shirt and jeans and hiking boots, and I'll look much younger than fifty-two. I'll look thirty-five, no more than forty.

My teeth will be white, and I'll have all my hair, and will seem calm. People will trust me. I'll be good at small talk, at introductions, at engaging strangers. Women and kids will like me.

I'll go to suburban shopping malls, and I'll wear blue oxford shirts with my jeans, white button-down shirts, and sometimes I'll wear a sling, sometimes I'll carry a cane.

I'll see people in parking lots, in department stores, in the aisles of clothes stores. I'll nod and smile, I'll say hello. Shy and friendly at the same time.

Or near schools, parked half a block down from the crosswalk. Near the junior high, the grade school, sometimes near the high school. I'll get out of the car and lean against the fender, the hood, half sitting, half standing. I'll seem to read the newspaper, I'll check my watch.

When a kid goes by, I'll look at my watch. I'll frown. Excuse me, I'll say, and they'll pause.

I'm sorry, but I'm waiting for Dawn Goodwin. You know her? Blonde hair. Fourteen, real tall.

The girl will smile, will shake her head.

My niece, I'll say, and I'll look at my watch again. She was supposed to meet me here ten minutes ago.

The kid will smile.

Dawn what? she'll say. Dawn who?

Goodwin, I'll say. Real pretty. Tall.

This will be in Nashua, New Hampshire, or Des Moines, or just outside Orlando. It will be sunny out, or cool and drizzling.

I'll have a Pontiac or Oldsmobile. A recent year. Waxed.

Or this will be Berkeley or Madison or Boulder or Austin. Lots of college kids, plenty of coming and going.

I'll wait in bars, in diners, in Laundromats, on the stairs to the library. I'll carry around *The Second Sex*, *The Catcher in the Rye*, Baudelaire. I'll smile, I'll seem to squint and read and not quite know what to say.

Hi, I'll say. How you doing?

They'll say, Okay.

They'll sit down a few steps away, on the next stool, near the chair by the dryers, in the adjoining booth.

Tired? I'll say. Exams coming up? Papers due?

They'll smile. Wearily. Gratefully.

Someone who'll listen.

She'll have blond hair and she'll wear a man's shirt. She'll wear a jean jacket, a tweed suitcoat, or sweats. She'll wear running shoes or boat shoes or sandals.

Sure, she'll say. She'll have lunch. She won't have eaten in days, it seems.

And in my car I'll say, There's a place out of town, on route 71, on Willow Road, on the old ferryman's turnpike. A place with beer, with catfish, believe it or not, with a view of the lake, the river, the mountains.

She'll shrug. She'll say, That sounds interesting.

We'll be four or five miles out of the city by then. We'll be near the state park, the state forest, and even though the road is posted, says, Closed, it's not. A shortcut, and the gravel will seem to spit at the underside of the car.

She'll look over at me, and suddenly she'll know, and she'll start to cry. She'll say nonononono, but it will already be too late.

eleven

The summer was hot that year, was in the eighties and nineties nearly every day, when I was eighteen and just finished with high school. Three, four, five days would go by and the temperatures would reach ninety-two, ninety-six, ninety-nine, and would drop into the upper seventies at night.

The radio and television said, Hazy, hot and humid. The radio talked about a Bermuda high, about a stagnant air mass, about a front coming through later in the week, a front that could cool things down a little, maybe into the eighties by the end of the week.

I wore shorts and sneakers without socks, and my grandmother and grandfather sat in rocking chairs on the front porch. My grandfather smoked his pipe, and a shade hung over the railing and partly blocked the sunlight. The sun was red in the west, over the tops of houses, and Bamp smoked, and Gram sat and watched the cars that passed and the people who walked slowly by.

Gram asked me if Eden, my girlfriend, was coming over, and I said maybe.

Dad came down the steps from the front hall and stood behind the screen door. He said it was too hot for humans upstairs, and he didn't remember this kind of heat in a long time, maybe since he was a kid.

Gram said the heat when she was a girl was worse. She said there weren't fans and refrigerators and air conditioners. She said there was just ice from the ice man, and lemonade. Real lemonade. Not the powder from a package. Squeezed lemons and sugar and plenty of ice.

She said her mother used to make ice cream and put fresh strawberries and blueberries in it, and she could taste it now, it was so good.

Dad said he'd seen an item in the paper about people in the Philippines, in a mountainous section of the jungle, who were living in caves and never had contact with the modern world. They were in the Stone Age. They were called the Tasadays or something. There were only a hundred or two hundred of them, and the government wasn't sure what to do. They'd brought in helicopters and camera crews, and it was believed by scientists that they had had no contact with anyone but themselves since long before the time of Christ.

Imagine, Gram said.

And Apollo 16, Dad said, had two men on the surface of the moon. For sixty or seventy hours.

A man walked by out front. He wore a blue tee shirt and his back was dark with sweat.

Gram said she worried about the colored, and the ones with the hair and drugs and beads.

She said when she was growing up there were no problems with the colored. There was a family of them in West Newton, and they were the nicest people you'd want to know.

Walter Washington, she said. Great big colored fellow. Had beautiful teeth. That's one thing she admired. They had beautiful white teeth.

Mom, Dad said. Please.

It's true, she said.

She said she didn't understand why they had to riot and burn everything down. She said they stole television sets and stereos, and they always ate cake.

Mom, Dad said. What're you talking about?

Don't tell me, she said. I've seen them on television. Sitting on the curb in front of the stores over in Roxbury. Eating those Hostess cakes all the time, the ones with white icing.

She said they should learn to eat better and then they wouldn't want to burn everything down.

EDEN SAID THERE WAS a party in Cambridge, and she said we ought to think about it. She said it was someone her friend Debbie knew from her job at the Chestnut Hill Mall. It was in North Cambridge, where all those factories used to be.

She took the leather pocketbook off her shoulder and put it down on a chair in my room. She set a bag of beer next to it.

I brought you cigarettes, she said. And something else. Something you'll like.

She was wearing tan shorts and sandals and a black tank top. She wasn't wearing a bra, and she'd put black makeup around her eyes.

She took a container of pills from her pocketbook. We start with black beauties, she said. One each. She handed me a black capsule and took two cans of beer from the paper bag.

This is to lift us up, to give us energy.

We snapped open the cans, took the pills.

Takes about a half hour, she said. You'll feel jumpy and excited. You'll have tons of energy. You won't be able to sit.

She sat on the side of the bed next to me. She held up the container of pills.

Then we take Quaaludes to ease out the jumpiness, to make you calm. She said, Trust me. The beer kind of slides

168

over the top of everything. It takes you up and down, and the cigarettes give you something to do with your hands.

This is a wonderful country, she said.

THE MUSIC WAS LOUD, was coming from speakers high on the brick walls. There were exposed beams, and white partitions to make a bathroom and kitchen, to make bedrooms. But mostly it was a huge open space, with small trees in pots, and couches and tables with food and bottles, and young men with blond hair, wearing white jackets, were waiters. They took away empty bottles and plates and filled the tables with more food, with sweating bottles, with clean plates.

A hundred people sat and stood around the room. Tall people in suits, with gray hair, and women in beaded dresses and pearls. A man went by in a ruffled blouse, with pierced ears, with sparkles in his hair. There was a man in a dress, in a red wig and high heels, and he kissed me when I walked by.

Sweet, he said. Honey and sugar. Maple syrup.

He smiled and I could see makeup hiding where he'd shaved.

A woman with frizzy blond hair stopped in front of me. She wore an orange jumpsuit, and her zipper, in front, was open to her navel, and I could see the sides of her breasts.

She said, Hey, and the music was loud, and there were fans near the windows. Two blocks away, over the rooftops, was the river, the Longfellow Bridge and Boston on the other side.

Hey, she said. Don't stare, don't keep looking.

Her face was damp and she had brown eyes. There were drops of moisture on the blond curls at her face and neck.

She said, People keep staring at me. They're trying to look at my tits.

She sipped blush wine from a snifter.

They all want to fuck me, she said.

She put her hand on my chest. Do you want to fuck me?

She had white teeth and silver hoops in her ears.

A thin man with a ponytail stood next to us. He had red arrows on the sides of his jeans. He had a long face, wet eyes. He said he was sad because of the destruction of the Indians. He'd been thinking about it and it was a clear case of genocide.

Fuck off, the blond woman said.

The man nodded and was gone.

Asshole, the woman said.

Who'd you come with? she asked. You one of Bill's collectibles? You from Cambridgeport?

I took two Valium from the watch pocket of my jeans.

You want one? I asked.

She put her tongue out and I put a yellow tablet on it. She swallowed and sipped wine. She lifted my hand and licked my index finger.

You're a boy, aren't you? You're just sixteen.

Eighteen, I said.

A young eighteen, she said. From the suburbs. Nice white boy.

She sipped.

Ever fucked a thirty-year-old woman? she asked.

She lifted my hand and put my index finger in her mouth. It was warm, was wet. She slid my finger in and out of her mouth. I could feel her mouth pulling on my finger.

The music swam, grew louder. I was swaying.

Eden slid her arm around my waist. The blond woman was gone and I could feel the sweat, on Eden's arm, on her side.

She said, You doing okay? You want to leave, you tell me. I sipped from a can, and some people were dancing, drifting like the music, like a leaf on water. They moved their arms in long wavering circles.

A woman's voice was somewhere in the music, but was whispering and sighing, was not singing.

A man said, What's your name? Your name Lincoln? Rad? Shannon? You a friend of Ryan's? You know him, don't you?

I was sitting on a couch and there were people on each side of me.

He was squatting down, and he wore black, and he had blue eyeliner, had rouge on his cheeks. His lipstick was black.

He was Lucious, he said. Bringer of light. Not Lucifer, the dark angel. Not luscious.

You're very pretty, he said. You're a dark Irish flower. You bloom at night, he said, and he was kneeling in front of me. His breath was minty like gin. He had clear liquid in a glass.

He said he was Lucious, but in Paris he was Percival. That was the Grail, he said. That was pierce the veil of the valley. Pierce the veil of religious mystery.

Was I Catholic? he asked. Had I gone to school with the nuns?

His mother was Jewish, he said. His father a Catholic.

He was dead now. In Morocco or Tangiers somewhere. He had dysentery, and surrounded by all those beautiful children in turbans. Like brown angels. Can you imagine? Halfway around the world.

He laughed.

There was new music on. Something harder and faster. Something that pounded.

You have beautiful eyes, he said. Do you know that? And hands.

He lifted my hand. Long fingers, he said. Long and strong.

He bet I didn't know that. He said he wasn't shy about some things. He didn't mind telling me.

You been to the beach? he asked. Roarke has a place on the beach. There were gulls and the surf pounded day and night like it meant to cleanse the world.

Did I ever feel like that? Like everything was filth?

My arms were itchy. I had to scratch a place on the back of my neck.

I was laughing, and Lucious said my laugh was wine. He said he could drink it.

Everything was warm, and outside, the river held the lights of Boston.

The blond woman walked behind Lucious. She waved.

All the songs of a night, Lucious said. All the songs of the skin and the sky and the rain.

His eyes were gray, were almost crossed eyes. They tilted toward each other.

He said he wanted me to come to the beach with him, but then Eden was on the couch. She laughed and she had sparkles in her hair.

Two men were kissing beneath a speaker. A woman with black hair was dancing by herself, and she had taken her jersey off, had tied it around her waist. Her breasts were small, her nipples dark, and sweat ran between her breasts.

The music was louder, was like the breeze from the windows. It drifted in and around us. It raised the hair on my skin, on my back and chest and legs. The music swayed, and people were tilted as they stood near the couches, as they leaned against the walls. They'd fall over.

A woman with red lipstick laughed, and her teeth were white, her tongue pink. She looked at me from all the way over, from the other side of the room. She winked, she lifted her glass to her mouth. There were silver bracelets on her wrist.

Eden said, I need smokes. I only have one left.

C'mon, she said. There's a store near here. At a corner somewhere.

The stairs were iron and concrete, and they clanged, and Eden's hair was damp and her eyes were raccoon eyes, were circles.

The street was hot. There was no air. There were silver

trash cans on the sidewalk, and steam was coming from a pipe in a brick wall, in an alley.

The windows were rolled down in the cars, and there were blasts of radio as they went by.

New England Dragway, a voice said, and the voice echoed like a cave, and the walls would drip slowly down. Bats squeaking, only it was the street.

A black guy said, Hey, pal. Hey. How you doing.

He was short and wore an alpine hat. He said, You got the time.

Eden laughed. She said, Night, and the man laughed.

He was sitting on the hood of a car. He took a pack of Kools from his shirt pocket. He held the pack out and I took a smoke. He flicked a lighter.

How you doing, Joe, he said to me. How come you and Jane're walking around? You lost in the woods? Can't find your way?

He wore glasses with heavy black frames.

Show us where the store is, Eden said. We need cigarettes. We'll buy you a pint.

You'll buy me a pint, the man said. Now that's sweet, he said.

Eden said, Then you come to the party. All the music in the world, and gin to make you like music, and gin to make you like everyone there. Everyone dancing and talking shit.

The store was bright like sun, was full of bottles, and Eden bought Kools for us, and two pints of gin.

Then we were walking near a warehouse and smoking cigarettes, and we sipped gin. We were in a neighborhood with small front lawns, and Mary on the half shell—in half-buried bathtubs—and behind the curtains we could see the flickering light from televisions.

He was Phil, and his voice was soft, his voice was a whisper, and he laughed.

The party's on Richmond Street, Eden said.

Richard Street.

Richford Street.

She laughed, and the gin was cool and warm, was menthol like Kools.

We went left and right, and there were streetlights and store lights and cars, and Phil said, That's where we started.

Then we were at the party, and Phil was standing near the speakers and he was talking to a woman with gray hair. Then it was much later, back in Newton. Me and Eden, and she said we could park near her house, we could pull in the driveway even.

The houses were quiet, and were set back on deep lawns and there were bushes and trees. Crickets were twitching, and over on Commonwealth Avenue, two blocks away, a car went by every ten minutes.

We lay on the grass in the backyard, and she said her mother and father were in New York.

Make all the noise you want, she said.

The crickets and cars were far away and there was a breeze in the trees. The grass was cool and the sky was full of pinlights.

Eden said they were like pills and booze and shit. Corks popping from champagne bottles, and then you closed your eyes, and in the darkness you could see streaking light and tiny spots way off.

She said it was like that for her, and then we didn't say anything, and the crickets were there and no cars anymore and the winking sky a million miles away.

BAMP SAID THE SNOW could be as much as eight or ten feet tall, would come halfway up the windows. He thought about that in the summer because it was so hot, and thinking about it was like a lake in Maine or something. The owls whooing in the pine trees and the moon in the water.

He worked there one summer, up to Maine, near York,

but maybe somewhere else. He wasn't sure. Maybe New Hampshire or Vermont. He and his brother George, who was gone, who died when he was twenty-three of a heart.

The Sox were playing in California on the radio, and every few minutes a car would pass. It was after ten and the game was just starting in California.

Bamp sucked on his pipe, and said he thought of the snow because he worked for an undertaker once, and they had an old lady die and the snow was so high they had to take the body out from the top of the window. Raise her up, wrapped in her sheets, and out the top half of the window, then slide her over the snow.

That was the most snow, he said.

But people were different now, put them in special places. Put them in homes and buildings, just the way they put his mother away.

Eleven brothers and sisters, and all she could do was cry anymore. Working in a laundry and coming home so tired she fell asleep at the table. Red face and red arms from washing all day. Her arms up to her elbows in bleach and water.

Maybe his mother went out the top part of the window, wrapped in a sheet like that. Maybe he was mixing the two up, whoever the other one was.

Someone was in the hospital. His sister May, and Grace who was married to his brother Andy. May had her arm taken off because of the gangrene. Infected, and they couldn't do anything for her.

May or Grace. May had the appendix out, and died, or maybe the teeth that were infected.

He couldn't remember. He couldn't keep track, but he thought it was his mother in the mental hospital in Waltham, and all of them in white, and the special jacket where her arms were wrapped around.

Weeping and wailing after George died, or May. May with her leg like that, and Mom crying at the table.

The windows had bars and she went to ninety pounds, and Eddy, his brother, couldn't go see her. It was terrible seeing her like that. The windows tall, like Frankenstein in the movie, and covered with bars and the long rooms with beds and all of them moaning. The straps and the water. Put them in water, because that would calm them, but she'd hardly look up or say a word.

Used to be a great big lady, and had kids. Had eleven, and then washed sheets and diapers all day, and he kept thinking of the snow and if that could have been her, sliding over the top of the snow.

Maybe she had come back, and was living with Grace and Andy, in Watertown. Maybe that was it. In 1940 or somewhere. Here in Newton or over to Watertown. Back before Parker was in the Navy, and out on a ship in the Pacific.

Sometime, he thought, and nodded.

THE PAPER SAID THERE WAS a body of a young woman in the woods.

The beer was warm.

She had dark hair, was five three, weighed 115 pounds. There was a small, blue, cross-shaped tattoo on her right forearm and ligature marks on her neck.

The police were asking for people who may have been in the area Sunday night or Monday morning.

I swallowed beer and turned the page.

Outside was gray and damp, was Tuesday or Wednesday, and everyone had gone to work.

The refrigerator hummed, and birds made noise and traffic was muffled, traffic was far away.

There were seven more cans under the bed. I finished one and set it on the windowsill. I cracked another, and the house was quiet, the house was empty.

I turned back the page. The woman was discovered Monday by men working on a nearby road.

There were no signs of struggle.

She had been walking, or she had been at a party, or she had been at a bar. On Friday or Saturday or Sunday.

She had a kid, from when she was sixteen, and her father called her a slut.

A car stopped on the street. Parked. The engine stopped. A car door slammed.

Her mother was nicer. She understood what it was like, and school sucked. She couldn't put her baby in an orphanage. All those people in white uniforms and cribs lined up like the Army.

The doorbell rang, and I sipped, and the walls and rooms were cool and the doorbell rang a second time, and maybe the man at the door drove a Chevrolet, a blue or black or brown sedan, and he had a dark suit and white shirt and skinny tie. He had short hair, and a notebook in his suitcoat pocket, and his gun at the chest and underarm, on the right.

He stood on the porch, and shifted his weight from one foot to the other, and looked down at the name and address on a piece of paper.

This eighteen-year-old fuck-up without a job or anything.

Fucking dirtball. Fucking useless scumbag.

The doorbell rang again, and I sipped and almost didn't breathe.

Was it Sunday? Monday?

He'd been in the Marines, and then college, and then the Academy, and those assholes pissed him off. They really did.

Fucking perverts and sickos.

He noticed the house next door, the green one with drawn shades, and the cars passed in front.

The second can was empty, and the third one didn't even taste warm anymore.

There were footsteps on the porch, and then a minute later the car started, was leaving.

In bed was the newspaper, and the third or fourth can,

and there were five left.

So that made it four? Five?

Fuck.

Didn't matter.

Sunday she left the kid with her mom, and the old man was in his chair in front of the tube, his face gray as the picture, his Coke and Luckies. Barely looked up. Said, You again, and she was wearing the white blouse with the gray stitching at the collar and sleeves, and it did bring out her eyes, her green-gray cat eyes.

And her mom in the kitchen kissed her, and she noticed the brown spots on her mom's hands and arms, and the blue veins in her legs, and thought, She looks like shit. She looks fifty-five, was forty-one; had her when she was eighteen, so she couldn't say anything about Tiffany.

Tiffany was fussing, was wiggling like a fish, and probably was wet.

The linoleum was cracked and there were dirty dishes in the sink. White grease in the frying pan still, the smell of old hamburger.

Jesus Christ.

The fourth beer was gone, and she had to leave, had to get out of there, bad as she felt for Mom, she wanted to run.

She got to Jackie's, and Jackie knew some guys renting on a pond out by Route 495, and they'd fished together and would maybe grill burgers and fish.

The place was nice. The pine trees and the little dock and water slapping the piles, and she must have had four or five beers, and thank God Jackie was driving.

Jackie was standing by the grill, wearing pink lipstick, talking to someone's wife. If she'd just take off twenty, thirty pounds. She wouldn't be bad at all.

You went over there, the place was full of Yodels and Devil Dogs and Swiss Rolls.

God, she had a Swiss Roll once, and felt like she was on

coffee and diet pills. Must have been five hundred calories.

The guy named Red was sweet, was kind of funny. Had that white white skin redheads had.

Wore cutoffs and no shirt, and no hair on his chest. Had a brown birthmark like a third nipple, and he said he didn't like the fishing so much, but hanging out and talking shit with guys.

Pardon the French, he said, and they laughed, and she could feel his eyes on her chest. The second button undone, and she didn't mind him looking. She knew they were full, and they didn't sag down and wrinkle from Tiffany the way she thought they would, and her legs were great. Maybe a little thick at the ankles, but good. Not perfect.

The phone rang, and I counted to nine and then it stopped, and afterwards, for three or four minutes, it seemed like the rings were echoing.

Then they were in a car, and Jackie hadn't seemed to mind, had said she'd talk to her, and gave her one of those smiles, and maybe Tiffany would grow up and go to college and Mom would be okay.

He was sweet, but he had this way of putting his hands on her, too heavy and hard, and she wanted to tell him no.

Knock it off. Please.

Everything was slow, and the paper was spread out on the floor, was lying open and lopsided next to the bed, and my legs were long and white and thin.

I leaned over to see how many were left, and there were four, and I almost tilted off, tilted over, like I was in a boat and a big swell came, and I could feel it under me, all those trillions of gallons of water.

Laughed. Almost laughed, because I was way way over, and could have gone, but caught myself, and the can on the table next to the bed was more than half full.

Ten twenty-one on the clock. Red numbers behind the can. The numbers changed every minute. Became 10:22, and

I looked away, and there were pictures on the wall and cars going by.

Eden with her raccoon eyes, and her mother screaming that her father didn't build a business and have her and love her so that she could be an ingrate, a spoiled brat, a princess who never worked a day in her life, and Eden said, You fucking cunt, and her mother stood with her mouth open, trying to breathe, and Eden wouldn't have said it if it wasn't for the phenobarb and her mother being such an asshole.

So she went to her room and slammed the door, and twenty minutes later her father called her from work, called on Eden's line, on her number, and said he was very sorry and very disappointed and didn't quite know what to say anymore. Her mother was devastated, and she loved her very very very much, and wanted what was best for her, and he worked his fingers to the bone.

She started to cry. She felt it in her nose and eyes, and said, Daddy, and she didn't even mean to hurt him, and then the tears were filling her eyes and falling on her nose and cheeks and falling on the front of her blouse, and she said, Daddy, I'm sorry, I'm sorry, I don't mean, I didn't want, and he said, Sweetheart, Sweetie, don't cry, don't be that way. We love you.

I swallowed, and then the woman was with Red, and my father was at the table, or at his desk in his room, his face in his hands, and saying, Don't you think you could go easy on that, and pointing to the glass, and saying, What about September, what about when the summer's over, and everyone I knew was gone to college, or went to the Army.

The walls were cracked in the back hall, going downstairs, and plaster was coming out, was white powder on the floor, on the stairs, and there was an extension cord plugged in the light socket in the middle of the ceiling, and he couldn't sleep at two a.m., in his undershirt and boxer shorts, his thin white arms and legs, pale and shining in the dark.

It was hot. It was eighty degrees at least, at two a.m. It was humid as the tropics.

So the woman was in the car, and Red who was so funny and nice at the house, and had a blue tee shirt on, said why didn't they stop at his apartment, he had some numbers rolled, and he had a bottle for special occasions, and she thought, Tiffany, and Mom with the brown spots and blue lines in her legs, and only forty-one.

The old bastard, staring at the gray light. His chair.

Slut.

Red's place was neat like she couldn't believe, neat like a nurse or an old lady lived there. Everything in place, and the stereo and records all lined up, and the glass top of the coffee table, and he said, Sit down, take a load off, relax, it's still the weekend.

It's just Sunday yet.

She said, What do you do, and he looked at her like he didn't understand, like she was talking in some language from outer space.

He looked more, and for a second it was like he had a glass eye, an eye from a laboratory.

The one on the left.

Like it was made from something else. Didn't focus right and didn't seem to see, and she could look at it and there was nothing there.

Job, she said. What kind of work.

And his look went away, and he said he worked for an undertaker, believe it or not.

She said, You're kidding. Honest to God, she said.

He nodded.

People might think it's strange, he said. People gave him a look when he told them, so most of the time he just said he worked in the human service field, just worked with people, even though the people happened to be dead.

Deceased, he said.

Passed on.

He smiled.

He said, You think that's strange, don't you. You think you'd like to go.

She shook her head. Really, she said.

He said it was strange how beautiful it could be. The brass handles, the polished wood, the burnished metal. And the linings. They were amazing. The workmanship. It was an art.

A buried art.

He handed her a drink and I cracked a can and the phone rang.

Once. Twice. Three, four, five, six, seven.

Then it stopped, and the house was still. The house was air, and nothing moved. I was a wall and a floor and a rug.

He said people didn't realize how important it was to make the deceased beautiful for their last journey.

He lit a number, and handed it to her, and her lungs were full, were almost burning. Her eyes watered.

He said the body was absolutely naked and white, was almost blue, and still as the darkest night. Just lying there on the table, and he had to make an incision, and fix the tubing, and he said people didn't realize.

There was something white in his hands, something long and thin and white. Something coiled.

He said people had nothing to be afraid of, if they only knew. If they could see how beautiful it could be, how quiet and white and final.

The phone rang again, and I listened and listened, and my eyes were closed, and I didn't breathe. I was still as dust and dirt and stone.

twelve

At thirty-two I waited on the third floor of Goldwin Smith Hall, and they came to the office that had no windows, that had slanted ceilings and five gray metal desks, an office I shared with five other graduate students.

They were seventeen or eighteen, and they wore shorts and polo shirts those first weeks of the semester in 1986, they wore sneakers. They had earrings and bracelets, and some wore bands around their ankles, bands of bright cloth, and they couldn't deal, they were flunking physics, flunking chem, they got a fifty-seven on a quiz in government and everyone else was smart, everyone else was fine.

A woman with black hair said someone on her hall was calling home every night, and it was only September and she couldn't believe the amount of work. It was incredible. High school was never like this. High school was cake. High school was cake with ice cream.

Angel food cake. Fudge ripple. She smiled. I don't know, she said.

She said, I sit down and there's nothing there. I get the

pens lined up and I get a dictionary ready, and tell my room-mate to leave me alone. And then I sit there. I hear footsteps in the hall, I hear a stereo somewhere, and I look at the page, and then I look at my watch.

I watch my watch, she said. Now I know why they call it a watch.

I'm talking like a crazy lady, she said. I'm heading around the bend.

She was from a section of Philly, but not a nice section. Not a place with big trees and long driveways and white picket fences.

You know. No station wagons and Volvos and shit.

Sorry, she said. She looked down.

She said it wasn't that kind of place, though there were rich parts not too far away.

Right, she said.

On her street there were little front yards, postage stamp yards, and millions of kids. Toys and big wheels and strollers spilling onto the sidewalk, and she and her mother lived on the first floor of a house her aunt and uncle owned. They lived upstairs, the aunt and uncle.

Mom's brother.

Speed, everyone called him.

Dad was gone. He was long gone, from before she was even born. Fuck and run, she said. That's what Mom said when she was drinking on Saturday night, and watching the shit on TV. *Dallas* and *Knot's Landing*. Crap like that.

She said she was sorry, but that's how she talked. That's how people where she grew up talked, and she used those words too. That language.

She said there were always kids hanging out, older kids, and girls her age with babies, and she said her mother went out and had her tubes tied. She didn't want anything to get worse than it already was. She called it drawing a line in the sand.

She worked in an insurance office in downtown Philly, and she pushed her in school. She kept saying she'd kill her if she ended up dumb and fat and broke like her mother, and she wasn't that way at all, but she knew what her mother meant.

She said she worked weekends in the produce department at the supermarket.

I know iceberg lettuce, she said. You want some nice tomatoes, some carrots or broccoli. I can get you some nice bananas, she said. Straight from Brazil, from Argentina. Just off the boat or the plane.

So it was a big deal, she said, her getting in here, and getting scholarships and loans and stuff. She said she couldn't believe the place when she visited. Quads and trees and hills and gorges. She said she thought this was Colorado or TV or something.

And everyone with blond hair and summers in Maine or on some island somewhere.

She said, Are you kidding. Are you shitting me.

All she knew about islands was that they were surrounded by water, and all she knew about water was that you drank it. That's what the mayor said, but it was true. Open fire hydrants, and those aluminum chairs from K-Mart on the postage stamp.

And these blond people with teeth, and the Rolex watches and kids her age with BMW cars.

Can you imagine? she said. Some eighteen-year-old with a car like that? With a two-hundred-dollar sweater? And I keep thinking how my mom rolled down her nylons to her ankles, and sat with a can of Bud watching JR and Sue Ellen and Bobby.

She said, And I keep thinking they'll know. They'll find out and send me back.

Back to Philly with all the screaming babies, and guys out on parole and coming back to the neighborhood and saying this time was different, this time they had plans, this time they'd do all right. You didn't have to worry about them.

ANN WAS THIN AND BLOND and wore a green cardigan she'd had since high school, that was more than ten years old. She sat in the big chair at the foot of my bed, and she said that Africa, after college, was strange and beautiful, like something—at twenty-two—she woke up to. Something she had dreamed about, had read about, had seen in movies.

Drums and tall African people whose skin was so black it was almost blue. Mangoes and oranges and cloth dyed red and green and yellow, like feathers.

The earth was red, and she said she'd always think of those wide flat trees, trees that looked like they were being blown in a storm, acacia trees, she thought they were called.

And chattering sounds from stands of trees. Birds and monkeys, high yammering sounds—whack, whack, whack. But quicker.

Whackwhackwhack, waaaaa.

Then clicks. Then more.

She said she thought of these sounds sometimes. At night, just before she fell asleep, when she was lying there, and it was like veils wafting across her face, and strands of silk and sleep—and she'd remember the birds and the monkeys, in Kenya, from eight, nine years before.

And it would seem strange to her—that she had gone there and spent a year at a girls' school in the countryside. Without knowing anybody, with only two semesters of Swahili, from this small city in east Tennessee where the hills were everywhere and the whine from the sawmill and the trains heading north punctuated the days. Were commas and periods and question marks.

A colon, she said.

A dash, a hyphen, an apostrophe.

She thought of corrugated roofs that caught the sunlight,

and in rain, drummed like a kettle. Roofs of houses and huts and buildings. Cinder block and concrete.

Unbeautiful, she said. Squat and functional.

But that was okay, because the people and the country-side were spectacular—were long and smooth as a curve, and the sky there was like nothing she'd ever seen.

She said in Ithaca sometimes, she'd look out the window, and say the trees were bare, and it was November, and there was rain, and she'd be staring at bare branches and she'd catch herself thinking about the sky in the evening in Kenya, just before dusk, and how in the west it lit the horizon with pink and purple and a deep deep blue, and she'd be amazed at how she arrived there, in Africa, in Ithaca—so far away from the sound of the sawmill and the trains in Tennessee.

She said all this stuff, it swirled around her at night, when she was trying to go to sleep, and she wasn't sure what to do with it.

She smiled and looked at her hands. Her fingers were moving, were fretting.

So, you, she said. What about you?

How you been, pal? she wanted to know.

What's your story?

HE HAD BLOND HAIR and bad skin, and he was from Gary, Indiana.

Built on sand and made of steel, he said. City of broad shoulders. Lunchpails and time clocks, and he thought about that, even though his dad taught history at the high school, and had gone to college and everything, it was something he thought about. At night and during the day.

It was different. Especially here, he said, and looked at the slanted ceiling.

I had my feet on the desk.

He said he wasn't sleeping, and he didn't know why. He felt like he was tired almost all the time, and all this stuff was

crowding him. Tests and reading and lectures and oral pre-
sentations, and every time he tried to look up and breathe,
tried to get a clearing, something would roll in and fill the
clearing.

Had to see someone. Had to read something.

And his work-study job too. Fifteen hours in the agricul-
ture library. Filing and hybrids.

He didn't know. It was getting to him. If he could only
sleep. Just six or seven or eight straight hours. Deep sleep.
Deep and refreshing.

Like a lake somewhere, a quiet place in the woods.

Just bird sounds. Light filtering down and maybe wind in
the trees.

Did I know what he meant? Just a few days, a night or
two.

Then everything would get better. He'd be able to handle
it.

It's not a movie, he said. He put his hand in front of his
face.

I know that. I'm absolutely sure of that.

But I lie in bed. At eleven or twelve. And I start to think,
and everything starts to speed up. It gets faster and faster,
and everything whirls and swims, and I just want to stop it,
to shut it off. It's like the gears have gone crazy, and this
engine's going too fast, and the oil's almost burned off and
everything's getting hotter and hotter. There's smoke, and I
wait for a fire or an explosion, but it doesn't happen.

He crossed his legs and looked at me. He was wearing a
white hooded sweatshirt and a watch with a broken strap.
He'd used wire to fix the strap.

He said he had friends from Gary, from high school, and
he thought of them a lot. Two or three of them.

Bill and Lenny and Chris.

They hadn't gone to college. They were either working
or in the Army. Chris was probably getting married at Christ-

mas. His girlfriend was pregnant, and he worked for UPS, and he guessed they'd go ahead and get married and have the kid.

Have a life. Furniture and an apartment.

He said senior year they used to drive around town, two or three of them. Lenny had a van, and at night he'd swing by and honk and they'd cruise.

They never said much. There was music—the Pogues and the Clash and Little Richard.

Bill was crazy for Little Richard. He'd say, Richard knows what the fuck he's doing. Richard's mama didn't raise no fool.

He said they always drove slowly, through the neighborhoods with the cars lining the curb and TV lights flickering and dogs snuffling trash bags.

Then they'd get on one of the strips, and all the lights would glow, would be selling burgers and booze and stereos and money. The streetlights were sodium, were yellow and weirdly bright like some concentration camp, and when they passed warehouses with chain-link fence around them and razor wire on top, he had this amazing feeling—like dogs would snarl and he'd see death's head patches on sidewalks and doorways and he'd wait for something.

It didn't come, of course. It never came.

It was just him and Lenny, maybe Chris, maybe Bill, and it was just Gary, Indiana. The Hoosier State.

He said they'd pass the strip and then it was a gas station, a car dealer with those colored flags flapping, and two three four miles later, the light would be gone, and they'd roll down the windows and they'd be able to smell the earth.

Corn or soybeans, and if they kept driving a while, they'd see a silo, and maybe the moon and stars and shit, hanging in the sky like a jewel shop or something.

He said they had a few beers between them. One or two. Or maybe a pint of Tango or Ripple or MD. The wino shit.

Passing it back and forth, and Lenny smoked his Pall Malls, and his eyes—Lenny's eyes—would flick from the road to the rearview and side mirrors, and then ten, fifteen miles out of town, past Hobart and Wheeler, there'd be hills, and turnoffs, and Lenny would always find roads that wound around in the hills, past trees and rocks, and they'd come to some clearing where there were smashed bottles and soggy cardboard and burn circles where someone had a little fire.

They'd cut the engine and turn off the music and sit there on some hill, and way the fuck off, if the night was clear, they'd see the lights of Gary, and past that, Chicago, and maybe even the lake, which was just this darkness past the lights. Just this flat black space where the wind blew and where wiseguys dumped bodies and shit.

And they'd sit and sit, sometimes for hours, not saying anything and hardly even breathing.

It was always a school night. Tuesday or Monday or Thursday, and he always thought about people at home, making their lunches for the next day and laying their clothes out and doing homework or watching TV.

He'd look at the lights, way off there, and he'd imagine living rooms and bedrooms, Wally Cleaver, and Ward and June, and Ricky and Dave from cable.

Black and white TV, and Harriet always smiling and Ozzie in his cardigan and tie. Then Ricky would sing, and his fat friend would come over.

They always had fat friends. Fat and jovial.

Wally had Lumpy, and Ricky had someone too.

Waldo or Rhino, Biff or Butch or Chuck.

Like Chet Morton, only that was much earlier, wasn't it. Chet and Frank and Joe. The portly chum of the Hardy boys.

He looked up at me. He had dark patches under his eyes.

He said, Listen to me. Jesus.

You're fine, I told him.

You remember Frank and Joe, he said.

Tony Prito, I said. Fenton G. Hardy. Aunt Gertrude.

He laughed. Excellent, he said. Awesome.

Bayport and roadsters. Sleuths, he said. The swarthy criminal, the gang of car thieves. The house on the cliff and the cave at the base of the cliff. The cave on the water where they brought boats in, and watery tunnels and stairs that rose through the cliff to the house.

Shit, he said.

And it was a counterfeit ring or jewel thieves or smugglers. And they got in there, late one night, Frank and Joe and maybe Tony Prito. At two in the morning they got their boat in close—the *Sleuth*, they called the boat—and they found the cave, and that was the secret, wasn't it? That the cave existed, and that it was connected to the house on the cliff?

He said, *The Tower Treasure. The House on the Cliff. Footprints Under the Window. The Shore Road Mystery.*

Aunt Gertrude and her cherry pie, and Chet always looking for a piece.

Fucking Chet, he said. And Chet's sister Viola.

Or Violet.

Something, he said.

Had the hots for Frank. Or Joe.

And Fenton G. Hardy, Bayport's world-famous detective, was always off somewhere, on some famous case, in Singapore or San Francisco.

Except for a few times. Frank and Joe came into the tower room, or the room in the cellar, and Fenton was tied up and gagged and shit, and Frank and Joe rescued him.

Then went home together, the three of them, and Tony and Chet and Aunt Gertrude and Mrs. Fenton would all be in the kitchen. Viola too, and the other babe. Joe's girl. Whatever her name was. Maybe the police chief too, and a dog.

Chet would say something about cherry pie, and they'd all laugh, and Aunt Gertrude would do the honors.

Wally Cleaver would be there, and the Andersons too. Kitten and Princess and Bud and what's his name.

Marcus Welby. Only younger. Before he became a doctor. *Father Knows Best.*

He said, Charlie Fucking Manson.

Frank and Joe and the Beaver meet Squeaky and Tex and Charlie. Go to Disneyland together and learn the value of being honest. Ward gives them a talk. In the bedroom upstairs.

And even Eddie learns too. Even Eddie doesn't say anything.

Eddie. Who's a cop in California. Highway patrolman.

Dan Matthews. Ten four.

Over and out, he said. Adam twelve, I'm on my way.

He said it was endless. He said he had to sleep. He said it'd be better after he slept for a little while.

Eddie and Chet and Ozzie.

Sitting on the hill in Gary, just last spring. Seeing the lights and knowing he'd be gone in a few more months, and that was strange. How you thought things and knew them, and then they happened. And you could go back in your mind, and it was like you could actually be there. On the side of the hill, in the van, and nobody saying a word.

ANN SAID MANHATTAN, after Africa, was not what she expected, though she wasn't sure what she had expected. Maybe some kind of glamor, but not that either. Maybe doormen in white gloves and snow falling outside Lincoln Center, and the scent, the aroma, of French bread and saffron from restaurants, and cab rides through the park. The trees and grass and huge lit buildings on every side.

Canyons, she said.

We sat on the side of a hill near the museum, and down below was the city and the lake, and the trees were beginning to fade, were turning a dull green. In a few weeks they would be orange and yellow.

She said after a year in Kenya she went for a few months to Tennessee, and that felt pretty strange too. After college and Africa, then back to the house where she'd grown up.

The news on television at six, then dinner with ice water and napkin rings.

The summer there was pretty amazing, the humidity just rolling in and settling into the valley, and she'd forgotten what that was like.

Maybe it was just an unusually hot summer and she hadn't expected that, especially after Africa.

But the long whining sound of that insect—the one that sounded like an electrical wire, she remembered that. And the haze, and she took two showers every day, because a shower seemed so luxurious and wonderful.

And she wrote letters to places in New York City, to get editing jobs. Wrote two or three letters a day, maybe thirty or forty in all, and then waited. Addressed them to places like East 57th Street, to Madison or Park Avenues, to West 34th, to East 72nd, and then looked out the window of her mother and father's house, and could see the foothills of the Smokies in the distance, and she said she tried to picture the addresses in New York City.

She thought of steel and glass towers and ferns in the lobby, and vendors with pushcarts on the sidewalk in front. Selling hot dogs and pretzels. And the offices would be on the nineteenth floor, the thirty-second floor, and the elevator was always silent and bonged like an airplane when it reached her floor, and the doors slid open and the carpeting, she imagined, was always dark.

And in Tennessee the temperatures in July were ninety-six and ninety-nine and a hundred and four one day, and she'd listen to her mother and father, and her sister, who still lived at home even though she was twenty-five.

They talked about what they'd have for dinner, and how

the zinnias and pansies and roses were doing in the yard and how much gas cost and what Mary Sue Madden was doing since her husband Lee Wayne had a heart attack and died back in February.

Everything should have been different after she'd spent a year in Africa. They would talk differently, and not watch the news, and Billy Ray Deeb would not go into the coffee shop downtown and pull out a roll of bills, and most of them looked like twenties and fifties and hundreds, and Daddy would say, Billy Ray had a good night at cards in Knoxville, and everyone laughed and said, Well, yes, and the yes was drawn out into two syllables.

That would all be different because of Africa, and because she spoke Swahili most of the time for a year, and she hiked partway up Mount Kilimanjaro, and saw zebras and giraffes and ate peanut butter soup and cornmeal, and was five or six or seven thousand miles from home.

She thought at least her brother would understand, would know what some of this felt like, but he didn't. He was still tall and thin and careful and quiet, and now he was married to a thin blond woman who grew up on a farm in Strawberry Plains, and she was pregnant, and the heat didn't seem to bother her at all.

She walked to the mailbox at the end of the driveway and nothing came. She wrote more letters, but after a while there was nobody else to write to.

Or Christmas in Africa, and imagining home from thousands of miles away, on December 25, and no snow or bells and an ache in her chest that hurt and was wonderful at the same time.

It was too strange, too weird beyond words.

She looked at me, and I looked at the grass.

Then Manhattan, she said, and her eyes were blue.

Things got real strange, she said.

Amazing, exotic.

She didn't even like to think about it.

SINGAPORE WAS STREETS and motion, Mae said. They lived on the ninth floor, and even as far back as seven or eight, which was how old she was when they finally left, she thought of things from high up, from the ninth floor.

People down below like ants, or at least dolls or toy soldiers, and toy cars and trucks, and the sounds muffled up there, like in a cloud.

But down below was amazing, was thick with people and cars and noise. Birds clucking and dozens of languages, and streets so narrow it felt like the buildings were lonely and had feet and were inching closer and closer all the time. Pretty soon they'd want to hold hands, the buildings, then do more than hold hands, and walking around would be like navigating through a jungle of legs.

Wasn't that strange, she said. Wasn't that an oddball way to see things.

She smiled. She wore a white blouse and black jeans and there was a red band holding her hair back.

She said she always thought of the window in her bedroom on the ninth floor, because it was one of her earliest memories, and all through childhood, all the way through those early years, she'd sit in a chair in front of the window and she'd watch outside.

There were other buildings, but at that height they didn't seem so close and crowded, and she could see the water, and there was no noise.

She said she loved the air up there and the light and space. There were times, she said, when she was sure she could fly. Up above there, and all the honking and yelling would be down on the street, but she'd open her wings and drift over everything, like sleep or dreams or swimming.

And that was some of the earliest stuff, and in a curious way, even though it was farther away in time, she could remember that more clearly and vividly. Like it wasn't ten or twelve years ago, but only last summer.

Did that happen to me? she wanted to know. Did I know what she meant?

Then India, she said, because her father worked for the State Department, and then Washington, D.C., and that was all. That was the sum total of the parts of her life.

India was wicked hot and totally dusty, and the food was really cool.

Not cool cool, she said. Kind of hot and spicy, but delicious cool, strange and wonderful cool.

They had a house with this giant garden, full of trees and bushes and flowers, and there was this little pond with lily pads and a bridge that crossed over it.

She used to climb the trees in the garden, and it was totally different than Singapore.

It was wicked wicked hot, and pretty flat, and there were no tall buildings at all. Nothing over four or five stories and that seemed incredibly sad.

India wasn't as poor as she'd thought it would be, at least where they were. Nobody had real fancy cars or houses, none of the regular people, she meant, but there weren't beggars on the streets and people with huge eyes.

At least that she was able to see.

But what she remembered best was her friend Kayla, whose father worked for the British government. Kayla had dark hair, and almost the exact same birthday as her, only a month off. November 7 and December 7.

They used to sleep over and talk all night, and Kayla's mother was a great big fat lady who sat on this fancy couch in the living room all day, and read romance novels. The ones with the beautiful woman, the raven-haired governess or something on the cover, standing near a giant house, and a single window on the third floor was lit. There was always a man with white teeth holding her or standing behind her.

She'd sit there on the couch in her robe, and read, and she laughed like there was a barrel in her chest, and she and Kayla, Mae and Kayla, went upstairs, and lay around on the bed and on the floor, and they'd talk about Keefe or Nevin or Page, kids in their class, and they'd almost be afraid to look at each other.

It was like eating ice cream or fresh donuts. It was delicious—there in the afternoon in India, for hour after hour.

Page told Tracy who told Kayla that Keefe liked Mae. Really liked Mae, and wanted to meet her on Saturday, only Kayla had to promise not to tell anyone except Mae, otherwise he'd never talk to Kayla again.

Keefe was tall for his age and very thin, and he had blond hair that grew long on top, and fell forward, and he was always brushing his hair out of his eyes.

Kayla thought Keefe was probably shy, and that was why Mae had to go up to him and say hello. Talk about blue jeans or the weather. Talk about Madonna or something, about David Bowie.

Keefe had already taken the first step, and now it was Mae's turn.

It would be fine. Keefe really did like her, Kayla said. Page wasn't making it up.

ANN ARRIVED IN MANHATTAN in September, and she remembered it rained half the time. Rained so often the streets were always wet, and at night they held the color of lights and looked like spilled paint.

She stayed at a rooming house off Forty-sixth Street, on the second floor, and she went to work during the days and looked for an apartment at night.

Her job was mostly typing at first, for an encyclopedia, and then they moved her up to checking statistical tables, then to writing occasional obituaries for the encyclopedia's yearbook.

Obits for physicists who had won the Nobel Prize years ago, and emigrated from Germany to England to the United States during and after the Second World War.

She said they always seemed to end up in California, as though that was the place where the land ended.

She'd sit there on the twenty-second floor, writing some poor physicist's obit, and think of a white-haired man on the beach in Santa Monica or Big Sur, standing and looking across the water, amazed that there was no place left to go.

She looked at me from the other side of the bed. Her head was on the pillow and her hand was on my arm.

Hey, she said. How you doing?

She said, Am I boring you? Am I putting you to sleep?

I said no. I said, Go on.

She got up for the bathroom. She was undressed and her back was long and white.

When she returned she was wearing a blue tee shirt.

She sat on the side of the bed, and said that at night, when she looked for an apartment with the rental agent, she couldn't believe the places.

Rooms with no closets, with crumbling plaster, with graffiti on the walls. MOE in giant red letters on a living room wall.

They'll paint over that, the agent said, and when they snapped the light on in the kitchen, dozens of roaches scurried for cover.

She found a place finally on Ninety-first Street on the east side, a studio. Bedroom, kitchen and living room all more or less in the same room. When she wanted a change of scenery she'd sit in the bathroom.

She said it was work from eight to five, and mostly she walked there. Twenty-six blocks each way and an hour for lunch.

There was a deli near their building, and she got a salad and sat in the lobby, next to the trees. She'd watch the elevators and the escalators that went up to the second level in the lobby, and she was always amazed at the numbers of people. People in suits, people wearing glasses, people with brief-cases, with mops, people in uniforms.

Then at night she'd go back to her place, and she'd cook rice, would cook pasta, and would read or watch TV while she ate.

She talked to her mother every Saturday, and once in a while, once every month or so, she'd go somewhere with one of the people from work. To a movie or a museum. Maybe to a play or a concert.

Other women, mostly. Once in a while with a guy.

She said weekends were tough. She'd dread Friday be-cause she had to leave the office and go home to her apart-ment.

On Saturday or Sunday, in the morning, she'd walk to places. To the Museum of Modern Art, or to bookstores or galleries, and she'd walk around.

Her back was to me, and I watched her shoulders, the tilt of her head.

I'd walk through the rooms at the museum, and I was always afraid that people would look at me, would know I was by myself. I was going from one painting to the next, from one room to another, because I had nowhere to go and couldn't be in that apartment even an hour more.

For three years, she said. I always had to go back there later in the afternoon. To my books and my TV. And I'd tell myself I was stupid, I was ugly, and that was why. Why I was alone.

She said she'd pick up the telephone and listen to the dial tone. She'd call the weather number, the number that told the time.

Then she didn't say anything. I waited, and there was only the tick of an insect against the window by the bed.

I listened for more.

thirteen

She thought about it all the time, when she was getting dinner ready or sitting on a chair in the living room, looking out onto California Street through the filmy curtains, arms folded across her chest, her eyes behind the lenses of her glasses moving from side to side.

I was twelve and home from school because of a cold, and she said it was nice not to be home alone all day, thinking, and going over and over things, again and again and again, even though she didn't want to, even though she tried to stop.

Maybe she should stop reading the paper every day and listening to the radio and watching the news on television. Maybe that would help, even though she didn't much think so.

She'd probably end up walking around with earplugs and blinders like some old plowhorse, or maybe with a bag over her head.

She smiled and chuckled.

Imagine, she said, and put her big hands at the sides of

her head, the way a bag would fit. Cut out some eye holes, and walk around all day, looking through the holes.

You want some orange juice? she asked. You want some toast, a dropped egg?

I shook my head.

She said colds were no fun. Colds were a cross, but if she had her choice, she'd rather have a cold than a toothache or earache. She'd rather have anything than have to go through labor again. Childbirth. Having a baby.

She said I should count myself lucky I'd never have to go through with that. Men didn't know, and that explained a lot of things. The world would be different if men could have babies.

That's why she wondered about items in the paper, about the things on the radio and television, the bodies in the trunks of cars, behind bowling alleys, in parking lots at the airport.

She said she didn't understand all this gangland business. All this killing and bloodshed. And what for? What did they hope to accomplish?

How many was it now? Fourteen? Or more?

She tried not to listen, tried not to read or look at the pictures, but she almost couldn't help it, and that made no sense.

Tied up in the trunk, in Brighton or Chelsea or Revere. The triple-decker houses pressed together, and laundry on the back porches. Babies screaming and televisions.

Queen for a Day, and the one with cancer, with the daughter in the wheelchair, was wearing the robe and the crown and was walking down the aisle to the stage, and everyone clapping, and crying big silver tears. Got a television and a freezer, and a trip to Bermuda, and her daughter in the wheelchair would get the best treatment money could buy.

But she thought the one with the husband who lost his job and had amnesia was more deserving. Because at least the cancer one had a husband with a job.

She said people didn't realize how important it was to be married to someone with a job. Whatever your grandfather didn't have, he always worked, and he brought the paycheck home Fridays, and didn't drink or gamble or run around.

She said she couldn't say that about all the people she knew. She had no intentions of naming names or pointing fingers or casting aspersions, but there were certain people, certain men, who stayed home on the couch all day with a bad back or a sore this or that, and expected their wives to wait on them hand and foot.

Get me this and make me that, and my poor sore back, and she made her baby face, and her voice got high.

Please, honey, she said they said, and that would last for about five minutes in her house if anybody knew what was good for them.

It was beyond her, she told me, and she refolded her arms and watched the street, her eyes moving more slowly behind the lenses.

Her eyes were blue, her eyelids heavy.

She said it made her think of the Strangler, back there a few years, killing poor old ladies in their apartments with their own nylons and such. Over to Commonwealth Avenue and Beacon Hill, practically next door to the State House, for the love of God.

Poor old ladies who lived by themselves and maybe had a cat or a poodle. They watched one of the stories in the afternoon, and then some person had to come along.

She still thought about that, even though it was three, four years ago. They said they caught him and he was in Bridgewater for the criminally insane, and he'd never see the light of day again. But she wasn't so sure. She didn't know if she believed any of that, even for a minute.

They were always saying things, and trying to get you to believe things and stop worrying.

We're here to help, they always said, and that was the

biggest lie since the Indians sold Manhattan, poor devils. How come there was never a trial, she said. If he was the one like they say. Kill thirteen or fourteen women, strangle them in their beds and leave them there, and not even arrest the man, and let the facts come out.

Albert something, she said, and for all she knew he was just some guy who liked to look in ladies' bedrooms because he was lonely all the time.

For all we knew, she said, the real Strangler was out there this very minute, walking through backyards, standing in hallways in apartment buildings. Standing in front of doors and saying hello and smiling and looking like a choirboy.

That's the thing, she said. You could bet he was a nice-looking man. Had blue eyes and fair skin, and combed his hair. He always wore pressed shirts, and tucked them in, and had a crease in his trousers.

Probably wore glasses, she said, seemed shy.

HEAVENLY FATHER, the priest said. Heavenly Father, grant us the wisdom and the patience to know Thy will for us, and the lower church, the church in the basement of Our Lady's, was full and hot, and there were people on both sides of me, and the hot and cold feeling went through my stomach, and down lower. Then cold, then icy sweat, on my back and arms, and I blinked and there were bright spots, and the man on one side looked at me, and the spots went away.

When Jesus rose again, the priest said, when he had gone through the agony of thorns and crucifixion and hours on the cross, in the blazing sun, between two thieves—when Jesus died and was reborn again, and when God, through his infinite love and mercy for all living things, had given his only begotten son to mankind, to redeem the sins of humanity, then might we—each of us—know finally how great a love this was.

There were spots, but I kept my eyes open, and the woman

in front of me had a red hat on, and had gray hair. She moved her lips, and she seemed to be praying the way Jesus and the monks prayed. Praying all the time, so that if they died, if a thunderbolt struck them, or they had a heart attack or died in their sleep, they would go straight to heaven. They could even pray in their sleep, could pray while they cooked dinner or watched television or wrote a letter.

Imagine the resurrection, the priest on the altar said. Imagine the morning in spring. Imagine the days, from Wednesday to Thursday to Friday. The walk through the streets, the cross of heavy beams, the sword in the side. Imagine the curses and the laughter and the mockery. The spitting and hissing and jeering crowds, the barking dogs, the cackles of old men and women.

There's blood on his head from the crown of thorns, and the heat is tremendous. Just a glaring sun and no drop of water, no shade.

Imagine the cruel words.

King of the Jews.

Messiah.

Prophet.

Then howls of laughter, of execration.

He said, You spend a long long night in the garden with your friends, with men you love and trust. You pray all through the night, in the dark and in the silence. One friend sells you for silver, the others fall asleep and pretend when the soldiers come not to know you. Then later, the hill itself, a dry barren hill, a treeless, comfortless hill.

Imagine the spikes, he said, in the hands and feet. Imagine the sun, and the eyes of the mob, the sounds of curses, of laughter.

His voice echoed, his voice came from a thousand miles away. The sweat was on my scalp, and my stomach clenched and heaved, and I bumped the man on my left.

His hand was on my shoulder, and the spots were bright,

were dancing, and my head banged against wood, and a voice said, Fainted, and someone lifted me and my head was bobbing, and faces went by upside down and stared and looked away.

Then up the stairs there was air, and I said, Okay—and my voice slid sideways, past trees and past the side of the church. Red bricks and gray stone, and the branches from underneath the tree were like the veins of a peeled leaf, and then blue blue sky beyond the branches, and the air was cool, the air was clear like the blue sky.

CHUCKIE SAID EDNA had big ones. He knew because he heard Sam tell how he touched them, under her sweater and shirt. Under her bra even.

Bare tit, Chuckie said, and they were wicked big, like grapefruits, like melons, like watermelons even. Huge, he said, and she was moaning and asking for it, and he would have gone farther, would have probably porked her if Renee hadn't walked into the room in Sully's basement and almost turned the light on.

Renee wasn't so bad herself, Lee Murphy said, and Chuckie said he wouldn't mind porking her.

Yuh, Lee Murphy said. If you had anything to pork her with.

Chuckie said, Fuck you, Murphy. You never saw anything so big in your life. He had to strap it onto the side of his leg when he wasn't using it; otherwise it would hang so far down it'd get in the way.

You need tweezers to find it, Lee said, and Chuckie said Lee wouldn't know what to do with a broad anyway. Renee or Edna, or Beverly Ansen.

Beverly Ansen, he said. Don't you wish.

She was in the grade ahead, and she had really big ones, and she was pretty too. Had curly hair, and she smiled and was nice to everybody, and she was a cheerleader even though she was only in eighth grade.

Chuckie said we didn't know shit, didn't know a thing about broads. Had never seen one naked, and wouldn't know what to do if we did.

And you have, Lee said.

Chuckie said not in person, but he'd seen plenty in his brother Anthony's magazines.

You're full of it, Lee said, and Chuckie said he'd show us if he thought we'd be able to keep a secret, but he was sure we wouldn't be able to.

We said, C'mon, and Chuckie said on second thought he didn't think so. Didn't think it was a very good idea. Said we'd get scared and run home crying or want to go to confession.

Lee said he was full of it, didn't have any pictures. Everyone knew his brother Anthony was a Twinkie anyway.

Fuck you, Murphy, Chuckie said, and we didn't say anything for a minute.

Anthony's room was next door.

Chuckie, Lee Murphy said, and Chuckie ignored him.

He said, Maybe I'll show Will, and then he said it was amazing to see what they had down below. All this hair, this fur. That's why they called it a beaver, and then underneath this crack where you put it in.

Lee said he didn't believe it, so Chuckie got up and went out and came back with a magazine. He sat between us on the bed, and he said if we told anyone he'd fucking kill us, and I could hear our breath.

He opened the magazine, and turned pages, and then there was a lady on a bed, and she had big ones with brown nipples, and her legs were spread open, and it looked like a cut, like a wound without a bandage.

There was hair, and she had her mouth open, and she was looking down at her hand, which was near there, on her thigh.

THE WIND WAS SOFT, was high in the trees, and the sky was blue as eyes. Mom and I sat on the back porch. Mom said she felt sometimes she was the only person left in the world, that everyone had gone away or died of some mysterious disease. She pictured all the streets and houses empty, and she could take any car, could go through any house or building or store, and that was all right.

Maybe there had been a nuclear war that killed people and left everything else the way it was. Not even a broken window.

She said she'd drive to downtown Boston, and go to Filene's and Jordan's. She'd get hats and coats and dresses and shoes. She'd get jewelry and perfume. Ten or twenty outfits, because what would it matter then. Nobody else would ever need anything.

Sometimes she lay in bed and she thought about it. Thought how all the streets would be empty, and she'd picture New York City when she was a kid, only the streets and sidewalks would be there without people.

That's what it felt like. Back in the late twenties and thirties. Not totally empty of people, but almost. Especially when it was cold, or when it was snowing or raining.

Men would light trash barrels on fire and stand around with their hands to the barrel, in long coats and hats. In vacant lots, or near highway or train bridges. All these men, and flames flickering and their faces lit up like they were in hell or something.

Her mother took care of other people's kids, and cleaned houses, and was gone most days, and sometimes left a note at the desk downstairs for when she came back from school, and the skinny man with the gray hair would knock on the door, would say, Your mom's staying the night, and he wore white shirts all the time that were yellow at the collar, and his eyes were large and soft like something that was never in sunlight.

She kept the door locked, and at Seventy-ninth Street, near the river, the room had a dumbwaiter from years ago, before they were single rooms with a toilet down the hall.

She imagined people coming up through the dumbwaiter. Peter Pan and Mickey Finn from the comics and Little Orphan Annie and Oliver Twist, but not Fagin or Bill Sikes. But Nancy would come.

She said she'd picture Peter Pan in his green suit and tights, and Mickey Finn looking like Dick Tracy in a suit with big shoulders, and Annie with her hair and red jumper.

Oliver she knew from the book her mother read to her, and Fagin had greasy hair, but she wouldn't let him in. Oliver and Nancy would come, and they would be grateful to her.

There were sirens and cars and trucks down below, and the walls were so thin she heard voices and conversations all the time. From the walls, from the heating vents and air shafts and the door where the dumbwaiter was.

A man and woman yelled, and an old lady prayed, and there was a room where the radio played all the time. There was a man who lived with his daughter, and she heard him tell her to be quiet, to wash the dishes, to clean up and brush her teeth and polish her shoes, and she was glad her mother wasn't like that.

She'd think about the building before it was broken into single rooms with thin walls. She'd be like one of the girls her mother took care of, girls who had fathers who were doctors or who built buildings for a living, and had another house upstate, in the Adirondacks or near the ocean in Connecticut.

She had a beautiful room with a white bed, and a closet so big she could walk inside. She had windows that looked onto a garden, and her own bathroom where nobody forgot to flush and clean the black hairs from the tub.

Then one day, while her father was away, the new cleaning lady came. She heard the new lady open the door, and stand in the hall, waiting for her to say, Come in. And she looked up, and it would be her mother, and even though they hadn't seen each other in five years, when she was only three or four years old, they knew each other immediately.

They shouted and cried and wrapped their arms around each other. They sat on the side of the bed, and she gave her mother lace handkerchiefs to cry in.

Her hands were raw and red and blistered from cooking and cleaning floors and toilets for other people. She and her father thought Mom was dead. That she'd drowned or been kidnapped and killed, or sold into the slave trade in Cairo or Baghdad.

She'd been out shopping, and a tile came loose from a roof. Or she slipped on ice and hit her head, or had been hit by a car. She came to in a bed in a hospital, or came to in a cot in a kindly old woman's basement apartment.

The old woman said, There, my dear, when she tried to stand up. She handed her a cup of warm tea, a cup of soup.

She had a white bandage around her head, and for the first three or four weeks she could barely speak. She could say yes and no and please and thank you, but that was all.

She dreamed at night of a tall handsome man in a coat and tie, standing by a window and weeping. The man wore glasses and his face was dark as clouds, and she thought somehow the man was a person she knew. And there was a little girl with dark hair, a girl in a room alone.

Mom said you could go on and on like Chinese boxes, or like going from room to room and house to house. There were stairs and rooms and windows and hallways. There were closets with secret passages and doorways, and some rooms had mirrors or beds or clocks or couches. There was a green bird in a cage in one room and a black cat in another room. His name was Zeke, she said, but she didn't know how she knew.

It was like floating, and she wasn't sure how you got there

or came back. Maybe on wings or trains or on the giant hands of clocks.

She thought sometimes there was something wrong with her, or this was because she spent too much time alone when she was a girl.

Because the rooms were always empty, and there were scars on the bureau, and paint was chipping from the radiator and window frames. The radiator made noise in the winter. It clacked and hissed and hummed and banged. She used to think there were people inside, people who went down the bathtub drain, or got flushed down the toilet, and were trapped inside the pipes, trying to get out.

She did that all the time when she was young, she said, and she still found herself doing it.

It was traveling, even though she didn't go anywhere. It was going away for as long and as far as she wanted, any place in the world, and any time. At least that's what it felt like.

She'd be making dinner or ironing clothes, and she'd start thinking of the ice age or the stone age. She'd think of woolly beasts and plumes of steam rising off mountains of ice. Cracking and groaning sounds as loud as thunder. Or the stone age, and there were people in caves who would squat around a fire.

Did I ever think like that? she asked. Did I know what she meant?

When she was with the nuns, she said, in Tarrytown, she didn't tell anyone. She was afraid there was something wrong with it. She should have been praying, they'd say. She should have been saying the Rosary.

Her head was in the clouds, Sister Alice said. She never paid attention. Couldn't sit still. A hen on a hot griddle.

A rolling stone gathers no moss, Sister Alice said, and she knew Sister liked her.

Sister sat on the bench in the hall with her, while the other girls were inside writing their numbers. Sister put her arm around her and said, Child, I know God loves you very much.

I know that for a fact, young lady.

Sister looked into her eyes. Sister wore glasses and her eyes were pale gray stones. Sister smelled like soap.

Sister Alice knew how hard everything had been. Her mother sick, and never being able to visit, but Sister knew God chose her to bear this cross. God had a special love for her, had a special place in his heart.

Mom imagined God as a little green man, maybe two feet tall, wearing a white suit and a little hat with a feather in it, and tights, and maybe a miniature bow and arrow.

God would be shy like a bat. God would be afraid of sunlight and noise and people. But God would leave hints about where he was, would leave footsteps going in different directions.

She said she was very ashamed to think like that, and she'd lie in bed afterward and pray. And God would be sitting on a gold throne, and he'd wear silver robes and he'd have a white beard as fleecy as clouds.

Maybe that was why the sky was like that, Mom said. That deep blue like the Virgin Mary's eyes, and the clouds like God's beard.

She said she didn't know.

Who could tell, she said.

GEORGIA GRANT HAD BROWN EYES and she sat two rows over, and lived on Brookside Road in a house with a garage for two cars and a picture window.

She told Lee Murphy she liked the blue sweater I wore, and she liked me, and Lee said he wouldn't tell Chuckie if I didn't want him to. Chuckie would talk about Georgia, and say what I should do, and that she barely had anything, had any knockers.

A pirate's dream. A carpenter's need.

Lee said he thought Georgia was okay. He said she was embarrassed and nervous about telling him, and he thought she might run away.

Then after school she was with her friends on Walnut Street, and I was with Lee, and she lingered behind, without her friends, and Lee Murphy said, Go ahead.

We were side by side on Walnut Street. We said hello.

Then nothing. We stopped at a curb. I looked at her for less than a second. I felt her eyes on me. Cars went by.

Her arms and legs were long and white and thin as the fingers of a rake. She looked over, and said it was nice to be able to walk together, without Mrs. Vara hanging over us like a rug. Mrs. Vara taught seventh grade, and was as old as my grandmother.

We crossed the street, and she said she hoped her mother would be all right. Her mother was in the hospital in Boston, at Mass General, had been there two weeks. There was something bad about her blood. Something that didn't work right, that made her sick. She got bruises from practically nothing, and was tired all the time and was always getting colds and infections and junk.

She fell down back in October, and couldn't get up till Dad came in from the garage and found her on the bedroom floor.

It was just her and Dad for now. She'd hear him in the kitchen and living room late at night, in the middle of the night. Walking around and trying to fall asleep on the couch. She found him one morning asleep at the kitchen table, his head on his arms like rest period in second grade.

He had bags under his eyes, and she thought he cried too. His eyes would be red.

Sometimes she felt worse for him than she did for Mom. Mom was in the hospital and had all the nurses and doctors. Dad didn't have anyone but her, and she didn't feel she was much use. Mostly she tried to stay out of the way. Tried not to worry Dad. He had enough to worry about.

If she could, she'd be invisible. Just there around the edges, in the corners and stuff. But close enough to watch out for him, to see he was okay. That's what she'd do, she said. If that was possible.

THE TREES AT NIGHT, when I was twelve, blew and waved and rustled, and when I walked home from the Boys' Club, there was almost nobody out. Just an old man, or a woman with a scarf over her hair, and the houses were close together and lit up and quiet.

Mom was working, and Dad would be asleep in a chair in the living room, so I walked the long way home, and watched cars pass, and went straight on Watertown Street, past the bar and the bank and the donut shop, past the car dealer, and the building where the phone company was.

The wind blew in the trees, and beyond the branches I could see the black sky and stars winking. The longer I looked the more stars I could see, and pretty soon, after a minute or two, there were a hundred stars, then a thousand, then ten thousand.

Past the fire station the houses became bigger, and there was a man on the other side of the street, walking in the same direction. He crossed over, just behind me.

His footsteps were loud and quick and kept pace with mine. He wore glasses and a dark raincoat and had a brief-case in one hand.

I began to jog. On my toes, my chest full of air, my arms high. At every other telephone pole I ran for a hundred feet then walked till I reached the next pole, ran at the pole after that. Then the houses were set farther back from the street and there were fewer lights.

I looked back, and he wasn't behind me by then. But I kept running. I ran for two poles, walked one, then three, then one. Then I ran without stopping, ran easily, my arms and legs loose, my sneakers like pads on the sidewalk. The wind was moving the branches in the trees, and the stars were overhead.

I took a right into the Albemarle, a long park with a school at one end, a brook, a pool and a half dozen baseball and softball and football fields. The Albemarle was maybe a third of a mile long and empty as far as I could see. At the other end was a patch of woods, and then Crafts Street, and houses. There were lights near the school and the pool, but everything else was black.

Halfway across I thought I heard things, thought I saw shadows move. I stopped and crouched and froze. There was wind and darkness, but nothing else.

Past the pool and the fenced-in softball field, I lay down on the grass. It was cool, was almost cold.

The sky was bigger there, was darker and brighter. I found the Big Dipper, and thought of the song, from Camp Union in the sixth grade. The song that slaves used to sing. Follow the drinking gourd, they sang.

They would travel through woods and swamps, and the dogs were barking and baying, and the men on horses had guns.

The woods were a black clump, maybe five hundred yards away, and the woods had been there since the Pilgrims, since the Indians even.

Nonantum was the name of that part of Newton. Nonantum was the Lake, after Silver Lake. The lake was gone now, was a puddle behind a factory building, but the word Nonantum was from the Indians.

So was Norumbeiga, on the other side of Newton. Where the Charles River circled around, and Indians traveled in canoes. Indians wore moccasins and had soft feet like cats and could move without being seen or heard.

The lights of cars went by on Crafts Street. The wind was moving, and at home Martha would be on the phone and

Greta and Seamus would be in bed early. Mom worked till eleven, and then she walked home. Walked the mile up California Street, near the river.

She said she was usually tired, and sometimes she'd imagine things. But mostly she liked the walk, liked the quiet, the dark. The first time all day she'd be able to hear herself think.

There was a light in the sky that moved. A plane way up there. Leaving Boston. Going to Chicago or Denver.

What if there was a flying saucer? A gray plate in the sky that hovered, that had tiny green or blue lights on its edge. It could go faster than any jet in the world, and could stand still in the sky. Maybe music would play, music like no one on earth had ever heard. And creatures with soft gray eyes. Eyes like God. Eyes that knew and understood.

The grass was cool under my head, and the wind was high in the trees, was moving. There were a hundred thousand lights in the sky. Shining lights, blinking lights. There were five hundred thousand. There were ten million.

fourteen

At seventy-four my hair will be white as clouds, my hands will shake and my eyes will be more gray than blue. I will be a tall, stooped, friendly old man, thin and smiling. The kids in the neighborhood will come to my door—laughing—for Halloween candy, to sell Girl Scout cookies, to sell chocolate bars so their class can go on a trip to Washington, D.C., to New York City, to a nature preserve in Canada. I'll joke with them and will always buy two boxes, two bars. Then I will ask how their mothers and fathers are, their brothers and sisters. I'll remember names, occupations, ages. An eighteen-year-old brother will be stationed in Greenland with the Air Force, a sister will be a gymnast on the junior high school team. A mother will have been promoted to partner in the law firm, and they will always be surprised by how well I remember.

My wife will be Ann, and she will still run in the mornings, even at seventy-one. She'll be thin and tan, and her gray hair will be cut short, and she will work half time as a psychotherapist in an office in downtown Boston.

Uh huh, she'll say. I see. Could you share that, she'll say, and nod and look for a long time into her client's eyes.

She'll hear stories—about lying awake at night and thinking a husband has cancer, about a daughter's obsession with food, about a childhood filled with humiliation and doubt and fear.

She'll always have tissues in her office. A box near the chair where the clients sit and a box near her chair, just in case.

There will be moments when she'll feel the pinch in her nostrils, when her throat will constrict. She'll be amazed by the things people carry around. Carry all their lives.

She will tell me about the girl who speaks in a whisper, and the man who says nothing's wrong, even though a nerve in his face jumps and he blinks his eyes almost constantly, as though someone is about to hit him.

We will eat on the porch off the kitchen, and we will have trees and bushes and flowers all around us. We will hear birds and we will see the light as it filters through the leaves.

I'll spend my days working in the garden, and will take photographs too. I will go out for an hour in the morning or the evening with my camera, to the woods, or to neighborhoods in Newton, where I grew up, and take pictures of houses and streets and trees that seem familiar, that seem to look like something I knew sixty or seventy years ago.

The giant pine with broken branches at the side of a house on California Street, the long brick building on Nevada Street that still has a bell tower and has been sandblasted and has offices and luxury apartments now.

I will squat down on the sidewalk, and look through the lens, and the tree, the building, will be framed for me. I'll focus through chain-link fence, through or past the leaves on a bush, or I will sit on the curb and look down. At the sand, the tiny rocks, the piece of rotting paper, the twigs at the base of the curbstone. I will find an old Popsicle stick, and will rub it on the curb until it has a point, and will remember that this is how I spent time when I was six years old. Looking at pieces of shiny mica embedded in concrete, seeing ants cross over pebbles that must seem the size of boulders to the ants. I will take photos of the curb, the bit of grass or dirt or stone.

People will walk by. People in suits, people with grocery bags or pocketbooks or backpacks, and they will look at me. Will smile.

Someone who just got out of the home. Someone who wouldn't harm an ant or a mosquito. A sweet old man who means well, but for whom things don't come easily anymore. Who slipped away while his wife was out shopping, while the nurse had gone to the bathroom, and he forgot where he was.

Later, I will go home, and I'll develop the photographs in the darkroom in the basement. There will be the smell of chemicals, the dim red light, and when I lift the paper from the bath and a picture is fixed, it will look nothing like what I saw or what I remember or what anything was like.

AT TWO OR THREE in the morning the pain will wake me, pain in my chest or lower back or deep in my bones. A dull ache, or sharp stabbing pain, or something thin and fast and deep like needles.

I will open my eyes and will feel the tube that goes into the hole in my throat, and will hear the suck and hiss and click of the ventilator, and my wrists will be in restraints, will be tied with padded straps to the side rails of the bed.

I will have pulled tubes out. I remember them rushing in, saying sharp words, and they will be angry the way Mom and Dad were angry, the way Gram was angry, long ago.

Mr. Ross, you could hurt yourself.

Or they'll call me Will. The twenty-three-year-old nurse,

the thirty-four-year-old resident with the white sneakers, with the aquamarine tie.

Will, they'll say. And they'll order a sedative that will make me less likely to pull tubes out. The tube in my penis, the tube in my throat, the tube that goes into my stomach. Pale tubes and pale liquids, except when there's a brief red stream of blood in the tube. A leak somewhere, a broken capillary, a spot under the skin.

At two or three in the morning the room will be dark except for the thin light from the moon. There will be light too from the hall, and somewhere far away blips from a monitor, a jagged red line crossing a blue field.

It will be my kidneys or my liver, or something with my lungs. I'll be sad and shy, and when they talk to me, when they tell me things, they'll speak slowly and loudly, like I am very young or very old and don't understand much.

One of them will be called Dr. Andress, and he will have a beard and brown eyes, and he will keep his hand on my arm as he talks, and his hand will feel like everything to me, will mean the world.

You're a very sick man, he'll say. You don't have much time. We've done all we could, he'll say. Science can only do so much.

Later in the afternoon a woman named Mildred will come in, and she will kiss me on the forehead, and I will think this is a mistake. She has the wrong room, the wrong person, the wrong time.

Not me, I'll think, and I'll wish I could speak, I'll shake my head.

She will be seventy and overweight, and she will have a voice like fifty years of whiskey and cigarettes, and she will tell me about Bob, our son, and our daughter Mandi—that they are well, that they plan to visit, from Kentucky, from Austin, Texas.

No, I'll want to say, but won't be able to, and I'll keep

shaking my head from side to side, and Mildred will look puzzled, then frustrated, then angry. She'll ring for the nurse, will say I need another shot.

He's agitated, she'll say. There's something wrong with him.

AT SEVENTY-FOUR I WILL LIVE in Pittsburgh, in two rooms above a shoe repair shop, above a Thai restaurant, and my television will stay on all day and night. Its gray light will flicker constantly, and its hum, its drone, will cover everything in my life like dust.

Late at night, I'll wake up and the television will be on—police shows and talk shows. People with white teeth talking about their new movie, their new tape, their new book. People in New York or Philadelphia or Washington or Los Angeles, and I'll know them better than I know myself.

My sister Greta will be the only other one still alive. Martha and Eric and Seamus will be dead from cancer or AIDS or car wrecks. I will have learned of their deaths through letters and phone calls from Greta, who stays in touch.

When I hear her voice on the phone I will picture her at seven, at sixteen, at thirty-two. I won't have seen her in forty years almost, but her voice will be familiar to me, when she asks if I'm getting out much, if I got her last letter, her package of gloves and underwear and canned goods. If I got her check.

She'll say, You have to take care of yourself. You have to take charge of your life.

Greta will have a daughter named Margaret Rose, whom I have never met, but whose picture is taped to the mirror behind my bureau. Margaret Rose lives in Canada. In Ontario. She has two sons, who Greta says are beautiful.

Wayne and Walter.

Carey and Casey.

They'll play baseball, will have girlfriends, will be growing like weeds.

Someday, Will, Greta will say.

Or I will live in Florida, on the gulf coast, in Red Level or Fort Myers or Naples, in a one-bedroom bungalow for seniors. There will be palm trees and trips in vans to the supermarket each week. I will wear sneakers and shorts and shirts the color of tropical fruit—lime and banana and kiwi.

My third wife, Chandra, will be gone two years, her ashes scattered from a boat off Boca Grande, but I will think of Ann and Irene, my first and second wives.

I will want to call and write, will want to say Hello, and Remember, and Please be good to yourself. Get rest, eat right, exercise.

The bungalow will not have a view of the water, but will be clean, and a social worker from the state will visit once a month. A woman named Cheryl, who has a briefcase and is overweight, and has three kids and no husband.

She will ask me questions, will fill out forms, and then will lean back in the armchair next to the window, and will say, So how are you, Mr. Ross? How's your sister? You heard from her? You feeling well?

I'll say yes, and tell her a little of my news. Greta called, and her grandsons are visiting her during spring break, and she was in the hospital briefly for her eyes, for a lens implant at Mass Eye and Ear, but she's done well. She can see better already.

Do you want coffee? I'll ask. Soda? Anything?

Cheryl will smile. No, she'll say, and I'll wait. It's been a month, and I'll be able to tell she needs to talk.

Nathan, she'll say. Her ex-husband.

He moved to California and remarried, and his stepson has something wrong, has some disease where he falls asleep all the time. Nathan wants to send the boy to New York, to the doctors there, but he doesn't know if he can get the time off from work.

And Mel, the girl, the oldest, has a boyfriend, and

Nathan's afraid she'll get pregnant. She's fifteen. She doesn't realize, doesn't know, doesn't understand. This is her life, Cheryl says Nathan says, and all he can do is stand there and watch her ruin it.

And my kids, Cheryl says. My God. You don't want to know.

THE AIR IN SANTA FE will be amazing. Will be clear and dry and cleaner than the sky in the mountains.

Ann will work as a potter and our house will be on the side of a hill, near the mountains. It will be a low house, with wood and tile, and cactus in heavy pots, and our three children, Jan and Wesley and Tom, will visit often, will bring their wives and husband and children, and there will be plenty of room. Five bedrooms and three bathrooms and places for the kids to play.

I will be especially close to Jan, who teaches English at Boston University, and is married to Michael, who has a beard and is an architect. They will have a son and a daughter, and while they visit, Michael will take the kids on hikes in the mountains, and Jan and I will go into the city together. Jan will hold my arm sometimes as we walk. She will be tall and will have strong shoulders, a thin face.

I will see lines at the sides of her mouth and eyes, and when she squints in the sun, I'll remember she is in her late thirties, is middle-aged, and I will think of the years. Jan in diapers, screaming because Ann had gone back to work.

I tried to give her food, toys; I rocked her, walked around the apartment with her squirming in my arms, I tried singing. Finally I put her in the car seat, and went for a drive, and she became quiet. Her red face became still, and the tears dried, and she was watching things. Watching houses and trees and cars, and soon she was smiling.

Jan calling from college, at midnight, saying she didn't understand anything, didn't think she could do anything, didn't know why she'd gone there in the first place.

Jan on the phone after her first baby, Jan on the couch with a book.

In Santa Fe I will be a good cook and will make my own bread and have an herb garden. I will be tan, will wear straw hats outside to protect myself from the sun.

MUCH OF THE TIME I will drift, and will not always be sure where I am, or what day it is, or if my name is John or Will or Jack or Ray.

The pain will be mostly gone. When they put needles into my hip or upper arm it will be as though it is happening to someone else, someone who is lying next to me. Someone who looks the same.

When the nurse comes in to change tubes, to suction the tracheotomy, to empty the containers of urine, to move me from one side of the bed to the other, I will barely notice her. She will be familiar to me, but I won't be sure where I've seen her.

She'll look like someone I knew in Cambridge, years ago. Someone I once went on a date with—saw a movie with on a rainy night in Harvard Square, and she had a red umbrella, and the night was warm and rain hung from leaves and telephone wires, and she had dark eyes and blond hair.

But that will have been forty years earlier, and couldn't be her. She'll be seventy now, will have grandchildren, may well be dead.

Or she'll look like someone in an amusement park, walking in a crowd in the other direction, and there was noise and the smell of popcorn and hot dogs and corn dogs was in the air, and I saw her for a half second, for five seconds. She had freckles and eyes that were almost black. Or eyes that were green or gray or blue, and met mine, and held, and I felt something, knew something.

They will wheel someone by in the hall, someone old,

someone with white hair. Someone on a stretcher, on the way to x-ray or surgery. Two men and a woman will walk by and then a woman and child. Red hair, black sweater.

My side will hurt, and then something in my chest will seem to move, will almost be pain and will spread out to my stomach, my arms, my neck.

My legs and hips will be bone, and my hair will be gray, and when I look at my hands tied to the side rails, there will be brown spots on them and my fingernails will be yellow.

How long, I'll think, and I'll want it to happen fast. I won't want to stay too long, like something in an aquarium, something behind glass, moving slowly, moving in clear fluid.

Hey, I'll want to say, but won't be able to.

And I'll imagine tall trees in a forest somewhere and high mountains. I'll imagine walking slowly beneath the trees, and crossing streams and gorges, and seeing snow—in July—on the peaks of mountains.

Or a beach or lake, and I won't know what month or how old or where in the world. California or Russia or Chile. Maine, near the coast, and I am with Jan, who says, Hey, Dad, and I look and she is holding up a silver fish. Or Wayne, who is Greta's grandson, and has blue blue eyes and is ten years old, and will be crying quietly because his brother said something, or he thought of something or lost something. He will have brown hair that falls on his forehead, and thin arms, and he'll wear shorts that nearly touch his knees.

Wayne, I'll try to say. Wayne, I'll say. But the words won't carry, the words won't get to him. He'll look up and see a strange old man mouthing words without sounds. A man wearing a bed sheet, a man with tubes in his throat and penis and stomach. A man who looks like he rose from a slab in a hospital, and Wayne will scream and the sounds will echo and echo, and I will reach for him, will want to pat his shoulder or put my arm around him, but his scream will rise to a shriek and he will think I'm a bad dream.

Dr. Walters, the speaker will say. Dr. Walters, line four nine nine.

And a man will be standing there, a man with a long face and old eyes. A man in black, with a clerical collar, and he will put his hand on my shoulder. He will put a small black kit on the table next to the bed and will take out a cross and rosary beads. He'll take out a small bottle of oil and one of water, and he'll start speaking in a slow, incantatory voice.

Dear Lord, the Father, he'll say, and people will walk by, and then over his shoulder, in the corner of the room, my mother and father will be standing, and they'll look at me as though they are peering over the sides of a crib. They'll smile, and my mother will reach around the man in black and will adjust a corner of the blanket. She'll smile and my father will look at her and smile, and then Gram will be there too.

Oh Lord, who is most high, who is all-powerful, grant us this day, the man will say. Then he will begin to speak in Latin, saying words and phrases, and the small bells will ring, and I will smell incense. He'll lift the oil, and will say, Bless this day, when the trumpets sound and the heavens themselves tremble, and he'll make a cross—with oil—on my forehead, my hands, my feet.

Dear Lord, take the soul of thy servant, Will, and bring him unto you, so that he may sit with Peter and Paul and all the apostles.

Go with God, Mildred will whisper in her smoky voice.

Go with God, Ann will say.

Someone will lean close, will have a hand on the side of my face.

You're in Newton Corner, the voice will whisper, and it's a long time ago. You're with your mother. You're going to Boston and she'll buy you a basketball, a baseball.

The voice will be Seamus, my brother, only Seamus will be forty-one years old. Seamus will have two daughters, and he will whisper, Will. Go to sleep. The movie's over. The dream's gone. There's nothing left.

Then Gram will lean close and she'll say she knew. She'll say you have to get up awfully early in the morning to put one over on her.

She'll say she knew all along, she understood long before I was even born. Before I was a twinkle, a speck, a shade of a thought. You must think I'm crazy, she'll whisper.

My head on the pillow will be cool, and feathers will flutter in my chest. They'll move up and down the inside of the wall.

There will be sounds. Music. Bits of the Beatles, the high sounds from the radio in the car. The car driving away and the chorus from Bach, from St. Matthew Passion—that deep deep voice, then the chorus rising, and I'll think that's where I want to go, to be with those voices.

Angel voices in movies. Clouds and such, and then someone laughing.

Kevin laughing, or the man lying on the sidewalk laughing. Looking up and saying, You know me. You know who I am. Don't pretend.

This isn't make-believe, the voice will say, and the man will have vomit on his front, and he will be on his back, smoking a cigarette and blowing smoke rings at me, at the sky.

I'll watch them rise, perfect white circles, then hover, then disappear.

THE HOME WILL BE CALLED Lakeside or Hillview or Elmwood. I'll share a room with four other men and two of them will wear diapers.

John, the aides will say. You had an accident last night, and I'll remember them coming in with flashlights and clean sheets, and John groaned when they lifted him.

We'll sit in a circle, and the woman from music therapy will blow into her pitch pipe and say, Ready.

White white skin and gray hair, and long hairless arms and legs and a hump on the back, and wheelchairs.

Not me, I'll think, and I'll close my eyes tight as fists and I'll hear their footsteps, their voices coming from five miles away.

Or a room somewhere, in Dallas maybe, or in Baltimore, near the water. Sirens all day and night, long peals, then bursts like quick bubbles, and I will hear cars and birds and bits of voices—in the backyard, out the window. Voices saying, Hazy and hot, saying, There were no survivors, saying, The police are not saying much.

The pint will be three quarters full, will be clear liquid, and I will sip slowly, in the chair near the window, the curtains drawn and hanging motionless, the room in dusk, in shadow, in gray film.

The sips will be short and small, tiny swallows, like birds' almost, and clean and warm as sunshine. I'll sip and sip, and sit forever, and outside will almost be dark and car lights will pass, and the lights on stores and banks, the streetlights, will glow like something that could shine for hours if the power failed.

Hey, I'll almost whisper in the dark, but there won't be sound. Hey, I'll say again, but so softly there still won't be sound.

The room will have a hot plate and a kitchen chair and a mattress on the floor in the corner. There will be one armchair and a toilet and sink, and I will hear people in other rooms.

I'll think of Mom and Dad and Greta and Seamus, of Eric and Martha, and nights in summer, a long way away, years and years ago. Gram and Bamp, and my seventy-four-year-old body will be strange to me, in Dallas or Baltimore.

We put sheets on the floor in the living room and slept there because the third floor was so hot, and all night the sounds from the street came in—the cars and wind—and

Martha said it was called California Street because you could drive to California on it, and you couldn't do that from anywhere else.

And outside, in Dallas, there will be haze forever, and fewer trees than there were in Newton, near Boston, sixty-eight years ago, and when I raise the bottle I will see my old man's hand on the glass and will think it looks like a claw, like talons, like white bones.

California with orange trees, Martha will have said, and sunshine all day and night. Cars everywhere—convertibles and woodies, and Disneyland, and hundreds of miles of beaches.

I'll picture the white sheets, the pillows bunched under our heads and Eric sleeping, his hand at his mouth.

Then I'll feel the aide's hand on my arm. John, he'll call me, or Jack or Ray. Will, he'll say, his voice loud. It's time. Let's go, he'll say, and he'll push me in the wheelchair toward the bathroom, toward the showers.

AT SEVENTY-FOUR nights will last forever, will seem a day or a week, and I'll get up and pace the house. Will go to the hallway, down the stairs, through the den, the kitchen, through the living and dining rooms. Out to the back deck, and I'll feel the night air, the breezes, and I'll feel the trees and the houses beyond the bushes, the garage, as though they're alive and breathing, as though at certain hours they could talk to me.

I'll want to say or do something. Take off my pajamas and lie down on the dark lawn. Feel dew on my old man's skin, on my withered back, my sagging behind. Grass and dew and the night's breezes.

Or pray. Say things to God or the sky, to the bush near the garage. Say thank you. Say I'm afraid. Say this has been long, much longer and harder than it might have been.

Say there's no backing out, no going backwards, no door or crack at the edge of time. Just forward movement, as of glaciers. And lying naked on the lawn in the backyard I'll say please let it be quick, and let it be quick for Ann. Let us die together, so that she doesn't wake up to find, so that I don't wake up to find, and we will be silent and still together, quiet as stone and forever together, like the heart carved on the tree. TLA. Me and Ann.

Somehow easy, brief, somehow graceful.

IN THE AFTERNOON my temperature will rise, will become 102, 103, and three of them will be there, and the blood pressure cuff, the Velcro crackling, the puff puff puff tightening on my upper arm—on his arm, because I will be outside myself, and his eyes will be partly closed.

One forty-six over one-ten, she'll say, and I'll know something, will know they're watching and waiting, and I'll want to back up, to get out.

To go back or sideways or something.

Find a green door, a gold doorknob, and reach, and it is there, is solid like gold or lead. And it turns, is unlocked, and I go through and there will be a long hallway, and everything and everyone is there in some other world, some other place.

Rooms and fields and whole continents of places and things.

I'll know them all, and they'll surprise me at the same time. People waving—Maurice from St. Jean's, who was fat. Maurice on a bicycle, and his mother will be jogging after him, saying Maurice, Maurice, my little cauliflower, she'll call, and Maurice will smile, will wave to me.

Other doors will lie within doors, and I'll feel a needle in my chest, but no pain, and through a red door there will be Susan Errent from Pace, from a long time ago, who was only there—at the school—four months, and had quick eyes and a low voice, and she'll say she was sad about it, about leaving so soon and sending only one thin letter in all the time after, and signing, Love, Sue.

Love you, Sue, I'll almost say, but will know it's not true.

Love Sue, not true.

And other places.

Mr. Ross, a man will say. Mr. Ross, he'll nearly shout. Can you hear me?

Will?

Mr. Ross?

I'll blink, and he'll be tall as a wall, and will have teeth like tombstones, in the west, where buffalo roamed, and Wild Bill and Lonesome Jane were.

Mr. Ross, we're trying to stabilize you, he'll say.

My head on the pillow will be heavy as stone, as lead.

My head is lead, I'll think.

My feet are sweet.

My hand is land.

Whole planets will whirl and swim like a movie. Music playing—a waltz, a polka, a ballet. White tights, a tutu. But no tattoo. The little man on *Fantasy Island*. Yes, Boss, he'll say, and look up.

Something cold and heavy. On my chest. Something wet and cold.

Then jolt. Then jolt and everything kicking.

Like a mule.

Duke of Flatbush, Duke of Earl, Duke Ellington—the A train and beyond. Clacking past, flashing station by station, and Ellen and I leaning on the rocking train and kissing, and her lips just parted—cool and liquid, warm and breathing too.

Breathing warm breath. Soft breath.

I'll open the door, but it will be the wrong one, will be a doorway I don't want to look through. A corpse laid out on a metal table, the trunk open—the Y cut from sternum to pubic bone. Just meat. Red meat and everyone around the table is masked and gowned, is double-gloved.

Not there. Somewhere else. Just not there.

Keep the door locked, in the basement. We know, but

don't know or remember. Out of sight. Behind doors.

Then wind. Wind pressing the leaves, the trees, the doors and hallways.

My father will whisper. Not here or there, he'll say in his papery voice. Somewhere besides, he'll say. Somewhere in the winter, in the north. Somewhere to the north. The Arctic. The open polar sea, the northwest passage.

I saw, my father will say, and he'll be young again, like the pictures from the Army.

I read a book, he'll say. About Franklin and Henson and icebergs a thousand feet tall. Four winters in the pack, frozen in for year upon year. No sun, and the wind a beast, and cracking ice. Long groans like pain, like giants in the dark.

The mate is seeing his mother on the ice. His beautiful young wife. Quarter rations, my father will say. Three ounces of hardtack. Scurvy.

Henry Hudson in a small boat, with some others. Cast off, and everything white.

How long, I'll think, and there will be a needle in my stomach and four or five of them around me. In gowns and masks, and the vent is clicking, clicking, clicking. Breath won't go in. Clicks again.

Then suck and hiss.

On a stretcher, moving fast. The machine—the vent—a bottle on a pole.

Five or six of them, and doors and windows and a slice of sky outside. Blue as ocean, as eyes. Clear clear blue.

Someone saying, Hold.

Please, someone will say. If you could just hold.

And no way out. No other way to stop this. The way everything moves forward and forward, and seems to race at times, seems then to slow, but always and forever moving.

Can't stop. Can't go back, or step aside, or make the hair turn dark again. The skin firm, breath sweet as Ellen's on the train.

An orange door and a long hallway. I'll run for a long time, for as long as the hallway goes. Run like a boy, run like the man in Kenya, under mountains. Kip, with twenty kids and wings for feet.

And Bob with a cigarette will say, Okay. From high school. Whom I haven't seen in thirty years.

In Australia. He went a long time ago. Not on the boats. The transport ships. Stole bread, stole a few coppers, and they sing down below. Roll me over, boys, and send me far.

AT SEVENTY-FOUR I WILL LOOK UP and everything will be upside down. The tiles in the ceiling, with the tiny holes in them, the tubes of light, the faces. All twenty-five or thirty-five or forty-five. None older. And all in whites, in masks like a holdup.

My eyes open, my hands free.

Mr. Ross, we're going to the OR.

We'll fix you up, they'll say.

A little glue. A patch here and there.

They'll smile. The woman with glasses. She'll have brown eyes and she'll pat my hand as we move down the halls.

You'll be fine. You'll be good as new, as fit as ever.

A boy again.

A baseball glove on the handlebar, toeing grass in left field.

Hey, I'll holler. C'mon, I'll say.

Then the bright circle of light on the ceiling. Silver circle, white light. A puffing, hissing sound.

A cone on mouth and nose. A voice whispering, Easy there. Steady, Mr. Ross.

Then metal on trays, and the cold air, the smell, like mint and basil, like rose leaves.

Easy there.

Just relax.

Breathe slow and deep.

232

There, they'll say. You'll be asleep. You'll dream a long time.

Mom and Gram, and Mom's mom and dad.

Dead somewhere, in New York City. In a room and the police coming in with the desk clerk. A passkey.

There's a kid somewhere, the clerk will say. Up to Tarrytown. With the sisters. In a home. A place there.

And the father, later, in Paterson or Newark. White hair and eyes that were gray. In a room too. Like he'd fallen asleep.

Ann will live by then with someone else. Someone with dark hair and a suntan. Someone who plays golf.

She may pause for a moment. In the car. On the way to the dentist, the mall. Have an odd feeling. Something she feels or thinks. A brush of wing, a cool bit of air, a sound.

Ping, whirrr.

Or she will be holding my hand and they will be around me. Wesley and Tom and Jan will lean forward, will kiss my waxy forehead, my near-blue lips.

Go with God, they'll whisper.

Easy, Dad.

Soft.

Slow.

And there will be soft light in the room. No more tubes and needles, no more taps on the arm or hand or shoulder.

It's time, they'll say, but that will be okay.

Maybe Martha with her beautiful daughter Alycia. Standing with Mildred, or Chandra, somewhere in Florida.

Or Dad smiling, Dad saying it doesn't take forever and won't be hard.

Sister Mary Boniface said God will not give you a cross you cannot bear, in Johnstown or Kansas. And her mother crying under the covers. Her father gone.

Okay, then, I'll want to say. I don't mind. I'll do okay, I'll think.

And the man in black again. A priest or rabbi or minister.

Came from downstairs. Happened to be visiting. Lucky thing. Has done this before.

Will say, Bless us father and these thy gifts, like grace a long time ago.

Dad will say to bow our heads and be grateful, and Greta squirming in her highchair, Eric looking from behind his folded hands.

Provide for the wants of others and the faithfully departed, and the other side of the river, the place above and over.

Ann saying, Okay, and holding my bony hand, and there will be no other way out. No escape.

But then ahead, a gray door, with red etching like poppy or rose, and I'll go through, into light and air—and slowly I'll go, and the door will close behind me, and will grow more and more distant and that will be all. I'll be surprised I hear wind and leaves—the way they rustle late at night— and that will seem lovely and strange, and then nothing. Then over.

Again. Like that.

fifteen

It's quiet tonight. It's still as heaven, as Eden. All green outside—leaves and bushes and grass, and a black sky and a slight breeze moving all of it, the curtains in here and leaves out there, and Ann breathing slowly and deeply, and I can hear the air moving in and out of her. And me here at thirty-seven, halfway through the year, the summer, the night.

One a.m. Maybe later, and all the green out there like the middle of a jungle, and this is only Ithaca in upstate New York, with waterfalls and a lake, and I hear a car pass and no voices, and blackness, and pale squares of light—through leaves and branches, light from the streetlamp, and nothing else.

Ann asleep for two hours already, wearing a white tee shirt five sizes too big, and under a quilt her Granny made years ago. Granny now dead, in the South, in east Tennessee, fifteen years. Fell in her apartment, lay there hours; finally taken to the hospital, and dead before her family could reach her, there on the other side of town, there in the seventies. Granny was Mrs. Taylor all her life, and Grandmother to

Ann, and said the WPA was made up of loafers leaning on hoe handles, and on the floor at the foot of the bed, unable to move or talk. Could barely breathe.

Gram in Newton, at ninety-five, falling too, falling near her bed, on the first floor, and now in Newton in a wheelchair in the nursing home.

Can't remember, she says. Can't remember at all.

Get me out, she says. They're trying to do things.

Her hands still big, but everything else shrunk down to sinew and tendon, to sagging flesh, frail bones.

Older than the century. Older than mountains or God almost.

Ann breathes, a liquid sound in her throat. On her back, her arm flung out on her right. Hailing a cab. Hitching a ride.

A dream on a street maybe, everyone whispering and pointing. Fancy dinner, and she's been jogging, is soaked with sweat, is wearing her red tee shirt with torn-off sleeves. The women in gowns, the men in tails. Pointing. Laughing.

No.

Quiet as stone, as wood. Quiet as one a.m.

Red numbers flick by. One oh seven.

Red glow like sun at the last instant—then it falls past the hills. Streaks of light.

Ann at thirty-four. Much longer hair now; blond in summer. Fair fair skin.

She's on stage, is singing, and the voice is like nothing she's ever heard. Like opera, like records.

Just opens her mouth, and something comes from deep within her—like cream, like honey. Then birds flying toward the balcony. Red birds and blue birds, and the men are weeping. Too lovely, too like something they heard somewhere. Heard late one night, walking on Seventh Avenue, on Park Avenue, in Kenmore Square in Boston. Past the neon, toward Fenway Park. Coming from a second-story window, it seemed.

And they were happy then, in love, or a little tired and a little drunk, but it was clear and sweet and deep, and they stopped and listened for two, for three minutes, and then it stopped, and it hurt not to hear it, hurt like pressure in the chest, like something died.

And thirty-seven, which is not young anymore. Gray strands of hair in the mirror. And not one or two. Maybe twenty or thirty, maybe more. And so fast. So quick.

Like a thief in the night, Gram said.

Back then.

The pillow is warm and cool under my head. The clock glows, flicks again.

Light blanket. Tan.

Ann has a separate blanket so we don't get tangled up.

A tan blanket she bought in New York City years ago.

Ann in the Museum of Modern Art. Walking slowly from room to room. Huge canvases splashed with paint.

Jack the Dripper.

Ann at twenty-four. Ann ten years ago, and who's to know where she might go. Tennessee to North Carolina to Africa to New York.

Then what?

Maybe California or maybe London.

She thought about it.

My hand brushes her side. I touch her hair. Light as air.

Soft hair. Soft like cloth. Even more so.

Water.

Wind.

Soft as cat fur.

Zeke the cat has black fur, giant white teeth. Zeke in Florida maybe, some other time.

Some other room or day or color. Not the same. Not what we think.

Was so long in there. Long as days and weeks, and they said, Wait, said, Be careful, be calm.

Watch out, they said, and long long halls. Shiny.

Someone came in and shined them at night.

Ann looked at me on the back porch, at a party, and thought not for her. Thought not something she'd care to explore, to get involved in.

Thought not.

Shy and thin. Had nervous mouth, fretting hands.

And Gram looking for a long time, and saying, You're Buzz, and I shook my head.

Eddy?

Ray?

Eric?

Seamus?

But didn't have a beard like Eric or Seamus, and she said, Will, and smiled her crooked smile, and she didn't have teeth. A crone's mouth. Sunken hole at the bottom of her face. Will, she said, and she's in there tonight, on the second floor, in the room with two other women.

They stare at her. They look at her funny. What's wrong with them?

And Mom alone in the house. All the rooms, and three floors, and the cat moving from room to room. Clocks ticking and glass catching night light from outside.

Cars on California Street, and the river down Bemis Road, and downtown. The towers visible from the third floor.

Hancock. Prudential.

She sighs, and I can feel sleep all the way to my feet. My back and arms. Legs, hands, groin.

Dad lying there week after week. Dad lying there, and his eyes marbles, his skin paper.

And then cremated, and the hole, and the stone with his name and dates, with Mom's name and the year she was born.

The pond and ducks. Lying there even tonight, in Newton. Three hundred miles away.

Moonlight and trees and flowers whispering. His ashes lying there. Gray and white and black. Chunks of bone.

I turn to my side, hand at the pillow, Ann behind me.

White wall, like stucco almost. Clock, books, flashlight, nail clippers, penknife. Walkman too.

Stations from all over. Stations from Canada in French, from Chicago, Detroit, even Boston.

The Bosstown. The Hub. The Athens of America. The city on a hill.

Ted Williams and Tony C. Bill Russell and Cousy and Hondo. The Bird. Bobby Orr. Yaz.

Come in if you can hear me, he said.

Hello. Hello. Are you there? Is anybody there?

Hip hurts. Onto back again.

Ceiling like stucco too, and the light in the center of the ceiling is like the moon, only not much glow.

Leaves outside. Curtain, lift, billow, wave, sway. Leaves some more.

Lovely sound, Ann said. Late at night.

Hear, she said. Listen.

Careful.

Like when she was six or seven, and at church camp. Tents, a fire, stories.

Lizann and Sue Ellen, and pine trees high as the sky. Pointing to God like a church steeple, overhead. Scudding black clouds at night, and then later, when she woke up, she was the only one awake, under the trees and stars.

Pine needles, and pine smell like something Mother cleaned the bathroom with. And all the clouds gone by then. In five, ten minutes. In an hour maybe. She wasn't asleep long. Just closed her eyes and slithered down in the sleeping bag.

Mama's prize. Mama's jewel.

Her precious thing, and church camp was nine days, and under the stars with Lizann and Sue Ellen, and Jane from Georgia had two-tone shoes with rubber soles to prevent slippage.

Prevent slippage was what Mother said, and there were

five million stars overhead when she woke up and was the only one awake.

All of them lying over the ridge, in sleeping bags. Vicki the mean one who made faces behind people's backs, and Elsie was nice and wore pearls even when they were hiking.

More than five million. Maybe a billion, up there, past the tops of trees. Suddenly so black, with small spots glowing, like white coals or something.

Even then she needed glasses. Glasses in the first grade. Cat glasses. Pointy at the sides.

Ann smiling in those pictures from first and third and fourth grade. Freckles, and small white teeth, and those eyes shining, just smiling behind the glasses.

Happy kid. Light hair, combed off the forehead. Her mother with the comb in the morning, wetted down from the bathroom sink.

Don't fuss, Mother said. Sit still, young lady, she said, the bobby pins in her mouth, in her other hand.

And Ann on the side of the tub, then in the photograph. Third-grade class.

Say cheese, and that smile. The eyes lit like all the world was a joy. The third-grade classroom, and red clay earth outside, brown-green lawns, stunted trees.

All the voices that long southern syrup.

Y'all, they said, and called her honey.

Kid with cat glasses, and a sweater with snowflake patterns, with deer on the front. Her favorite black shoes with the straps across the top.

Read books all the time. Mrs. Taylor, Grandmother Taylor, said she had her nose in a book all day if you let her. A bookworm.

Lying in her corner of the couch in the den, not moving for hours. People walking by, and her turning a page, wrapping a strand of hair around her finger. Wearing shorts and white socks with her black shoes. A pale blue jersey. Hair in place. Reading half the day in summer.

The boy who swallowed the sea. Could take the whole sea in his mouth, and left the boats and the fish on the bed of the sea.

Or the creature in the closet, and if she walked through late at night—couldn't sleep—and there was a ship on the other side, painted sails, an ocean as big as the world.

And playing the piano, down there in east Tennessee, a thousand miles away from Newton or Boston. Quietly playing the piano an hour every afternoon. Plink, plink. The Waltzing Parakeet and The Girl Who Sang. Hour after hour some days, and if Mrs. Hasson frowned at her, she worked extra hard.

She moves her arm, and touches my side. At the hip, the side of my stomach.

Strange the two of us, all these miles and years later. Amazing we landed here, next to each other at one thirty-three a.m., in the middle of New York state. At thirty-seven and thirty-four years old.

And now not using anything. No jellies or creams, no packet of pills. Eight a.m. every morning. The round silver packet on the night table, with her glasses and radio.

Not saying we would or wouldn't. Not saying, This is what we'll do after four, five years.

More that we wouldn't try not to. Wouldn't use anything.

Which is to say.

But maybe not either.

She's warm as a stove. Warm and quiet.

She sighed and said, Honey, said, Honey, and then that weak weak feeling. Then just lying in the tangle, in sweat, and touching idly, touching lightly.

Not like before.

Maybe in there now.

Maybe not.

Would have dark hair. Would have to wear glasses.

Ann can't see to go to the bathroom in the middle of the night. Wears contacts all day, then at night brushes her teeth, takes the contacts out, cleans them, puts on glasses with amber frames. Thick glass. Embarrassed.

Bookworm. Librarian.

But not so either.

Endearing. Vulnerable. Oddly sexy. Like underneath this proper exterior. Hidden inside.

He'd have black hair, and would be quick like Ann. Have blue or gray eyes. Skinny like when I was a kid. Knobby knees, ribs showing.

Play catch in the backyard, hour after hour. That lovely smell of leather, the smack of the ball hitting the glove. Like Eric and me in the yard. Reach back, fingers on the seams. And then throw. A frozen rope. Then a knuckler, a bender. That spin like something in orbit, whirling around the sun.

Curving down and away. Strike three. The tenth strikeout. Final game of the World Series. Standing near the garage, toeing the rubber, and fifty thousand in the stands.

The buzz and hum of the crowd.

How long? Maybe another day or week or month, and then nine months.

Maybe walk on the beach, or sit on the deck in the summer. Me and Jack. Me and Harry or Sam or Bob.

Ray too. That's a good name.

Ann might like that.

Those tiny fingers and toes at first. Diapers all the time. Screaming at all hours. Screaming there at the edge of sleep, and please stop.

Drift, then even louder screaming, so stagger in, and lift him, lift her, and she's heat, and she's wet, so lay her on the table, and unfasten, wipe, dry with powder, put on a clean one.

No longer screaming, but the hands balled into fists, and she's squirming, is tense, so sit on the rocker, her head on my shoulder, and rock back and forth and back and forth.

Maybe two or three a.m. Maybe later. No sound anywhere in the world. No cars or voices. Maybe beginning to get gray at the edges of the window, and she's quiet, she's breathing slowly. Her hand no longer a fist. Her hand on my tee shirt.

Such tiny fingernails.

Maybe ten, twelve pounds. Nothing more than that. Everything inside stirring. And so tired it's like being drunk almost. Eyes don't focus, and that deep deep feeling. Underwater and beyond the glass.

Just lay me down somewhere. No lights or noise or movement.

She's heavy then. On the shoulder or arm.

Helen maybe.

Ruth.

Martha.

Two-fourteen. Numbers flick.

All of it so fast. Thirty-seven years old already, and that's not possible. Halfway to something.

In the cold ground.

Stretched.

Ann sleeps so deeply at first. Till four or five, then she stays at the edge of sleep. Hearing things, aware of the air, the shade flapping.

Is that rain? Rustling. Wind, leaves, patter.

Not much rain in months. The grass brown, the farmers hurting. Could use it. Could use a week of soaking rain. Day after day. Cool and dark, and all that moisture in the fields.

Boston the week Dad was dying. All that rain. Day after day after day. Standing at the window in the lounge, there on the sixth floor. Looking down at Cambridge Street, farther down, at Brighton Center. The bars and the hardware store. Ice cream, eyeglasses.

And traffic, and everything wet and shining. Water on the glass. Drops, dripping into tiny streams and rivers, down the face of the glass.

At two in the afternoon and ten at night. Lights on the street, in the puddles, on the wet pavement.

Thought it would never end. The rain, and Dad not dying.

Unbelievable how long. No food or fluids anymore, and the vent breathing.

Please, Dad. Let go.

He couldn't have known, couldn't have felt much.

Eric and Seamus, Greta, Martha. Dark eyes, with pockets under the eyes. And Mom. Poor Mom. Must have been so sad for her. Alone in that house. All those years and hours.

And Dad at the end. The doc coming in. Just a kid. Couldn't have been more than thirty.

Dad dead. Skinny like a cancer victim, like AIDS or something. Like death. Claims them. Says this isn't life anymore.

Never imagined he could look so dead. The skin yellow and almost blue and waxy. The mouth and eyes partway open.

Six a.m., Sunday, and the rain stopped. One of those clear shining mornings.

She pats my arm, turns to her side.

Slow rain, but steady. Quiet. Hope it lasts. Falling into the grass, onto the roofs and trees. Onto the streets and sidewalks. Streams in the gutters. Falling on the lake, the parks, into Fall Creek.

You'd hear it, sleeping in a tent.

Patter patter.

Have to do laundry tomorrow, but that could wait. Wouldn't dry on the line.

Diapers. Cotton or those other ones. Clogging the landfills, killing the earth. No ozone layer. Greenhouse effect. Global warming. Melt the polar ice cap.

All those crazy Brits in ships stuck on the ice. Heaving and groaning.

Was awful in there. Feel tears in my eyes sometimes. Thinking of then. Like I belonged, deserved. That and cockroaches.

Ann just looked, said she could not imagine, could not

picture me, and it was a while ago.

Thirteen years this summer, this month even.

Is that true? Thirteen?

Already. Quick, but slow as death too.

Have to make money. Buy the kid a baseball glove. Even a girl. She could play. They do that now, more than years ago.

Baseball glove, and bicycle to cruise the neighborhood. Go swimming under the waterfall. Beautiful town to grow up in. Ithaca, New York. Trees, not much traffic. Get used to the cold.

Not so many sickos.

But that boy in the woods last summer. Maybe spring. Just fourteen, hands bound, naked from the waist down. Dead two, three days. Kid from western Massachusetts.

Awful. Mother and father. Would cry a month. Would have trouble breathing, thinking.

Would watch all the time.

Would be tough too. Maybe he'd hate me. Big bastard like me. Over two hundred pounds. Not small like Dad.

Have to be careful. Gentle as Jesus. Kind.

Tenderness. Otis Redding from twelve. Loved Otis. Live from Europe. Paris maybe.

Borrowing the car. Asking for money.

See them with kids in stores, and they want everything. Gimme, gimme, gimme.

Whining.

Have to say no.

Sleep.

Have to sleep. Won't be much good tomorrow. Laundry, get groceries.

Ceiling white like paper.

What holds it up? Could fall, smack in the face. Suppose the sky could too. Sun might not rise. Chicken Little.

Stuart Little. A mouse or a weasel.

The pig was Charlotte. No, the spider.

Pig was Arthur or something. Close.

High hat, and a pince-nez on a velvet string. Or some old bastard in a picture with a pointy beard and a grim face. A life sucks and you die face. Die painfully. Die screaming.

Gram in the nursing home, even tonight. Lying there, and probably not sleeping well. Probably staring at the ceiling, or waiting for someone to do something to her. Come in and steal her teeth or her nice white sweater. The one Jane gave her for Christmas four, five years ago. All of them out there.

The aides. From Jamaica and Haiti. Down there. Working all the time. Working fifty, sixty hours. Working till their feet ache, till their ankles swell. Rooms full of kids at home.

Not easy. Not fun. No streets of gold. No free lunch.

Ninety-five and counting. Pain in her back, her legs, her hands and sides.

Talking about one thing and another. Talking shit. Talking trash.

All those years of things to remember. Her brother carried down the hall by the doctor, his arms and legs dangling down. And the cone on his face on the kitchen table. Saying breathe deep. Breathe deep and slow.

Couldn't have been more than seven or eight. Nineteen oh four maybe, 1910.

Somewhere in there, around there. A million years ago.

Happens like you wouldn't believe. You blink your eyes, look away for a second, and you're an old lady. An almost dead lady in a home. Strangers coming in with your teeth, coming in to give you a bath with sponges. Coming in to wipe you.

The rain's steady, is slapping leaves, and the roof outside the window. Roof over the front porch.

Should get up maybe and see that it's not getting in. Getting Ann's shoes, lined up under the window.

Probably not. Too slow and steady. No wind really. Would

hear it on the screen. Maybe in a while, in ten minutes if it seems.

She must be awake there. They never sleep much—get to be that age. It's all like sleep and waking. Just gliding along, gliding over the tops of things. Dreams and voices, and then coming in and setting the dinner tray on the table, and pushing the wheelchair in.

Tastes like sawdust and tin cans and dog food. Tastes like cardboard.

Thinking of when there were hardly any houses around, and almost no cars. Just one or two on the streets. Big tall black things. Could have your car any color, Mr. Ford said, as long as it was black.

Pigtails and bloomers and gaslight. Sputtering at night, making wavy shadows. Ma said get home before dark, before the goblins come. Men in coats, with candle flames for eyes. Liked little girls.

Have brown hair maybe. Not as dark as mine. Like Ann's. Lighter.

Eyes like mine. Mostly blue. Black center.

Would be tall and gangly. Hair falling into his eyes. Skateboard and old tennis racket. Would eat frozen yogurt out of a coffee cup.

Hey, Jack, I'll say to him.

Come out to the back deck, on a summer night. Crickets, and a fan going in someone's window nearby.

He's ten, fourteen, nineteen and home from college. We don't say much, don't need to.

Or she has pierced ears and long tan legs, sandals.
Ruth.
Hey, Helen.
Mom in bed too. In Newton, in that house with all the rooms. Downstairs where Gram was, and empty now. A lamp, a few cans of soup in the pantry, a footstool in the bathroom. Echoing. Water dripping.

Rooms seem big. A shade, a curtain.

The third floor full of books and bags of old clothes, broken chairs. Eric's weight bench, Seamus's hockey equipment. Piles and piles of junk.

Windows rattle at night. Radiators hissed and clanked. Man downstairs. Cellar man.

Mom in New York City, and all those lights at night. Like some huge party, some boat in the middle of the ocean. Every window a light, and lights strung on wires on every deck. Music and ballrooms.

Sad how her mother.

All the people and streets. Men in long coats. Holes in shoes. Wear socks for gloves. Stamp feet, rub hands.

Ann so smooth. Cool skin like paper. Pale and cool. Touches like small feathers, like petals.

Peach.

Two-ten, two-eleven, two-thirteen.

Car goes by. Not real fast. Maybe from work. Two jobs, kids to feed.

Food on the table, roof overhead. Food and fuel.

Hierarchy of needs. Air, earth. Warmth.

Not hit or humiliated.

Would be powerful. Something deep.

So small. A tiny thing. A dusting of hair on the head.

Skull bones not even fused at first. Plates of bone, like the continents drifting.

Imagine. Great winged creatures and mountains of ice. Explosions of volcanoes, of earthquakes, suns and moons colliding.

Expressway at rush hour. Don't miss Boston for that. For other things.

Seamus with his beard. Wonderful way he laughs. Throaty. Heh, heh, heh, but deep.

Mom seventy this August. Long way from Bellevue, from Ninety-fourth Street, and the nuns with habits like wings.

Great scoops of starched white cloth on their heads. Thought they could fly.

Gidget. Flying around. Dumb. Like *Hogan's Heroes*. Sergeant Schultz. Knows nothing. Sees nothing. Nice old man. Beer and sausage.

Mom seventy. Could get her a book, mail it. Maybe a sweater.

Original.

Maybe drive there for the weekend. Me and Ann. Pull in, surprise her.

Always think how old she looks. Lines, everything drawn down.

I'm not old, she says.

Not twenty-six either.

Same here.

Thirty-seven, and Ann sleeping like a cat. Forever. Stretched out, almost hear her purr.

Dreaming of Tennessee, maybe Kenya. The sky an ocean of blue. Parrots and mangos.

Ann said, Honey, said, Oh, said, Oh.

Blue eyes, and tall, and very funny. Would love jokes.

Dad, tell the one about the guy whose car breaks down.

The one about the lady and her three sons.

The boy in the igloo.

The farmer's wife.

The elephant with sneakers.

Tell, Dad, he'll say.

A long time ago, I'll say. A long long time ago, before I knew your mother, and before you were born, of course, I used to lie awake at night and think. And one night, I'll say. In the summer, or in the middle of January, and snow was falling outside, the wind was howling.

The wind is slow tonight.

Just rain, just leaves. Feed the roots.

Ann's hair.

Soft. Light.

Gets blond in the summer.

July here. Past the fourth, before Labor Day.

How long?

How late?

Could lie here forever. The bed a boat, floating on a lake, a sea, an ocean. Bobbing along. Fish gliding underneath, long fronds, seaweed waving.

Or drift across the sky—a carpet ride, silent as air. No engine. Just toys below. Drift to the other side of something, like falling asleep.

What does she dream?

Gram? Mom? Ann?

Long white rooms and a fireplace and tall people in robes chanting.

Like church, in New York in 1927. All the streets and cars, and St. Patrick's with Momma.

Momma tired all the time. Momma pale and coughing. A thin coat in winter and blood in the handkerchief.

All the red candles, the ceiling a thousand feet high. Statues and paintings. God's house. Whisper, wear a cloth over your hair. Genuflect, kneel, touch the holy water to tips of fingers, to forehead.

God's home, so hush. Be careful. His white beard, the gold circle over his head. His bedroom and kitchen and bathroom, his voice like thunder.

Gram in pigtails, when there were no houses. Just fields that went all the way to the river. A stone wall, and she ran and hid, and stayed a long time, behind the tree, the bush, the rock.

Nobody looking, and the light turned gray, and she waited and waited. Waited for Ma or Pa, for someone. Uncle Willie, someone.

Then dark almost, and there would be men coming to find her soon. Men with lanterns that swung and made long shadows.

Giants, with fire eyes.

A long time, they looked. Long as days and nights. Months of nights, all strung together.

Ann said, Will. Said, Lovely.

Said, Okay, and she was tense and strong, was tired.

Said, Sleep well. Said, Sweet dreams. Then curled up, hand near her face, and soon she was still, was quiet.

Eric and Seamus and Martha and Greta. In Massachusetts and sleeping. In rooms with curtains, with faint light from the moon and stars.

And Rolfe somewhere, all these years later. A room with a television and hot plate. Rolfe with a cat who sleeps at the foot of the bed.

Light from the hall coming through cracks at the edge of the door. A radio somewhere down the hall. Someone talking, whispering, a few notes of music.

Rolfe dreaming.

A car, a thousand miles of road. White line, tank of gas.

Rolfe with wind pushing back his hair.

Shades.

Just looking.

Hey.

Hey.

Ann breathes quietly, breathes easily. One, two, three, four, five.

I count till ten.

How many breaths in a night? In a lifetime?

Eyes like mine. Blue eyes, and dark hair and a smile. Running toward me down the front walk. Smiling, in diapers.

Or wearing a tie at the side of the bed.

Dad, he'd say. Hey.

On a porch, in a room, in a booth at a restaurant. He'd have a thin face, high cheekbones, a narrow nose.

Keys in the door, rattling. Someone saying, no no no no.

Saying no a dozen times.

Then laughing. Will, she said. Sweetheart. Then quietly, she curled up, was still.

Mom in bed, and long shadows in the house in Newton.

He'll sleep a long long time. He'll sleep for ten, for twelve, for fourteen hours. He'll sleep on his stomach, his back, and his brow will be furrowed, like he's thinking hard.

Jack or Ray.

Ruth, Helen.

He'll have a rip in the knee of his jeans. He'll wear an old tee shirt of mine.

Too big, but he likes that.

Tell about the guy on the ice floe, he'll say.

About the big guy who never moved. The fly would land, and he didn't blink or breathe.

He'll look over. Blue eyes like his mother, and brown hair.

Long legs in shorts. Sneakers without laces.

Tell that one, he'll say. The things people said. The way they looked.

Years ago. In there.

To someone a long time ago. Someone with the same name. Someone you used to know.